D0282805

Where Coyotes Howl

ALSO BY SANDRA DALLAS

Little Souls
Westering Women
The Patchwork Bride
The Last Midwife
A Quilt for Christmas
Fallen Women
True Sisters
The Bride's House
Whiter Than Snow
Prayers for Sale
Tallgrass
New Mercies
The Chili Queen
Alice's Tulips
The Diary of Mattie Spenser
The Persian Pickle Club
Buster Midnight's Cafe

Where Coyotes Howl

Sandra Dallas

ST. MARTIN'S PRESS
NEW YORK

This is a work of fiction. All of the characters, organizations, and events portrayed in this novel are either products of the author's imagination or are used fictitiously.

First published in the United States by St. Martin's Press, an imprint of St. Martin's Publishing Group

WHERE COYOTES HOWL. Copyright © 2023 by Sandra Dallas. All rights reserved. Printed in the United States of America. For information, address St. Martin's Publishing Group, 120 Broadway, New York, NY 10271.

www.stmartins.com

Design by Meryl Sussman Levavi

Library of Congress Cataloging-in-Publication Data

Names: Dallas, Sandra, author.
Title: Where coyotes howl / Sandra Dallas.
Description: First edition. | New York: St. Martin's Press, 2023.
Identifiers: LCCN 2022052666 | ISBN 9781250277909 (hardcover) |
    ISBN 9781250277916 (ebook)
Subjects: LCGFT: Western fiction. | Novels.
Classification: LCC PS3554.A434 W465 2023 | DDC 813/.54—dc23/
    eng/20221109
LC record available at https://lccn.loc.gov/2022052666

Our books may be purchased in bulk for promotional, educational, or business use. Please contact your local bookseller or the Macmillan Corporate and Premium Sales Department at 1-800-221-7945, extension 5442, or by email at MacmillanSpecialMarkets@macmillan.com.

First Edition: 2023

1   3   5   7   9   10   8   6   4   2

For Bob . . . And when the world is through with us,
we'll have each other's arms.

Bury me not on the lone prairie
Where coyotes howl, and the wind blows free.

—"The Cowboy's Lament"

Where Coyotes Howl

Prologue

1945

A ragged curtain snapped against the broken glass of the window in the old shack, which had begun to list. Its boards, the paint scraped off by the wind and sand, were a splintery gray. The door sagged open, its white china knob cracked and yellowed.

The two women held on to their hats as the wind blew across the treeless prairie, bringing dirt and the scent of sage. The older of the two put her hand on the door as if to knock. "It doesn't seem right just walking in." She laughed a little. "Nobody's lived here in thirty years, but it still feels like I ought to knock. 'Course I never had to. Ellen was always outside at the door when she heard someone coming. She was that happy for company. Well, weren't we all?"

She pushed the door open and the two walked across the floorboards to a kitchen chair that lay in the dust. Two of its legs were broken off. The cracked chimney of a kerosene lamp lay nearby. "Everything left behind that was worth anything got hauled off long ago, not that there was so much."

"Stolen?" the second woman asked.

"Oh no, Martha. When folks moved on, they left things behind, and people just took them. It was expected." The woman picked up what remained of the chair, running her hand over the pressed-wood back. It was a design of roses. "I remember when Ellen got these chairs. The table was something he made, but she ordered the chairs from the catalogue, then had them freighted in to Wallace. She wiped them off and polished them with a dishrag every day. I should have taken them, but I couldn't. That was before I married, and I didn't have any place for them. Besides it would have made me cry to sit on one of them. I hope whoever got the other ones didn't chop them up for kindling."

The women glanced around the room, which was both kitchen and living room. A bedroom was in the back. Shreds of newspaper that had made do as wallpaper clung to the walls. The floor was warped, and weeds had sprung up in the cracks between the boards. A scrap of faded blue material was caught on a nail. The room had a moldy smell, like old pancakes, and the older woman led the way back outside. "It's been deserted all these years, but I still feel like an intruder. I hope you don't mind me stopping. I think of it like I'm paying my respects." She was lost in thought a moment, then said, "Thirty years! Look what's happened in all that time. She came here about the time of World War One and now we've had a second world war. We've got refrigerators and gas stoves and Hoover vacuum cleaners. There are motorcars going up and down the road. Whoever thought back then that airplanes would be flying over Wyoming?"

A murder of crows suddenly rose into the air and flew off over the prairie, which was covered with long, dry grass for as far as you could see. The blue sky went from horizon to horizon without a hill or a mountain to block the view. An early winter wind came up and rattled the grass and sent a chill through the women. "Kind of creepy, isn't it?" her companion said.

"No. It was always a friendly place."

"Did anyone move in after them?"

"Maybe a drifter or two, a cowboy looking for a place in a storm. But nobody permanent. I'm glad. It wouldn't have seemed right, somebody else in her house." The woman's shoe had come untied, and she braced her back against the house while she tied it. The shoes were the kind that older women wore, sturdy, with small heels, and laced up. She had on a long, heavy coat—a man's coat—although a smart felt hat with a veil and a feather was attached to her head with a long pin.

The woman straightened and put her hand to her face to shade her eyes. "Over there was her garden. It was a marvel. She could grow anything. And beside the house were flowers. Such flowers. Daisies, phlox, poppies, hollyhocks. She made the cutest hollyhock dolls for the Brownell girls. They lived north of here. Nothing's left of their place. Now alls that grows here are sunflowers and goldenrod. They're dried up now."

"She must have been lonesome out here on the prairie."

"Oh my, yes. We all were. You can't live in Wyoming and not be lonesome. I know that the coyotes scared her. Howling at night the way they do. She wasn't one to complain, but she did say the coyotes made her shiver. I remember when one of them got a calf. When she saw that half-eaten calf, she sobbed, just sobbed."

"She didn't like it here then?"

"Oh, I wouldn't say that. She loved the open prairie. I

think things would have been better back then if we'd just had a radio. Radios did more for ranchwomen than electricity. But it was too early for radios. And we wouldn't have got reception out here anyway. Shoot, we didn't even have rural delivery."

The woman smiled, remembering. "She had him, though. He made it all worthwhile. She wasn't one of those mail-order brides; it wasn't any heart-and-hand marriage. They fell in love the first time they saw each other. She was fierce about him, loved him more than the sunrise. And he loved her right back."

The woman stared off into space, then shook her head. "Now don't mind me. I get to remembering. I hope you can forgive an old woman for being caught up in memories. Not that I'm so old, but Wyoming ages you. I was thinking just now how it used to be when I came down this road and stopped here. Of course, we didn't have an automobile back then. That was 1915 or 1916, so it's been thirty years. Still, it just seemed as natural as anything to stop today. We can go on now." She picked off a strand of needle-and-thread grass that was caught in her cotton stocking and had drilled its way into her leg.

The two started for the car.

"What were they like?" the younger woman asked.

Her friend looked back at the shack, at the dead canes of an old rosebush. The wind came up again. She removed her hat and shook the dirt from it, then reached inside the Packard for a thermos of coffee and two tin cups. She glanced at a bench beside the door of the shack, but the seat was broken. Instead, she sat down on the running board and motioned for her friend to sit beside her. "Oh, they weren't anybody to speak of," she said, pouring the coffee, then settling in. "You could throw a rock and hit a dozen like them. Folks that were here for a time, and then they weren't. Packed up and left behind anything that didn't fit in the wagon. Except for the way they loved each other, they were just ordinary, everyday folks. Just ordinary."

One

He sat hunched over in the saddle as he rode up to the schoolhouse on the spotted devil horse he called Huckleberry, the reins held loosely in his gloved right hand. He was dressed in a broad-brimmed white Stetson hat, a leather vest over a boiled white shirt with pockets, and fifteen-dollar fancy striped pants that were tucked into high-heeled boots. Spurs with little chains dangled from his boot heels. A big revolver hung from a wide leather belt strapped around his hips. He touched the brim of his hat with his left hand.

He was just a plain puncher—wiry, because ranchers preferred small, tough men; big men were hard on horses.

She had read *The Virginian* and all of the Zane Grey books, and he looked to her like a hero straight out of one of those novels. She felt a shiver of excitement go down her spine.

"Ma'am," he said. He could be a talker and had practiced in his mind how he would greet her, but he was so tongue-tied he could barely get out the single word.

"Yes," she replied. There was a quiver in her voice, and she cleared her throat.

He drawled, "I work for the I. P. Gurley. I've come to fetch Pike."

"Pike?" was all she could say.

"Yes'm."

"Oh yes. Pike. Is everything all right?"

He nodded, not sure he could get out another sentence. She waited, and it was clear to him that she wanted an explanation. She couldn't know that cowpunchers were afraid of proper women, so damn scared of saying something wrong. He took a deep breath. "I came to town to deliver some papers to the lawyer. Mr. Gurley said I ought to ride home with Pike."

"I see. School is almost over. The children are writing down their spelling words. Pike will be done in a few minutes." She smiled at him. "It's such a lovely day that I came outside to stand in the sun for a minute."

He nodded.

"I'm the new schoolteacher," she said.

"Oh." Of course he knew that. Everybody did. The Wallace school board, such as it was, had advertised in Iowa for a teacher, had asked anyone interested to send a letter listing qualifications and references, along with a photograph. The pictures were pinned to the wall in the general store, above the applications, and everyone who came in was asked to mark which teacher they preferred. The names were blocked out to make the selection appear anonymous. Only the mothers of the future students read the applications and noted that the new teacher was less qualified than the others. The men studied the pictures.

He had taken one look at the photographs and put an X under her name—Ellen Webster. Then he'd paid the other Gurley punchers a nickel each to do the same. Of course, it wasn't much of a contest, because the other applicants looked like old maids. With one exception, the school board was made up of men, and they offered the job to Ellen.

He'd been taken with that picture and had a regular mash on her. And now he'd come to see if she was as pretty as the photograph. He was right pleased. She had blond hair and eyes the color of a piece of turquoise. He hadn't known from the photograph that she was tiny, barely five feet. She looked like one of those china statues he'd seen on a parlor center table. "You like Wallace right well?" he asked at last. Except for Mrs. Gurley, he wasn't used to making conversation with women. Most of the women he encountered worked at the saloons or bawdy houses.

"I like it *right well*," she replied, then smiled to take the sting out of her teasing.

He didn't know she'd teased. They both felt the awkward silence that followed and wished the other would say something more. "That's good," he said at last.

He dismounted as she came down the steps of the schoolhouse and held out her hand. "I'm Ellen Webster." She hadn't been able to see his face under the big hat, but now she observed that it was tanned, that the nose was straight, and that he had eyes the blue of the Wyoming sky. She figured him to be in his late twenties. In fact, he was thirty-three, ten years older than she was.

He wasn't sure what to do but finally switched the reins to his left hand and shook her hand with his right, barely touching her fingers. "I know."

She waited, and when he didn't introduce himself she said, "I don't know your name."

"It's Charlie. Charlie Bacon."

"It's nice to meet you, Mr. Bacon."

He smiled. "You can call me Charlie."

She wouldn't do so. That was altogether too familiar, but she liked that he offered it. This was only her second week at the school, and she was trying to make a good impression on people in Wallace. It wouldn't do to call a man by his first name. "I suppose I had better go inside. I wouldn't want the students to ignore their spelling. You don't think they'd do that, do you?"

Charlie considered that, as if it had been a real question. He tried to think of a clever remark but could only reply, "I couldn't say."

The schoolhouse door was flung open then, and a young man yelled, "Fatback! I seen you through the window. What are you doing out here?"

Ellen frowned. "Fatback?"

He shrugged, embarrassed. "It doesn't mean anything. It's what I get called on account of my name is Bacon."

"I see."

"What are you doing out here?" the boy yelled again. "You come to check out the teacher?"

The cowboy's face turned red under the tan, because, of course, that was exactly the reason he was there. Mr. Gurley hadn't said a word about bringing Pike back with him. "I came to fetch you, boy," he lied. "Your pa doesn't want you getting into trouble on the way home."

"I don't make trouble."

Charlie swatted at Pike, who ducked. "He gives you any foolishness, you whip him," he told Ellen.

"Whip him?"

"Yes, ma'am. It's the only way to keep him in line." He grinned at the boy.

"How can I do that? He's five inches taller than I am."

"You just send for me. I'll do it."

"In a pig's eye," Pike said.

"Try me."

The boy considered that. He turned to Ellen. "He beat up Chauncey Tatum last week, after Chauncey insulted my dad. Near kilt him. Broke his arm in two places. I wouldn't go up against him if I was you."

Ellen laughed. She felt more comfortable with the boy there. "That's good advice, Pike. I'll keep it in mind."

Charlie scraped the toe of his boot in the dirt and said, "I didn't have any choice. There isn't a man who's worked for him who wouldn't go to hell for Mr. Gurley."

There was a commotion in the school; then a dozen students ran outside. "Did you finish copying your spelling words?" Ellen called. There was a chorus of yesses.

Several of the boys came over to admire Charlie's horse. "You going to let me ride Huckleberry one day, Fatback?" one asked.

"Nope."

"Can't nobody touch that horse. Charlie Bacon's the best rider there is. He can turn on a dime and give you a nickel back," Pike explained to Ellen. "I guess you'd kill anybody who did, wouldn't you?" he asked Charlie.

"Probably."

Ellen had raised her hand to pat the horse, but now she dropped it.

Charlie looked askance. "I didn't mean you."

"I wouldn't want to tempt you." Now she blushed, wondering if he thought she had been too familiar.

Pike had gone for his horse, which was among several tied to a railing in front of the schoolhouse. He mounted and rode up next to Charlie.

Charlie was reluctant to go, but there was no reason for him to stay. He touched the brim of his hat again. "I guess maybe I'll see you sometime."

Ellen didn't want him to leave. She said suddenly, "At the box supper? There's one here at the school on Saturday night. The school board thought it was a good idea. They arranged it so that I can get to know the parents—and others." She blushed and glanced over at where two children were going up and down on a teeter-totter, which was a board placed on a stump.

"Box supper?"

"You know, the women prepare suppers; then they're auctioned off. The money goes for schoolbooks."

"I know what it is. I've never been to one."

Ellen threw caution to the wind. "Then you ought to come, Mr. Bacon. I can guarantee you'll get a good meal."

"Yes, ma'am," he said and mounted Huckleberry and spurred him just a little too much, so that the horse reared before he took off.

Ellen watched him go, Pike riding hard to catch up. She chided herself for being so brazen. What must he think of her, all but asking him to have supper with her?

She did not know that he grinned until he was only a speck in the distance. Or that he'd already decided she was a woman he'd want to get his rope on.

Two

Ellen had taught school in Fort Madison, Iowa, for only a year when she spotted the advertisement in a newspaper for a teacher in Wallace, Wyoming. The ad was in a big-city newspaper that someone had left behind on a bench in the depot, where Ellen was awaiting the arrival of a friend. She studied it for a moment, wondering where Wallace was, picturing it being near deep canyons set against pine-covered mountains. She hadn't considered that Wallace might be a flat High Plains town with so little vegetation to obscure the view that one could almost see the earth curve. Instead, she thought, there would be ranches with soft-spoken cowboys, feisty young women on fast ponies, maybe holdup men and saloons with scarlet women. Iowa was so sedate, and she smiled at the excitement Wyoming might hold.

She tore out the ad and slipped it into her purse. That night after a Fort Madison teachers' meeting that was so dull she had nearly fallen asleep, she took out the scrap of newspaper as she was getting ready for bed. She read it again, then crumpled it and threw it into the wastepaper basket. In the middle of the night, she got out of bed and retrieved it. It lay on her dresser for two days.

What harm would it do to apply? she asked herself. There was nothing to keep her in Iowa. Her parents were dead, and her sister was married and living in Illinois. Ellen hadn't the slightest interest in any of the young men she'd met in Fort Madison. With only one year's experience, she wasn't likely to be offered the position in Wyoming, and even if she was, she could always turn it down.

Two months later, a letter with the Wallace postmark was sitting on the hall table in the boardinghouse where she lived. A rejection, she was sure as she took it up to her room and stared at it for a long time, feeling letdown. She hadn't counted on being given the job, but nonetheless, she was disappointed.

When she opened the letter and saw that the school board had offered her the position, she was so surprised that she sat down hard on the bed. What had she been thinking? She glanced at her bedside table. Zane Grey's *The Last of the Plainsmen* was hidden under her Bible. Ellen wasn't sure it was proper for a schoolteacher to read novels, and the woman who ran the boardinghouse was a gossip. She picked up the book and stared at the cover of windblown clouds over a desert. The story didn't take place in Wyoming, but what did that matter? She pictured herself in a daring divided skirt, atop a bronco, watching the sky turn crimson at sunset, as she raced across mountaintops beside a cowboy. She smiled at such foolishness. She was being offered a position in a country school, not a romantic encounter with a cowpuncher.

She wondered what her sister, Lizzie, would think. The two were close. Lizzie was four years older, and after their parents died when Ellen was sixteen, Lizzie raised her younger sister. She'd even put off her marriage until Ellen was grown. When Ellen wanted to go to normal school to get a teaching certifi-

cate, Lizzie paid the cost. She encouraged Ellen to leave Illinois
for Iowa so that she could see a little more of the world—not
that Iowa was London or Paris or even California. Ellen ought
to ask for Lizzie's approval, but Lizzie had encouraged her to
be independent, to take chances. Maybe it was time that Ellen
made decisions on her own.

The dinner bell rang downstairs. Ellen started to slip the
novel back under the Bible, then changed her mind and set it
on top of the Good Book. At that moment she made up her
mind to accept the job. It was only for a year.

She wrote Lizzie right away, and her sister wrote back, "Of
course you should accept. What a grand adventure. If you
don't like it, you can always go back to Iowa."

EASTERN WYOMING WASN'T what Ellen had anticipated. The
land was flat as a flapjack, covered with sage and rabbit bush.
It was brown, not lush and green, and there were no mountains. The Great Plains seemed endless without a landmark
to break the monotony. Ellen had thought there would be elk
and moose, but instead there were antelope and jackrabbits—
and rattlesnakes. An old man sitting next to her on the two-
day trip by train told her all about the snakes, said she ought
to wear boots to keep her ankles from being bitten. "But you
ain't got to worry too much, because the ground's so rough,
those snakes get their bellies tore open just crawling over it."
She believed him until he laughed.

Wallace was an even bigger disappointment. From the
train window, she saw only two real streets, going east–west
parallel to the railroad tracks. One was two blocks long and
comprised the business district. Behind it was a collection
of houses, most of them unpainted. The area near the depot,

shaded by cottonwoods, looked to her more like a campground for horse thieves and bank robbers than stove-up cowboys down on their luck. Men lounged in the shade of the trees or were stretched out on blankets, sleeping. Just before she got off the train, she turned to the old man and asked, "Are you sure this is Wyoming?" For a minute she wondered if she ought to stay on the train until it reached California. After all, she'd read novels about California, too, and just then the idea of orange groves seemed more appealing than sagebrush. But she'd made a commitment. Besides, she could see a group of people waiting for the train and she was sure they made up the Wallace school board.

As she climbed down from the car, a man in a moustache that drooped to his chin approached. He swept off his hat and bowed, and she could see that his face was dark from the sun, but his forehead, shaded by the hat, was as white as a baby's. "You be Miss Webster?" he asked.

She wanted to giggle at the courtly bow and stilted language and wondered if she should curtsey, but instead she said, "I am."

"We are relieved to see you."

"Relieved" seemed an odd word, and Ellen wondered if they thought she wouldn't show up. He introduced her to three other men and a woman, who looked Ellen up and down. At least the woman was straightforward in the way she sized her up. "You are a little bit of a thing," she said. Then she introduced herself. "I'm Mrs. Gurley. I expect you're tired and would like to wash your face." She turned to a group of men who had been lounging around the depot—cowboys, Ellen decided—and said, "Go on with you, now. You've seen the new teacher. Don't scare her none." She smiled at Ellen, and Ellen liked her at once. "Men. You'd think they'd never seen a young woman that's decent before." She waved her hand at the other members of the school board. "She's tuckered. You can meet with her tomorrow." She pointed to a buckboard. "I'll take you to the McGinty place. I'd have you stay with me on the ranch, but it's too far from the school."

"Is that the boardinghouse?" Ellen asked.

"Close enough. We don't have any real boardinghouses in Wallace, and the hotel is . . ." She paused, searching for a word, then gave up. "You wouldn't want to live there. Mrs. McGinty's a good cook, and old McGinty, well, don't mind him."

Ellen hadn't thought about where she'd live. She assumed she would have her pick of boardinghouses, but then she'd assumed Wallace would be a regular town, not a drab collection of buildings that included a saloon, a pool hall, a general store, a livery stable, a blacksmith's, and a few other businesses—one of them a bawdy house, she thought. She took in all of them as Mrs. Gurley drove her down Main Street in a buckboard. Behind Main was the only other street in Wallace—the residential district, with some twenty houses. Other shacks were scattered along dirt paths on either side of town.

The woman studied Ellen as they rode along. "You might want to put away that bonnet. The wind and the dust'll ruin it." Ellen put her hand to her head. She had worn a white straw hat with a veil and a cluster of artificial flowers. It had been the latest style in Iowa. "It's awful pretty, though," Mrs. Gurley continued. "I remember coming out here thirty years ago with a white bonnet with satin sashes. I haven't worn it since. Sunbonnet's the best thing. It'll keep out the dirt and the wind and shade your face a little, not that it'll help much. Just look at me." She turned a tanned, wrinkled face to Ellen.

"I'm told buttermilk will keep your face white," Ellen said.

"Yeah, I was told that, too. Don't count on it." Mrs. Gurley laughed. "Ranching, which is what Wyoming's all about, is a hardscrabble life, but I wouldn't trade it for a mansion in Chicago."

"Hardscrabble?"

Mrs. Gurley stopped the buckboard in front of a frame house set on a path at the west end of the residential street. The building sagged as if it were leaning into the wind. "Rough. Hard."

"I know what it means."

"You don't know what it means out here. It's the worst life you can imagine for a woman. And the best. You fight blizzards in the winter so bad you can't see a foot in front of you. You can freeze to death walking from the house to the barn. And in the summer, there's the heat. They like to tell about a man that went to hell and asked for an overcoat because he came from Wyoming and was used to real heat." She smiled at Ellen, who laughed.

"You do whatever your man does—ride herd, brand, castrate." She glanced at Ellen to see if the last word offended her, but Ellen didn't react. "And you do the cooking and birth the babies, too."

Ellen was taken aback. "You said it was the best life."

The older woman nodded, a faraway look on her face. "I did. There's nothing like sitting on the veranda—if you've got one—in the evening, watching a sunset like God's set the sky on fire, listening to the cattle, looking out over your land, and knowing you did it all. Oh, your husband did his part, but you were right there. He couldn't have done it without you. He might not admit it, but you know, and down deep, he does, too. Likely he'll be a good man. Cowboys are something special. There's times Wyoming's the most beautiful place in God's kingdom. Sometimes I think He calls the toughest of us to Wyoming, because if you're not tough, you don't make it."

She started to get down from the buckboard, then turned to Ellen. "Last teacher—Frieda Lewis—wasn't prime. She left in February. I knew she would. You can tell right off if a person's going to stick. You . . ." She looked at Ellen a long time. "I'd bet a yearling you'll stick."

THAT FIRST WEEK, Ellen wasn't so sure. In fact, after looking around the house where she would live for the next nine months, she wasn't sure she would stay the first night. It was clean, but her bedroom was the size of a chicken coop and there were knotholes and gaps between the boards that made up the walls. Ellen could only imagine what it would be like in the winter when the wind howled and the snow sifted in. Two dogs scratching fleas lay in front of the cookstove, which provided the only heat in the house. Mrs. McGinty was a gaunt, nervous woman who took Ellen's hand and said she was welcome, but Mr. McGinty only sat in his chair with his hat on and grunted at her when she was introduced. He reluctantly unloaded Ellen's trunk from the buckboard and carried it into her room.

Ellen thought it was going to be a long winter in that cramped house with the two McGintys.

"You get a good night's rest. I'll pick you up tomorrow to take you to supper at the ranch. The whole board'll be there. You can get to know them," Mrs. Gurley said. When Ellen looked apprehensive, the woman added, "Oh, don't you worry. They're grateful you're here. Alls you got to do is show them you can read and write and count to ten and you got the job as long as you want it."

After Mrs. Gurley left, Mrs. McGinty said, "We live simple here, but I try to keep it as nice as I can. You let me know if you need anything."

"Don't coddle her," her husband said. He had sat back down in his chair and kicked one of the dogs. "You lazy thing," he said.

Ellen flinched.

"He meant the dog," Mrs. McGinty said.

"Maybe." He guffawed.

"Don't mind him," she said, then flinched when he waved an arm at her. "I'll help you to unpack."

Ellen had purchased an upright trunk with drawers and cubbyholes, which was a good thing, she realized, because the bedroom had no dresser, only nails in the walls to hold her dresses. In fact, the only furniture was a narrow bed and a small table with a kerosene lamp on it. She began shaking out the dresses and laying them on the bed, while Mrs. McGinty admired them, touching a lace collar with her hand. "Oh my," she said. "I ain't never seen such a pretty thing." She marveled at Ellen's hats and gloves, her shirtwaists and skirts and petticoats, then opined that they were too good for Wallace. "Didn't you bring no calico?" she asked.

Ellen had purchased her wardrobe before leaving Iowa, buying the latest fashions, and now she wondered if it was too fine for Wyoming. She did not want to appear pretentious. She took out two old dresses, and Mrs. McGinty nodded. "Them's better."

Ellen opened one of the trunk drawers. It held her jewelry, and she closed it quickly, hoping Mrs. McGinty hadn't seen the contents. It wasn't that she distrusted the woman. She wouldn't want to show off when she knew Mrs. McGinty likely didn't have jewelry, even a wedding ring. But the old woman had glimpsed the objects and put her hand on Ellen's. "Best you lock that away," she said.

Ellen started to ask why, then stopped. She trusted Mrs. McGinty, but maybe not her husband. She was glad that, not knowing where she would be living, she had brought a lock-box with her.

Mrs. McGinty watched as Ellen hung the dresses on the nails, then said she'd send her husband in with water so that Ellen could wash herself. She'd had a china basin and pitcher once, she said, but they had been broken. The tin basin on the table would have to do.

In a few minutes, McGinty entered the room with a pail of water. He looked at Ellen's dresses and smirked. "School-teaching must pay mighty well. Or maybe you got some other way of making money." She wanted to tell him that she'd purchased the clothes with money her sister had sent, but it was none of the man's business.

He stood in the doorway, until Ellen said, "Excuse me," and closed the door. She took off her jacket and washed her face and hands, then sat down on the bed. The tick was matted, and Ellen thought it must be filled with prairie grass instead of feathers. She hoped there weren't insects. Well, it couldn't be helped. She closed her eyes and was almost asleep when Mrs. McGinty called, "Supper!"

Ellen would rather sleep, but she did not want to be rude and went into the room that was both kitchen and parlor and sat down at the table, which was set with spoons. There were no forks—or napkins either. She understood. Doing laundry must be hard.

Mrs. McGinty handed a tin plate of food to her husband, then set one down in front of Ellen. She thought there might be a blessing, but the man began eating right away, holding his plate high and shoving the food into his mouth. Ellen waited for Mrs. McGinty to take her seat, but the woman stood by the stove. "Won't you join us?" Ellen asked.

"She don't sit down," McGinty said.

When Ellen sent her a questioning look, the woman said, "He'll want something more. You go ahead before it gets cold."

McGinty was finished before Ellen picked up her spoon. He held out his plate to his wife, who filled it again. He devoured the second helping almost as quickly as the first, then shoved the plate aside and slurped coffee. His wife picked up the plate and put a large piece of pie on it and set it down. He was half-finished before he looked up and gestured at the table with his spoon. "Sit," he said. She had barely taken a bite when he rose and went outside with the dogs.

Mrs. McGinty, her head bowed, glanced at Ellen. "He likes me to do for him."

"Of course," Ellen replied. She was appalled at the man's lack of manners.

"I'm glad you're here. I'm glad for the company. It gets lonely . . ." She didn't finish.

Ellen thought of the vastness of the land, how barren Mrs. McGinty's life was, and wondered how any woman could live that way. Could she stick, as Mrs. Gurley had put it? Ellen thought that over. She would prove she was prime, she vowed. It was only a year, less than that. How long had poor Mrs. McGinty lived on this awful prairie?

Three

The day of the box supper, Ellen worked in the kitchen with Mrs. McGinty. The woman was a plain cook, and except for a container of cinnamon, the larder was bare of spices. There was a barrel of flour and a sack of sugar, tins of baking powder and baking soda, salt and pepper. Strings of dried sliced apples hung from the ceiling. Outside in the dirt cellar, barrels of potatoes and onions and wrinkled apples were stored. On the cellar shelves were glass jars of pickles and tomatoes and green beans that Mrs. McGinty had bottled in the summer. Slabs of smoked meat hung from the beams.

Since domestic science was one of the subjects Ellen taught, she knew she ought to prepare a meal that was not only appetizing but attractive. She'd be judged on it, by both the men and the women. She would have to see if the general store had something she could add to make her supper appealing.

Main Street was only a short block away. As she walked down the dirt road to Wallace's two-block commercial district, she wondered if Charlie Bacon would bid on her supper, wondered if he'd even show up that afternoon. She'd be disappointed if he didn't, although there were plenty of other cowboys who would be happy to eat with her. She'd been checked out by a

dozen of them, men who had stopped at the school to water
their horses or inquire if she needed wood chopped or water
carried from the well to the schoolhouse. Now, as she entered
the general store, several punchers introduced themselves,
touching their hats and calling her ma'am, wishing her good
morning, asking how she liked Wyoming, telling her if she
needed something, just to ask them. She could tell they were
nervous by the way they blushed and stuttered and looked at
the floor. One muttered to his friend that she was as pretty
as a newborn heifer. They seemed in awe of her and she remembered Mrs. Gurley telling her they weren't used to being
around decent women.

Ellen wondered about the indecent women, whether she
would recognize them. But, of course, she would—the painted
faces and satin dresses. She'd seen the hussies in Iowa. Such
women didn't dress like that in Wallace, however, at least not
on the street, and Ellen might not have recognized the pair
who came into the store if she had not seen them come out of
the Columbine, an establishment across the street, the building she had decided was the whorehouse. They weren't dressed
as well as she was.

"Well, look who's here," one said. Ellen turned, thinking
the remark was made about her, but the woman was address-
ing one of the cowboys.

"Up kind of early, aren't you, Mutt?" the cowboy asked.

"Where was you last night? I thought it was payday. I was
waiting for you."

The puncher glanced at Ellen, then stuttered, "Over at the
Silver Dollar. I lost my wages."

"Next time come and see me first."

"Say, how's Gladys doing?" the second woman asked another cowboy.

"She's got herself in the family way," he replied.

"Knocked her up, did you? You tell her I said hello."

"Yes, ma'am, I will."

The storekeeper glanced at the prostitutes and motioned Ellen to come to the counter. "Don't mind them two. They're not so bad."

"No, of course not," Ellen said, although she couldn't help staring. She'd never been this close to a prostitute before and was surprised that the women seemed so ordinary—flirtatious maybe, but nice enough.

"That there's the new schoolmarm, come here from Iowa," one of the cowboys said, shoving a thumb at Ellen, who blushed.

The women looked her over. "Isn't that swell," Mutt said. "Next thing you know we'll have a church and electricity, and one day, maybe I can have me a telephone." She smiled at Ellen. "Any of them fellows give you trouble, you just take a horsewhip to them."

"I was a schoolteacher once," the second woman told her. "You tell little Spuddy Williams he owes Miss Frieda some homework." She laughed.

Her predecessor, the first schoolteacher! Ellen was stunned and did not know how to reply.

"I guess you heard of me," Frieda said. "I had a soft spot for Spuddy. He was my favorite." Spuddy was one of the youngest students and an imp.

The storekeeper stepped in. "Now you girls go on about your business and let her alone."

"Sure thing," Mutt said, then asked her friend in a loud whisper, "How long do you think she's going to last?"

Frieda glanced over her shoulder at Ellen. "You ever get tired of schoolteaching, you come see us," she said, then nudged her friend and laughed. "Pay's better, and you don't have to worry about old McGinty."

"WHAT HAPPENED TO the first schoolteacher?" Ellen asked Mrs. McGinty as the two put together their box suppers. The older woman was going to the schoolhouse, too, although her husband said he wouldn't bid so much as a dime for his own food prepared by his own wife. Ellen had been so nervous in the store that she had purchased only a jar of preserves, and at first she didn't know what to do with them. You didn't spread strawberry jam on a ham sandwich. Then she came up with the idea of making strawberry turnovers. She had assembled them, and now she put her arm into the oven to test the heat. The temperature was right, and Ellen slid the pastry in to bake. She turned to Mrs. McGinty, who had not answered her question.

"She didn't like teaching, I guess," Mrs. McGinty said.

"She lived here with you?"

Mrs. McGinty nodded.

"She moved on then."

"You could say that."

"Away from Wallace?"

Mrs. McGinty looked at Ellen sharply. "Why do you ask?"

Ellen wished then that she hadn't brought up the subject. "There was a woman in the store . . ."

"Then you know." Mrs. McGinty turned away, and that was the last of the conversation.

But not the last of Ellen's curiosity about Frieda. She wondered why the woman had turned to prostitution. If she hadn't liked teaching at the Wallace school, she surely could have found a position elsewhere. Perhaps she was just a loose woman who had pretended to be a teacher until she found something more to her liking. And what had she meant when she'd told Ellen she didn't have to worry about old McGinty anymore?

From the very first, Ellen had not liked the man, and during the little more than two weeks she'd lived with the McGintys she hadn't seen any reason to change her mind. He was not so unattractive the one time he had shaved and cleaned up, younger looking than his wife, but then, as Mrs. Gurley had suggested, women aged quickly in Wyoming. When she met the McGintys, Ellen had thought them to be in their seventies. Now she knew they were barely fifty.

Ellen could not warm up to him. He was surly, and it was clear that his wife feared him. He was lazy, too. While McGinty talked about *his* house, *his* food, *his* money, Ellen observed that it was Mrs. McGinty who did the work, chopping wood, hauling water, caring for the cow and horses, taking in laundry, and preparing fifty-cent Sunday dinners for the cowboys who were in town. Old McGinty claimed he had been maimed in an accident, and he never lifted a hand.

The turnovers were brown, and Ellen wrapped a towel around her hand to remove the hot pan from the oven.

"What you got here?"

Ellen hadn't heard the man come in, and she nearly dropped the pan.

"I guess I'll just try one."

"They're for the box supper."

"Well, I supplied the makings."

He reached around her, but Ellen moved the pan. "No, you did not. I bought the jam at the mercantile." She set the pan at the back of the stove where he couldn't reach it.

"Ain't you the feisty one." He had just returned from the general store, which also served as the post office. Ellen had been too flustered to ask for the mail when she was there, and McGinty had gone for it. He told her the mail was his business and neither she nor his wife was to fetch it.

He spread out the mail on the table, then stared at one of the envelopes for a long time. He lifted a lid on the stove and threw the letter into the fire. As it went into the flames, Ellen saw Mrs. McGinty's name on it. "Is there a letter for me?" Ellen asked.

"How should I know?" He set two envelopes on the table.

Ellen saw her name on one and picked it up.

Mrs. McGinty, who had been slicing bread, waited until her husband was back outside before she went to the table. "I'd hoped there was a letter from my daughter." She sat down and put her head in her hands.

Ellen had not known about a daughter. McGinty had not replaced the stove lid, and she peered inside the firebox. The letter was only partially burned, and she used the lid lifter to remove it from the ashes. "Is this it?"

Mrs. McGinty looked at the remains of the letter and bowed her head. "That cussed man," she said. "He won't even let me hear from Laura. He resents the least little thing that makes me happy." She plucked off the burnt bits of paper, then shoved the letter into her apron pocket. "Don't let him know I have it," she said. She began to cry. "Don't ever get married, Miss Webster."

Ellen sat down and put her arm around the woman. Lizzie's letters meant so much to her that she knew how much Mrs. McGinty must treasure correspondence from her daughter.

"He can't read. He tries to keep it secret—says his eyesight's no good—but I know. After all these years, he still thinks he's fooled me. He hates it that Laura writes me, and he don't know what she says. But he can recognize her hand, knows when a letter's from her. He just can't let me have that little bit of pleasure.

"I tried to teach him to read when we was first married, but McGinty, he claimed he already knew, and he backhanded me for thinking he was stupid."

"You've had a hard life," Ellen sympathized.

Mrs. McGinty blew out her breath. "Oh, no harder than anybody else. You don't have to feel sorry for me." She got up and used her apron to pick up the hot pan and put the turnovers into the pie safe to cool. "My! Some cowboy's going to think he's died and went to heaven when he tastes these." She closed the pie safe door and wiped her eyes on her sleeve.

THE BIDDING FOR the box suppers was sharp. Mrs. McGinty was known as a good cook, and her box brought a dollar. Others went for a quarter or fifty cents, one for as much as two dollars. Then the auctioneer—the man with the long moustache who was head of the school board—raised Ellen's supper over his head and said, "Now I wonder what little lady fixed this." He pointed at Ellen.

"Fifty cents!" a man yelled.

"A dollar!"

"Two dollars!"

Ellen didn't know who was bidding. The price went up. Women stopped talking to watch, and Ellen hoped people weren't staring at her.

The bidding reached five dollars and stopped. "Anybody else?" the auctioneer asked. "It's for a good cause. Money's going toward schoolbooks. How about one more bid?"

"Eight dollars!" a man called, and people gasped. A woman turned to Ellen and grinned. "Nobody ever paid eight dollars before."

Ellen blushed, and then she had an awful thought. What if the bidder was old McGinty? She boarded at the McGinty house, so what would people think? Then she heard a man say, "I. P. Gurley must pay pretty good. Eight dollars is more'n a week's wages."

In a minute, Charlie Bacon strode toward Ellen, her box supper in his hand. "Ma'am," he said, touching his Stetson. "I expect you are a good cook."

One of the mothers shook her head. "Lord, it's Charlie Bacon. He looks smitten. I hope we don't have to replace the schoolteacher again."

"Hello, Mr. Bacon," Ellen said.

Folks stared at them a moment, then dispersed, some sitting on the schoolhouse steps because it was a warm October day and the sun was high in the sky. Others went inside and set their box suppers on the school benches. A few spread blankets on the ground and unpacked the food. Charlie looked around, but the only place left to sit was the prairie. He took off his coat and laid it on the ground. "We can sit here," he said.

Ellen knew that parents were keeping an eye on her and it wouldn't do for them to think she was fast. She glanced around until she spotted Hattie Young. Hattie was sixteen, one of the oldest in the class. She was smart and loved learning and had confided to Ellen that she hoped to be a teacher herself. Ellen was fond of her because she was cheerful and helped the younger students. "Why don't you join us, Hattie. There's plenty of food," she said.

"Yes, ma'am," Hattie said, thrilled at the honor. It wasn't just that she liked being singled out by the teacher, but she had a crush on Charlie Bacon. She glanced at him and saw him glaring at her and added, quickly, "Yes, ma'am, I'd like to, but I have to eat with my family." She turned away, knowing her dreams of Charlie Bacon had turned to dust on that October afternoon.

Four

Both Ellen and Charlie remembered almost everything they talked about that afternoon. Charlie recalled that after he said Ellen must be the best cook in Wyoming she'd demurred and told him she had once decided to make a raisin pie. She'd been in a hurry, and when the pie was cut open she discovered she had reached for the beans instead of the raisins. And Ellen remembered that Charlie told her he'd had a trained pig. He'd fashioned a leash for it, and the pig followed him around the barnyard and even into the ranch house. He did that once too often, however, and Mrs. Gurley had her husband slaughter the pig. Charlie refused to eat pork for the next month.

He wasn't like the men Ellen had known in Iowa. Charlie listened to her when she talked and didn't try to impress her with what a swell fellow he was. He wasn't frivolous with pretty words like the boys she'd known in Iowa. Although he had gone to school only through the eighth grade, he was well-spoken and interested in what she had to say. Ellen liked his sense of humor and the fact he could laugh at himself. She loved the way he bragged about Wyoming, as if it were the grandest place on earth. Ellen thought there was a kindness to Charlie, too, in the way he talked about animals and the Gurleys.

Once their shyness was gone, the two talked so much that Ellen nearly forgot about the program the children had practiced for their parents and guests and had to rush to gather the eighteen pupils for the performance. The former teacher had never put together an entertainment, so the parents were impressed with their children's recitations—bad as they were.

Pike had demanded to say a poem. The request pleased Ellen so much that she hadn't even asked him the name of it. He stood up and grinned at the boys, then bowed and recited:

Oh God, above, look down below
Upon us poor scholars.
We've hired a fool to teach our school
And pay her forty dollars.

Some of the women gasped, and Mrs. Gurley admonished, "Pike!" Ellen was shocked but realized that if she was to be a successful teacher she'd have to be a good sport, and she laughed. Later Charlie told Pike if he was ever that disrespectful of Miss Ellen again he'd thrash him.

McGinty laughed at the recitation, too. He'd thought nobody would dare bid on his wife's supper, and he was furious that someone had paid a dollar to eat with Mrs. McGinty. "Next thing you know, you'll be working down at the Columbine," he told his wife as the three of them walked home.

Ellen thought Mrs. McGinty would lash out at him for the insult, but she only ducked her head and said in a low voice, "Don't shame me, Wesley. I couldn't help who bought it."

Ellen was not so meek. "That is a disgraceful thing for a man to say to his wife," she told him.

"Didn't ask you."

"No, but I take offense just the same. You dishonor us by speaking that way." She knew she should not have said anything. What if McGinty threw her out? If he did, he would likely tell a scandalous story about her. Besides, where would she go? There was no place else for her to board. She would have to move into the schoolhouse.

McGinty apparently was not used to a woman standing up to him. He snarled and headed for the saloon.

"I ought not to have spoken," Ellen said.

Mrs. McGinty turned her head a little, and Ellen could see that the corners of her mouth were raised. "It warmed my heart that you did when I couldn't. He won't take a poker to you."

"He hits you with a poker?" Ellen was shocked. She couldn't imagine such a thing.

Mrs. McGinty shrugged. "More often he just threatens. I know better than to provoke him."

"But sometimes it is more than a threat."

"Not often."

Ellen took the woman's arm. "Mrs. McGinty, I am so sorry."

"Ruth," she said, changing the subject. "You call me Ruth from now on."

"And I am Ellen." She wanted to pursue the conversation but knew her friend did not. Ellen wondered why being beaten was a wife's shame and not her husband's.

IT WAS A sweet courtship. The two did not see each other often. After all, Charlie was a cowboy and worked six days a week and frequently seven. He had been with the Gurleys for five years, and they depended on him. Still, he managed to find ways to call on Ellen. If he was in town on an errand, he stopped by the school to ride home with Pike. The children were onto him and yelled, "Fatback's sweet on Teacher!" When Ellen, embarrassed, blushed, they cried, "Miss Ellen's going to marry Fatback!" Both she and Charlie pretended they didn't hear.

One morning, Charlie arrived at the McGinty place, leading a saddled horse. "I thought you ought to see the country, and there's places a flivver won't go." It wasn't necessary to add that he didn't own one of the few Model Ts in Wallace and was more at home in a saddle than on the seat of an automobile anyway.

The horse was fitted with a regular saddle, not a sidesaddle, and Ellen changed into her divided skirt, ignoring McGinty's remark that it was scandalous for a woman to dress like a man. He said he wasn't sure such a female should live in his house. She could give him and his wife a bad reputation. By then, Ellen knew the McGintys needed the money she gave them for her board and room and it wasn't likely he would carry through on his threat to evict her.

She had ridden horses before. And while she was no cowgirl, she still managed to keep up with Charlie. Mrs. Gurley had lent them her horse, Red Girl, who was gentle. Ellen didn't know that the woman had sighed when Charlie asked permission to borrow the horse to take Ellen riding and said, "All I ask is that she teaches out the year."

Charlie blushed and said he was only taking the teacher for a ride, not asking her to marry him. "It's sinful to keep her cooped up in the McGinty place."

"Oh, go on with you. I've seen lovesick bulls before, and you aren't any different." She softened. "I got to say she's mighty nice—and a looker, too. If you're set on getting hitched, Charlie, you couldn't do better."

"Yes, ma'am," he said and grinned at her.

The two set off across the prairie, riding under a bluebell-blue sky, through clumps of silver-green sage that gave off a pungent odor. Ellen had thought of the land as a flat, brown expanse, but now she began to see the variation in landscape and color. By late October, the stands of grass had turned golden, whipping in the wind like wheat in the fields. She had believed that all grass was the same, until Charlie pointed out the variety—buffalo grass and blue grama, and needle-and-thread grass, which stuck to Ellen's clothes. He told her that the skeleton-like tumbleweeds that skidded across the prairie were really Russian thistle, mixed in with wheat seed that the Russian immigrants had brought to America years before. She loved the variation in color of the foliage but admired most of all the rabbit bush, which had bloomed earlier, its yellow flowers as bright as gold coins. As they rode across the High Plains, Ellen realized the land was not flat but undulated with hillocks and was cut with arroyos that meandered like the streams that had formed them long before.

Small birds flew up as they passed, and hawks and blue-winged and cinnamon teal soared overhead. Jackrabbits darted from where they were hiding under rock outcroppings, and antelope paused to watch them. They were the most curious animals on God's earth, Charlie said. The antelope were brown and blended into the ground, but Ellen could see their white rumps as they bounded off. She and Charlie passed a prairie dog colony, the little rodents sitting up beside their burrows, chattering. Ellen wanted to go close, but Charlie warned her to stay away since rattlesnakes lay in wait for the little dogs. Or a horse could break a leg if it stepped into one of the dozens of holes.

"Are there rattlesnakes?" Ellen asked.

"Some. But what you really have to watch out for are hoop snakes," Charlie drawled.

"Hoop snakes. I never heard of them."

"Dangdest things. They put their tails in their mouths and turn themselves into circles and just roll over the prairie, faster than a freight train." He turned away, then pointed in the distance. "Might be one over there."

Ellen looked but didn't see anything. "Are they dangerous?"

"You don't want to get close to one. It could whip you to death." He paused. "I've seen only one or two around Wallace."

Ellen shivered and kept a lookout. She was afraid of snakes.

They rode for a long time, Charlie telling her about the prairie. She could see that he loved it. Ellen did not, not yet, at least—the bigness of it made her wary—but she liked it better when she was with Charlie. They passed homesteads, and Charlie told her about dryland farming, how crops could be raised in the arid soil. Some of the houses—shacks, really—were deserted, the doors sagging open. Farming was hard work, Charlie said, and many homesteaders weren't up to it.

He stopped his horse at the dirt path to one raw-board house that looked like a dry-goods box, where a woman was hanging up the wash. She used her hand to shade her eyes from the sun, then recognized Charlie and waved him in. Charlie led the way, reining in his horse with one hand as he touched the brim of his hat with the other.

"Why, what are you doing all the way out here, Charlie?" she asked. "You 'light and set awhile. Morris's out with the cows, won't be home till dark. I could use me the company. It's been a time since I seen anybody." The woman's face was tanned from the sun and windburned, but then hers was, too, Ellen thought. She'd refused to wear a sunbonnet.

Charlie glanced at Ellen, who nodded. He dismounted and helped her off her horse. "This here's the new schoolteacher, Miss Ellen. I'm showing her around a bit."

"I just bet you are." The woman smiled at Ellen. "I heard you was here. I sure am glad for it." She arched her back and put her hands on her waist, and Ellen saw that she was pregnant. The woman put out her hand and said, "I'm Gladys Turnbull."

Ellen had reached for the hand but paused for an instant when Gladys gave her name. When Ellen had first gone into the general store, she'd heard one of the prostitutes ask about Gladys. If Gladys noticed Ellen's hesitation, she didn't react. Ashamed of herself, Ellen touched Gladys's hand and said, "I am happy to meet you."

"Come on inside," Gladys said. "Alls I can offer you is water, and it ain't too cold at that. In my condition, whiskey turns my stomach, and if I can't drink it, I told Morris he can't neither." She was pretty in a faded way. Her hair was yellow as butter but limp, and her eyes were a blue so pale that they looked washed out by the sun. Ellen wondered if Wyoming had aged her prematurely.

Gladys turned to the cupboard, which was really a wooden box nailed to the wall, for glasses, and Ellen looked around. The house was plain but neat—one room with a cookstove and an iron bed, a table, and two chairs. Red-striped curtains hung in the single window.

"You got it real nice here," Charlie said.

"I sure do," Gladys told him.

Ellen didn't think so. She was stunned at the barrenness of the place, which made the McGinty house seem prosperous. She wondered how the woman could be so content. Wouldn't Gladys die of loneliness out here? Could she love her husband so much that she could put up with this meager existence?

Ellen struggled to find something nice to say and finally added, "You're a fine housekeeper. Everything is so tidy."

"That's 'cause we don't got nothing." Gladys laughed. "But then we got everything we need, and lucky to have it." She handed around the glasses—jelly jars—of water and pointed to the two chairs, then seated herself on the bed. "Way out here, I don't get many visitors," she said, and Ellen wondered what in the world they would talk about. But she didn't have to worry. Gladys chattered away, pointing out the cradle her husband had made from a whiskey box attached to runners. "I hope you stay in Wallace awhile," she told Ellen. "There was another teacher, but she quit. Maybe you heard about her."

"I've met her," Ellen blurted out. Gladys as well as Charlie stared at her.

"Where was that at?" Charlie asked.

"In the store." Ellen fumbled, then recovered. "She told me she missed Spuddy. He's one of the students."

"That's Horace's boy," Charlie explained to Gladys.

"Poor kid. His daddy's no good. You think he'll be a troublemaker when he grows up?"

"Not if I can help it," Ellen answered.

Gladys studied her. "You're a good person."

Ellen blushed. "I'm a teacher. That's my job."

"Frieda didn't feel that way."

At the mention of the prostitute, the three were quiet. "You like Wallace, do you?" Gladys asked at last.

"I'm beginning to."

"It's a nice enough town. We don't get too many bears."

"Charlie told me about hoop snakes. I haven't seen one, though."

Gladys burst out laughing. "He did what?" She turned to Charlie. "You're a devil." Charlie looked sheepish, and Gladys laughed again. "There's no such thing as a hoop snake. It's just a joke the cowboys tell."

Ellen looked abashed. How could she have been so stupid? She thought to rebuke Charlie, but it was her own fault for being gullible. So instead, she asked, "When is the baby due?"

"I'm not just sure. Sometime in the winter."

"Is there a doctor in Wallace?"

Gladys laughed. "You'd have to go all the way to Cheyenne for one, although I heard a new one's about to set up. There's a woman not far away that acts as a midwife. That is, if the snow ain't too deep and Morris can get to her. Otherwise, I guess he'll just have to deliver it."

Charlie looked away, embarrassed at the talk of childbirth. But Gladys was taken up with the subject. "He's awful good at calving. I don't suppose birthing a baby's much different. Morris's a good man, not like old McGinty." She stopped and looked at Ellen. "You ever heard the story of when their girl was born?"

Ellen shook her head. She knew Charlie was uncomfortable and tried to change the subject, remarking that they must be going.

But Gladys would have none of it. "I wasn't here then, but I heard all about it. Ruth McGinty got the pains and knew the baby was coming fast. Old McGinty wouldn't do nothing, just sat on a chair in the yard. She had to go to the neighbors' and ask them to send a boy for the midwife. Then she went inside and near had to deliver that baby herself. The midwife arrived just as the girl was poking out her head. Old McGinty never stirred himself, just sat in the yard drinking whiskey."

As Gladys talked, Charlie sat with his elbows on his knees, staring at the floor, wishing he were anyplace but inside that shack. He'd never heard such talk before and couldn't imagine how Gladys could keep on jabbering. He didn't know if he could look Ellen in the face after that. At last, Gladys realized Charlie was out of sorts, but instead of making her guest more comfortable, she said, "You ought to hear about this, Charlie. You men never think when you're having a good time what it means to us girls." She slapped her knee and stood up. "You want to stay for supper? Morris'll be here then."

That was Charlie's cue to leave. "If we don't get back, Miss Ellen's reputation will be mud." He stood and led Ellen to the horses and helped her mount. They thanked Gladys and rode to the end of the trail, then stopped and waved. Gladys had resumed hanging up the wash but turned and yelled, "You come back anytime!"

"I'm sorry about that. Gladys talks too much," he told Ellen.

"I didn't mind. Maybe when it's time to teach biology, I'll have her come and talk to the class." Then she blurted out, "Was she a prostitute?"

Charlie's face turned red. "You might say that, but I just think of her as a decent woman."

Ellen admired Charlie for that. "Then I shall do the same."

Five

The snow came unexpectedly, swooping down on the schoolhouse from the west. "We better git to home," Pike told Ellen.

"There is barely an hour left of school. Surely you can wait," she replied.

The other children were already gathering their dinner pails and placing their books into oilcloth bags to keep them dry, putting on coats and mittens and hurrying for the door. "School is not dismissed," Ellen protested.

"Teacher, it looks like a blizzard. We got to go," one of the children replied.

"Surely another hour . . . ," Ellen said, but the children were already out the door, mounting horses, climbing into buggies, or running for home. Ellen shook her head. Anything to get out of school early, she thought. This was Wyoming. Weren't they used to a little snow? She stood in the doorway, arms wrapped around herself to keep warm, watching as the children hurried off.

The school was a challenge for Ellen, who had taught only one grade in Iowa. The eighteen pupils in the Wallace school ranged in age from little Spuddy (the favorite of Frieda, the former teacher) in second grade, to Hattie and Pike, who were in high school. She gave the older students assignments to do while she taught the younger ones. But when Ellen turned to the high school students, the grade school children grew restless. She solved the problem by asking some of the older girls to read to the younger ones or print letters on their slates.

Now Ellen sighed as she watched the children leave. She might as well make use of the extra hour to tidy the schoolroom. She took a broom from the corner and swept the floor, then found a rag and dipped it into the water bucket and washed the blackboard. She removed the Halloween decorations that the children had pinned to the wall and threw them into the stove, then straightened the bookshelf.

The kindling box was almost empty, and Ellen wrapped her shawl around her shoulders and went outside for more wood. The snow was heavy now, and the wind whipped it around so hard that Ellen could barely see. Someone had planted trees for a windbreak next to the school, but they were too stubby to block the gale. She realized then that the children had known what they were doing when they left and decided that she, too, should head for home. She locked the schoolhouse door and started off.

The school was located on the south side of Wallace, nearly half a mile from the McGinty house. Ellen had always enjoyed the walk, using the time to plan lessons or review the day's activities. Or to think about Charlie Bacon. Now she thought only about the snow. The morning had been calm, and she had worn a shawl instead of a coat. She had not thought to take boots, and her shoes were wet. She plodded through the snow in the direction of the McGinty house, the sodden flakes so thick that she could not see the sky. The wind howled and blew the snow around so hard that Ellen had to wait until it paused to be sure she was going in the right direction. This was only November. What would the snow be like when winter came?

Suddenly a figure loomed up in front of her—a man in a buggy. "I was afraid you'd get lost," a muffled voice said. Ellen recognized the horse and thought at first that McGinty had come for her. Then she realized the figure was Ruth. "I remembered you wasn't wearing a coat and didn't have no overshoes when you left this morning," Ruth said. "Get in before you freeze."

Ellen climbed into the buggy, and Ruth threw a blanket over her before turning the horse toward home.

"I am grateful to you," Ellen told Ruth. "But I could have made it home." This was Wyoming. It wouldn't do to have her landlady think she wasn't capable of dealing with a little snow.

"Sure you could," Ruth replied. "It was an excuse for me to get out of the house. I like the cold weather. Snow always seems so clean."

Ellen smiled at the way the woman let her save face. They reached the barn, and Ellen helped unhitch the buggy.

Inside the house, Ruth heated a teakettle of water and poured it into a basin, telling Ellen to soak her frozen feet to keep from catching cold. She hung up Ellen's wet stockings, then stuffed newspaper into the shoes to help them keep their shape and set them under the stove. She sat down in a chair beside Ellen and took out her quilt pieces. The bits of calico added color to the drab room.

"You like to sew," Ellen observed. It seemed that Ruth was always working with the scraps in spare moments.

"Lord, yes. I don't know what I'd do without my piecing." She examined a scrap that was nearly worn through and set it aside. "You can't make a new quilt with old material," she observed, shaking her head. "But mostly that's all I got."

Ruth had made tea, and the two women sat near the

cookstove, quietly talking. It was a pleasant scene, and Ruth seemed content—until McGinty came home. When she heard him stamping his feet outside, Ruth jumped up and thrust the sewing into a basket. She began preparing supper.

McGinty came into the house and remarked that the buggy was covered with snow. "You had to fetch her from the schoolhouse, didn't you?" He smirked. "What kind of teacher don't know about the weather? Likely they'll be looking for a new one by New Year."

Ruth started to defend Ellen but thought better of it. Ellen didn't reply either. But she vowed she would stick. No matter how bad the weather got, she would not leave. She was not a quitter.

AFTER A TIME, Ellen came to enjoy the snow—the clean white that settled the prairie dust, the brisk air so much drier than the winter air she was used to in Iowa, the sight of children pulling sleds or throwing snowballs. When Charlie came to see her, he had charcoal smudges under his eyes to keep from going snow-blind; the glare of sun on snow was that sharp. He visited more often now that winter was coming on and there was less activity at the ranch. At first, he sat in the house with Ellen, but that was awkward with McGinty in the room. The older man dominated the conversation or made snide remarks, and when Ruth invited Charlie to stay for dinner McGinty snarled that they were getting paid for only one boarder, not two. So when the weather was decent—or even when it wasn't—the couple went outside, where Charlie chopped wood for the cookstove. They went for long walks or for rides in the snow. There was no restaurant in Wallace, so they could not go out for a meal or even pie and coffee. The only establishment that served food was the saloon, and that was no place to take a schoolteacher.

Sometimes they stopped at the mercantile, where Charlie examined the hardware and horse blankets. Ellen looked at buttons and fingered the bolts of calico, which were as cheap as shoddy. No wonder Ruth's quilt scraps were so thin. Charlie bought a nickel's worth of lemon or horehound drops, and if the store was empty they sat on chairs beside the potbellied stove. Sometimes the storekeeper made a pot of coffee and set it on the stove for them. "You got three of my kids at that school," he said, explaining his gesture. Once he sat down with them and asked Ellen, "You planning on staying the winter?"

"Of course."

"We'll see, I guess."

Why was everyone so sure she would quit? Their skepticism only strengthened Ellen's resolve to finish the year at the school and maybe even stay on for another. Wyoming had been an adjustment, but now she was glad she had come. She loved the children, their self-reliance and lack of artifice. The parents were so glad she was there that they rarely interfered in her teaching. While she could not warm up to McGinty, she'd become fond of Ruth, who not only cooked and kept the house clean but had taken over Ellen's laundry. Ruth protested when Ellen tried to pay her for it, but Ellen insisted. She did not give the additional money to McGinty and wondered if Ruth kept it hidden for her own use. Lord knew the woman could use it, what with her two frayed dresses and patched shoes.

ONE MORNING IN early December, Charlie showed up with a note for Ellen. It was from Mrs. Gurley, he explained as he took the crushed piece of paper from his pocket. Ellen read it and smiled. "You know what it says?"

He grinned. "You bet."

"What do you think?"

"I think you better say yes. Leastways, I hope you will."

Mrs. Gurley had invited Ellen to spend Christmas on the ranch. Before Charlie left, Ellen had penned a reply, accepting the invitation.

She had already ordered Christmas presents, since she was not sure how long it would take for them to be shipped to Wyoming. Ellen's sister, Lizzie, had picked out a half-dozen lengths of calico in a Chicago store for her to give to Ruth, and Ellen had bought gloves for McGinty from Montgomery Ward & Co. in New York. She'd also ordered a $1.25 gold-filled watch chain for Charlie, because he used a leather thong in place of a chain. She'd liked the solid gold watch chains in the catalogue better, but they were $5.75 and she wasn't sure it was proper to spend that much money on a gift for him—or even to give him a gift at all. She'd decided to wait and see if he gave her something first.

She'd also ordered boxes of chalk to hand out to her students the last day of school before the Christmas holiday. Now that she would spend Christmas with the Gurleys, she sent away to Ward's for a blue bandana for Mr. Gurley and pocketknife for Pike. She would use some of the material her sister had sent to make an apron for Mrs. McGinty.

SCHOOL LET OUT early the day before Christmas. The children rushed off with their chalk, amidst shouts of "Happy Christmas" and "See you next year." As Ellen watched them disappear under a cloudless sky so clear that it made the snow sparkle, she heard the sound of sleigh bells.

"It's Fatback!" Pike yelled. He had stayed behind because he knew Ellen would be going to his ranch later that day and he wanted to ride beside them on his horse. In a minute Charlie stopped the sleigh in front of the schoolhouse.

"Snow's too deep for a buggy, and the sleigh's warmer, too," Charlie explained.

"It's a surprise," Pike whispered. "Fatback spent all day yesterday cleaning out that old sleigh. He'd have painted it, except it's too cold for paint to stick."

"How delightful!" Ellen said, clapping her hands with pleasure as Charlie put Ellen's packages and sack of clothing into the back of the sleigh. She had brought them with her to school that morning. "It looks just like Santa's sleigh in 'A Visit from St. Nicholas.'"

"Mrs. Gurley suggested it."

"No such a thing," Pike said. "It was all Fatback's idea. Ma forgot we even had the sleigh." He gave Charlie a sly grin. "Fatback just wants to sit next to you."

Charlie swatted at the boy, but he was in high spirits as he helped Ellen onto the seat. He threw a fur robe over her. The skin seemed to weigh as much as if it were made of bricks, and Charlie explained it was a buffalo robe. "Warmest fur there is. I had a buffalo coat once. It weighed me down so much I could hardly walk. But if you're out in a blizzard, it'll save your life.

Ellen was already bundled up in a heavy coat, overshoes, and a muffler her sister had sent her for Christmas. It was soft wool in a lovely shade of blue that matched her eyes, and Ellen was proud of it. Lizzie had written that Ellen should open the present early so that she could wear it to the ranch.

The Gurley place was an hour away, and Ellen wondered that Pike was so enthusiastic about school when he had to ride that far and back each day. When they reached the ranch, it was late afternoon. The sky was darkening and the wind had come up, and Ellen was grateful for the buffalo robe. Dogs barked, and the light from kerosene lamps glowed in the windows of the ranch house. The center part of the structure was log, but there were frame appendages. Gurley had built the log cabin first, then added on as he became more prosperous, Charlie explained.

"Do you sleep there?" Ellen asked Charlie.

"The bunkhouse," he said, pointing to a building near the barn. "There's only three of us now along with the foreman. He lives yonder with his wife, but they're away for Christmas. Mr. Gurley'll hire more in the spring."

Pike rode toward the door and yelled, "Ma, she's here!"

The Gurleys had heard the sleigh bells, however, and they stood in the doorway. "Charlie, you get her in here before she freezes," Mrs. Gurley ordered.

Charlie helped Ellen from the sleigh, and Mrs. Gurley hurried her into the house. "You must be froze. Come sit by the fire." She led Ellen to a huge stone fireplace where big logs were burning, then helped her remove her coat. As Mrs. Gurley unwound Ellen's muffler, she ran her fingers over it and said, "My, this is as fine as anything. Margaret, come and look at this."

Ellen noticed the young woman standing in the shadows of the room now and thought she must be the hired girl. She came forward into the light, and Ellen realized there was something different about her. The girl's face was odd, sort of concave, with eyes that bulged, and her arms were hinged in an unnatural way. She smiled and said, "Hi. Hi, Teacher." She reached out her hand and felt the muffler, and her eyes lit up. "Soft," she said.

She started to take the scarf, but Mrs. Gurley said, "No, Margaret. That belongs to the teacher."

"No," the girl said, reluctant to let go of it.

"It doesn't belong to us," Mrs. Gurley said firmly, removing the girl's hand. Then she said, "This is our daughter, Margaret."

Ellen was surprised. Pike had never said anything about a sister. She wanted to ask what was wrong with the girl, but of course she wouldn't. "Hello, Margaret," she said.

"We have a tree," Margaret said. She pointed at a Christmas tree in the corner that was decorated with strings of popcorn and ornaments made from pine cones and pretty paper. "Don't eat the popcorn," she admonished.

"Come and help with dinner, Margaret," Mrs. Gurley said. Ellen started to rise, but Mrs. Gurley put out her hand. "Supper's all ready. We were just waiting for you." She nodded at Pike, who went outside and rang a bell. In a minute, Charlie, Mr. Gurley, and two other men—cowboys—came inside and went to the long dinner table. One of the cowboys eyed Ellen, then nudged Charlie with his elbow. She remembered him from her first trip to the general store, although she wasn't sure if he was the man who'd lost his wages gambling.

Ellen had been used to leisurely suppers with plenty of conversation in the boardinghouse in Iowa, but here everyone concentrated on eating, hunched over, speaking only to ask for the bread or the gravy. Mrs. Gurley moved from the cookstove to the table, bringing more meat and potatoes and then pie. People in Wyoming didn't seem to like green vegetables much, Ellen observed. When they were finished, the two cowboys stood up and said they were going into Wallace and wouldn't be back until after Christmas. Nobody inquired just where they would spend their time.

Charlie and Mr. Gurley seemed ready to leave the table, too, but Mrs. Gurley told them to stay where they were. "It's Christmas Eve, and we have a guest. Those two boys will finish chores before they leave." She set a coffeepot on the table, then sat down with her own plate of food. Mr. Gurley leaned back in his chair until it was resting on two legs and took out a pipe and lit it. Charlie scooted back his chair. He held his tin cup by the bowl and finished his coffee and set it down. Ellen picked up the big pot and filled the cups, even Pike's and Margaret's. She thought how pleasant the scene was and how different from the McGintys' table, where McGinty always had something to complain about and Ruth never opened her mouth.

"Teacher gave me a box of chalk," Pike announced.

Ellen realized then that she should have brought chalk for Margaret—only she hadn't known about Margaret. She didn't have a Christmas present for the girl, and Margaret would be disappointed. Maybe she could order something from the catalogue and give it to Pike to deliver to her later. Of course, that wouldn't be the same as giving Margaret a gift on Christmas Day, but it would have to do.

Mrs. Gurley sat back in her chair and said, "Isn't this a nice Christmas Eve? Snow outside, that old sleigh with its bells, and company."

"Santa's coming," Margaret whispered to Ellen. She smiled at the teacher as if sharing a secret.

Pike shook his head at Ellen, as if to let her know he didn't believe in Santa, but he wouldn't spoil it for his sister.

"How old are you?" Ellen asked.

Margaret thought a minute, then said, "I forgot."

She turned to her mother, who said, "You are sixteen."

"Sixteen," Margaret said.

"I'm fifteen," Pike said.

"Fifteen?" Charlie said. "I thought you were twelve."

Ellen laughed when she saw Pike frown. She turned to Mr. Gurley. "He's one of the smartest boys in the class."

"And the worst behaved, most likely," Mr. Gurley told her.

The conversation was easy, and they teased one another until Mrs. Gurley rose and said she and Margaret had to wash the dishes before she set her bread for the next day. Ellen stood, too, and began clearing the table. Mrs. Gurley pumped water from a pump on the drainboard into a kettle, heated it on the stove, and washed the dishes. Ellen dried, while Margaret set the table for breakfast. The men went into the living room to sit by the fire.

When the dishes were done and Mrs. Gurley had mixed her bread dough, she said it was time for bed. Ellen would share Margaret's bed. "I hope you don't mind. I could fix you a place by the fire, but Margaret was so excited you would sleep with her."

"No, of course not," Ellen replied. "We'll keep each other warm."

"I thought maybe I'd show her the barn first," Charlie said.

"The barn?" Mrs. Gurley exchanged an amused glance with her husband.

"It's real pretty at night in the snow."

"Why, so it is," Mrs. Gurley said. "But don't be too long."

"We might see Santa out there. We'll tell him you're a good girl," Charlie told Margaret.

"I'm a good girl." She beamed.

IN THE MORNING, Ellen awoke to the sound of bells. "Santa," Margaret said, sitting up in bed.

Charlie had told Ellen the night before that he would ring the bells at dawn to wake Margaret. In previous years, the girl had awakened the house at midnight to see if Santa had come. So Mrs. Gurley had told her she could not get up this Christmas morning until she heard the bells.

"Get up." Margaret pushed at Ellen with her hand. "Presents."

Ellen would have preferred to stay in bed. She and Charlie had trudged through the snow to the barn the night before, and Charlie had introduced her to the horses. They'd sat on bales of hay and talked until Ellen's feet were frozen. On the way back to the house, Ellen had made a snowball and thrown it at Charlie's back. He'd turned, startled, then washed her face in snow. When Ellen tried to run away, she'd fallen, and Charlie had picked her up and carried her back to the house. By the time they reached it, they were both laughing, and Ellen had put her finger to her lips, warning him not to wake the Gurleys.

He set her down but didn't let go of her, and then he said, "Damn, I'd like to kiss you!"

"Damn, I wish you would!" Ellen said, wondering if she had been too bold or if her language offended him.

"I guess I will then." He'd given her a light kiss on the lips, and then he turned his head to the side, embarrassed, and said, "Good night, Miss Ellen."

"Good night, Mr. Fatback."

Charlie picked up a handful of snow and dropped it down Ellen's neck, and she shrieked and went inside.

Now she sat up in bed as Margaret said, "Come on!" Margaret, dressed in a long flannel nightgown, went to the door, barely able to wait for Ellen to put on her wrapper. Charlie came inside, stamping snow from his boots, saying he'd seen a fat old man in a red suit outside. The rest of the family emerged, half-dressed. They all gathered in front of the fireplace. Two stockings were hung on nails pounded into the mortar between the stones. Each contained an orange, a peppermint stick, and a sack of chocolate drops. Beneath Pike's stocking was a bridle, and underneath Margaret's was a rag doll. The doll's dress was made of material identical to that of the dress Margaret had worn the day before. Margaret picked up the doll and held it to her face. "Hello, dolly."

"It's a perfect present. She loves it," Ellen said.

Mrs. Gurley nodded. "Last year, she got a china doll, but she dropped it, and the head broke. Margaret was devastated. Before that, it was a wax doll that was left too close to the fire. This one should last longer."

"More presents," Margaret said, pointing to the Christmas tree.

Mrs. Gurley said they would have to wait until everyone was dressed and had finished breakfast.

Breakfast was eaten quickly. Ellen didn't know if that was because everyone was anxious to open presents or if ranch people always ate fast.

"Now?" Margaret asked, and Mrs. Gurley nodded, telling everyone to leave the dishes on the table and gather around the tree.

They opened the presents one by one, prolonging the excitement, because there were not many of them. Each of the children received socks and shirts. Mr. Gurley got a pair of boots, his wife a cast-iron frying pan the size of a washbasin. They gave Charlie a safety razor. Charlie pointed to a package under the tree and said, "Why, I bet that there's for the teacher."

Ellen opened it to find a solid gold horseshoe brooch with a green enamel four-leaf clover in the center. "Oh!" she said.

She knew it cost more than five dollars and wished she had bought the better watch chain for him.

"It's double good luck," Charlie explained.

Ellen went to the bedroom for the presents she had brought. They were wrapped in paper from the mercantile that she had saved and ironed to take out the wrinkles.

Mrs. Gurley exclaimed over the apron and remarked it was much nicer than anything she could make. Mr. Gurley told her that blue was his favorite color and that the bandana would keep the dust out of his mouth. Pike said, "Oh boy," when he unwrapped the pocketknife. Charlie grinned at her as he held up the watch chain and said it was the best present he ever got.

Ellen told Margaret that her present would come later. That way, Christmas would last a long time, she explained, but the girl didn't understand. Margaret was the only one who had not received a gift from Ellen, and she looked ready to cry. Ellen's heart went out to the girl.

Ellen had been sitting on the floor in front of the fire, and slowly she rose and said, "I forgot one present. I must have left it in the other room. She went into the bedroom, then came back and told Margaret, "Why, here it is!" She handed the girl the blue muffler that Lizzie had given her.

Six

It had been a lovely Christmas, and now Ellen snuggled beside Charlie in the horse-drawn sleigh. She thought he might have put his arm around her if he hadn't been holding the reins in both hands. Mrs. Gurley had invited her to stay longer, but it had begun to snow again and they were all concerned there might be a blizzard that could keep her snowbound for days. What if school opened the day after New Year's and the teacher wasn't there? Besides, with the foreman away and two of the cowboys gone and likely to use the storm as an excuse to stay in town, Charlie was busy with ranch duties. The family stood outside and waved—Margaret waving her doll's hand—until the sleigh was out of sight and the sound of the bells could no longer be heard.

"Margaret's a sweet girl. I suppose she was born that way," Ellen observed.

"I reckon," Charlie said. "She's always been like that as far as I know. I wasn't around when she was born."

"Children like Margaret, it makes you wonder where God is."

"Yes, ma'am." He added, "There's a lot of things in Wyoming makes you wonder where God is. Snow's one of them."

Ellen wouldn't let the subject drop. "Mrs. Gurley says Margaret can count to ten, but she has trouble recognizing numbers."

In fact, Ellen had inquired if Margaret had ever attended school. "I've been teaching her at home," Mrs. Gurley replied. "Pike took her to school with him last year, but the teacher didn't want her in class. She said my daughter couldn't learn and that she gave her the willy-wabbles." Mrs. Gurley shook her head. "Miss Frieda said she'd quit before she had to teach a dummy." She snorted. "Not that Margaret made a difference with that teacher. Miss Frieda quit anyway. I suppose you know what happened to her."

Ellen didn't answer, and Mrs. Gurley continued. "The children were mean to Margaret. They called her names. Pike came home every day with bruises he got from fighting the boys who insulted her. After a week, Margaret refused to go anymore, and we didn't see any reason to force her to."

"Maybe she could try again. She might not keep up with the others, but she would learn something. I could keep the children in line. She wouldn't have to worry about their taunts."

"Maybe."

Ellen didn't push it. She wasn't sure herself that it was a good idea. And she had to admit that she didn't know how to teach a child like Margaret.

Now she told Charlie, "Pike looks after his sister."

"That's a good thing. He'll have to take care of her when his folks are gone. It's a heavy burden."

Yes, Ellen thought. *Was God ever in Wyoming?*

THE SNOW WAS coming down steadily when they reached Wallace. The McGintys were not home, so Ellen asked Charlie if he would like to come inside and warm up. He wanted to, but the storm might get worse, and with the other hands away, he ought to get back to the ranch. Ellen watched him until he disappeared in the snow that covered the sleigh's tracks. She went into her room and hung up her coat and her good dress and put Charlie's present in her trunk, where she had stored the lacelike collar that Ruth had made for her out of store string. Ellen had been touched by the gift. With the cooking and cleaning and sewing and laundry, the woman surely had little time to crochet.

The fire in the cookstove was low, but Ellen did not add more wood, knowing it would have to be replaced, probably by Ruth. Wind blowing through the cracks between the boards on the wall made the room even colder. Snow had sifted onto the bed. Ellen was chilled and tired and lay down and covered herself with a worn quilt, thinking she might order a warm wool blanket from the catalogue. She wished she had the scarf her sister had given her to wrap around her neck. Well, it couldn't be helped. She'd have felt guilty if she hadn't given Margaret a present. Ellen put her coat over herself, pretending it was a buffalo robe, and drifted off to sleep.

She was not sure what woke her up. She sat up from a deep sleep, a little disoriented, wondering what time it was and how long she had slept. The room was dark. She brushed off the snow that had accumulated on the bed, then got up and started to light the lamp on the little table but was stopped at the sound of a cry.

For a moment, she wondered if it was coyotes. The howling of coyotes frightened her, although Charlie had said they were cowards and were more afraid of her than she was of them. He said she'd get used to them (although she never did). It was not a coyote howl that she'd heard, however. Maybe a wolf. She had never seen a wolf, but she'd read about them, how they attacked calves. She didn't weigh much more than a calf and knew she could never fight off such a vicious animal. The idea of a wolf lurking outside the thin wall made her shiver.

Then she heard the sound again and realized that it was coming from inside the house and that it was human. She crept to the door and opened it a crack. The big room was lit by a single kerosene lamp in the center of the table. It cast a weak circle of light that did not reach the corners of the room. Ellen glimpsed movement by the cookstove.

"No. Please, Wesley. I'm sorry." The words were low and pleading and filled with anguish.

Ellen opened the door wider and saw that Ruth was leaning over the cookstove, McGinty behind her.

"Not my hands." Her voice was a whimper.

"Teach you this time. You won't do it again. Stupid woman."

They must not know she was there, and Ellen wasn't sure what to do. It wasn't her place to interfere, but she couldn't ignore the fear in Ruth's voice. "What's going on?" she asked, wishing she did not sound so timid.

McGinty whirled around, and Ellen could see the anger in his face. "You! What are you doing here? You ain't supposed to be here."

"I came back early because of the storm."

"You get back in there. This ain't your business."

Ruth had backed away from her husband and slunk into a corner, and Ellen couldn't make her out. For an instant she wondered if the two had only had a disagreement and she had interfered. It was more than that, however. "Ruth?" she asked. She cleared her throat and tried to speak with the authority she used in the schoolroom. "Are you all right?"

"I said get back in there. Women ain't telling me what to do."

Ellen went to the table and picked up the lamp and held it high. She could see Ruth now and the terrified look on her face. The woman held her hands in front of her, not curled but the fingers extended, as if they hurt. "What did he do to you?" Ellen asked.

"He . . ." She glanced at her husband. "He didn't do nothing. It's my fault."

"Fool woman," McGinty growled. "I'm her husband. I got the right. I got the right to kill her if I want. It's her own damn fault, making me out to be a jackass. I ain't putting up with it." He was drunk and slurred his words. He reached out to strike his wife, then must have realized he couldn't do that in front of Ellen. He slammed the table instead—slammed it so hard that he would have knocked over the lamp if Ellen had not been holding it.

"You are shameful!" Ellen said.

He raised his fist as if to strike her but thought better of it and stomped outside, leaving the door open. The wind blew snow into the house, and Ruth came out of her corner and rushed outside. Ellen thought the woman was following her husband, perhaps to urge him to come back. Instead, Ruth thrust her hands into the snow and held them there, an anguished look on her face. After a moment, she returned to the house. Ellen closed the door and would have put the board through the brackets on either side of it to shut him out, but Ruth whimpered, "No. That will only make it worse."

The woman sat down on a chair at the table, her head bowed, her hands in her lap, palms upward.

"What did he do to you?" Ellen asked. She set the lamp on the table so that light encircled Ruth, who hid her hands.

Ellen gently turned them over. "What?" she asked. The hands were red and blistered.

"It was an accident. He didn't mean it."

"They're burned."

"It's my fault. I never should have gone with him, should have let him hit me instead."

"He pushed you and you fell against the cookstove?" Suddenly Ellen realized Ruth hadn't fallen at all. "He held your hands on the stove! He burned you on purpose! Oh, Ruth, how could he!"

"It was almost cold—the stove."

"It was no such thing. Don't you dare defend him. What kind of man would do this, and to his wife!"

"The snow helps. My hands feel better now."

Ellen went to Ruth's sewing basket and removed one of the lengths of calico she'd given the woman for Christmas and tore off two strips, wrapping them around Ruth's hands. Ruth protested, saying the material was too precious, but Ellen told her it could be washed and would be as good as new. When she was done, Ellen built up the fire and made tea.

"What made him do it?" Ellen asked at last. She could not imagine how a man could be so cruel to such a gentle woman.

"We went to the Silver Dollar. I didn't want to. I don't like saloons, and I know to keep away from McGinty when he drinks. But I was afraid to say no. He wore his new gloves, and when somebody asked him where he got them, he said you'd give them to him, that you was sweet on him. He said, 'Schoolteacher ordered them from the Montgomery Ward's. Only thing my wife give me was a shirt.'"

Ellen shuddered. How could anyone think she was sweet on McGinty?

As if knowing what Ellen was thinking, Ruth added quickly,

"Nobody believed him. Everybody thought it was funny to think you care about him, and they laughed. That made him mad." She looked down at her wrapped hands. "Johnny Dare— he's the bartender—asked what he give me. I said nothing, and Wesley told them, 'She don't deserve nothing.'"

In the lamplight, Ellen could see tears on Ruth's cheeks. Ellen put her arm around her friend and said, "That was un- kind. You have been a good wife to him."

Ruth shook her head. "Not good enough, I reckon. They told Wesley he was a cheap old skunk, made fun of him. He was mad all the way home, and when we got here, he said I'd shamed him." She shook her head. "I don't know what I did. He said he'd teach me, and that's when he put my hands on the stove."

"He should be horsewhipped."

"It's not his fault. He got stomped by a mule once. He used to be a good cowhand, but he couldn't work after that, and it did something to his head."

"When was that?"

"Three, four years ago."

Ellen remembered the story of how McGinty had refused to get a midwife for Ruth when she went into labor and knew Ruth wouldn't admit he had always been a cruel man.

Ruth didn't want to talk about the incident anymore and said she ought to be getting supper, but Ellen told her not to touch anything with her hands as bad as they were. She would prepare supper and breakfast, too, and do the cooking until Ruth's hands healed.

ELLEN NEVER CONFRONTED McGinty. She had said her piece when she called him shameful. He was a weak man and feared she might tell others what he had done to his wife. So he kept clear of Ellen and did not abuse his wife, not physically, after that. The three ate their meals in silence, and as soon as he finished supper McGinty went to the Silver Dollar, leaving the women alone. Ellen helped with the cooking, even after Ruth's hands healed. Then the two sat at the table in the lamplight, Ruth grading papers or knitting while Ruth pieced. Often they went to bed before McGinty returned.

Ellen did not care for her bedroom. She nailed pictures cut from magazines on the wall, but there was little she could do to brighten the cheerless room. Since it was far from the cookstove, the room was freezing, and along with a thick flannel gown Ellen wore stockings and sometimes mittens to bed. At first, she had left her door open to the big room in hopes the heat from the cookstove would penetrate, but she had awakened once to find McGinty standing in the doorway, staring at her. After that, she kept the door closed.

She didn't trust the man. She understood now what Frieda had said about enduring old McGinty. She didn't fear him physically. He would never strike her or harm her the way he had his wife. In fact, McGinty probably was more worried about Ellen than she was about him, fearing she would move out and leave him without the income she paid to board. Or she might tell the school board if he acted inappropriately.

Still, she didn't like the way McGinty stared at her or crept around the outside of the house when she was in her room. He never made any noise, but Ellen knew he was there. She hung her coat over the window so that he couldn't look in, but he could still peer inside through the gaps between the boards or the knothole that was across from her bed. In fact, it seemed the knothole had gotten bigger. She began dressing and undressing in the dark. That didn't stop the feeling she was being watched, however. She confirmed she was right after she went to the back of the house one morning and found footprints in the snow.

That night, Ellen waited until McGinty said he was going to check on the horse, as he often did about the time she went to bed. She said good night to Ruth and went into her room, taking her papers and her knitting with her, and closed the door. Instead of undressing, however, she blew out the lamp and sat on the bed until she heard a sound outside, the padding of footsteps in the snow. She waited until they stopped, then slid along the wall until she was next to the knothole. She took her knitting needle and thrust it through the opening. There was a cry and the sound of steps running away.

The next morning, McGinty's eye was red. He said he'd run into a nail sticking out in the barn. Ruth was sympathetic, but Ellen only smiled.

SHE WAS TOO embarrassed by McGinty's spying to tell Charlie, but she did complain to him about the way McGinty treated Ruth. "He burned her hands. I saw it. He did it on purpose," she said.

"That's not right. There's no cause for a man to do that," Charlie replied. "Ought to be taken down."

"You'll do something then? Talk to him, threaten him?"

Charlie shook his head and said much as Ellen wanted him to, he couldn't come between a man and his wife.

Ellen was disappointed, but after she thought about it she realized interfering might only make things worse. There was no law that said a man couldn't discipline his wife, and McGinty might be so mad at Charlie that he would take his anger out on Ruth.

Seven

The winter was long. It snowed often. At times, blizzards made it difficult to see more than a few feet, and once that year Ellen kept the children—even those who lived in town—overnight in the schoolhouse, rather than let them take their chances with the storm. The children played games as the snow blanketed the little building. The boys tied a rope around themselves and fastened it to the schoolhouse door for fear of being lost in the white when they went outside for firewood. They ate crackers and dried beef that Ellen had stocked in case of an emergency. In the evening firelight, she read poetry to them and they told stories. They slept on the floor, wrapped in coats, warmed by the blaze in the potbellied stove.

The children thought it was great fun until they woke hungry and cold, because the fire had gone out. They worried that their parents had gone out in the blizzard to look for them. The snow stopped, and not long after dawn, men on horseback arrived at the school. Ellen thought they might be angry that she had kept their children, but they told her she had done the right thing. She went outside to see that the snow had drifted to the roof of the school. The sun came out, and in a few days there was bare ground.

Other days the sun shone as brightly as if it were summer, making the snow dazzle and turning Ellen's face red if she was outside too long without a hat. She loved the crisp, dry air, although it made her skin flake, and she sent away to Montgomery Ward for jars of cold cream.

Folks might have holed up for the winter months, but instead, they used any excuse to gather. Ranchers invited their neighbors to Sunday dinners, the guests arriving on horseback or in sleighs or wagons. They attended potlucks and taffy pulls and dances held every month at the one-room schoolhouse, which was the only place in Wallace large enough to accommodate them. The tables that served the children as desks were pushed back, leaving a space in the center for dancing. Of course, it was a small area, so only a few couples could dance at one time. Johnny Dare from the Silver Dollar performed with a fiddle and most of the cowboys played the harmonica, so there was music of a kind. When they weren't dancing, the women sat on benches, gossiping, while the men passed around bottles and talked of crops and cattle prices.

Ellen was in great demand as a partner. All the single men—and a few married ones—wanted to dance with the schoolteacher, and she felt she had to oblige them, no matter how much they stepped on her feet. The first time she attended a dance, she wore her best slippers, but they were nearly ruined, so after that she put on boots. Still, when she got home after a dance, she had to soak her feet. To her disappointment, Charlie was no better on the dance floor than the other cowboys. Still, she liked the way he held her, with a certain possessiveness.

After the success of the children's performance at the box supper in the fall, people asked for more school entertainments. Ellen put on a holiday program the week before Christmas and a Valentine's Day performance, although she never again allowed Pike to recite a poem. Town meetings were held in the schoolhouse, too. Politicians came and talked, and women as well as men attended, since women in Wyoming had had the vote for a generation. Wyoming had been the first territory to give women the vote.

One Sunday, a minister asked permission to use the school for religious services. Wallace was growing. More houses had joined the twenty or so that had been there when Ellen arrived. A doctor had moved to town that winter, and now a group of Wallace women invited the minister in hopes he would establish a church. They would see if there was enough support, and they were gratified that not only townspeople but folks from throughout the area came to hear him preach. McGinty derided the preacher, but that didn't deter Ruth from accompanying Ellen to services. There was a look of rapture on Ruth's face when the preaching began. She told Ellen her father had been a minister and she had been raised in a church and had missed it. McGinty refused to give his wife so much as a penny for the collection plate, but she still put in a dime.

Ranch families drove as much as an hour to reach the church meetings, among them the Gurleys. Ellen had been to the ranch several times now, but she had never seen Margaret in a crowd of people and noticed how friendly the girl was, how much she wanted to be with others. When she saw Ellen, she ran to her and cried, "Hi, Teacher!" Ellen held out her hands and told her she was glad Margaret had come. Not everyone felt that way. Margaret approached a girl about her age, one of Ellen's students, who turned away. Two or three people frowned when they saw her, and one asked what she was doing there. Mrs. Gurley went to her daughter's side and took her arm, leading her into the church. The girl seemed to forget the slights when the singing started, and she joined in with a pretty voice. Her mother had taught her the hymns.

Ellen was disappointed that Charlie wasn't with the Gurleys. When she asked about him, Mrs. Gurley told her most cowboys were infidels. Well, maybe he could have come just to see *her*, Ellen thought.

The church services were so successful that after a month the minister was hired and his new congregation started fundraising to build a church.

SPRING CAME SUDDENLY in May. The snow melted, and the grasses turned green. Ellen had arrived in the fall, and she'd thought the prairie was always dull. Now she saw the colors in the earth, the green studded with the red and pink of wildflowers. Even the cactus bloomed. The cottonwood trees budded. Flowers that had been planted by women in the mud of Wallace bloomed in shades of purple and orange. The High Plains weren't lush like the towns along the Mississippi River that Ellen knew, but they were pretty in their way. After the dreary weather of winter, Ellen felt refreshed.

Spring was a busy time on ranches, and although he no longer had to break a trail through the snow to come to Wallace, Charlie visited less often then. Mostly, Ellen saw him when he came to town on some errand and stopped by the schoolhouse to ride home with Pike. The boy gave her a running account of Charlie. "Old Fatback near broke his leg when a mother cow knocked him over," the boy announced one day. Another time he told her Charlie had been bucked off a mean bronco and near stomped to death. Ellen worried, not realizing these were the hazards of ranching and nobody took them as seriously as she did.

When he could get away for an afternoon, Charlie brought Red Girl for her to ride and they loped out onto the plains, stopping at a grove of trees or a pond. Once Ellen picked a horsehair off her jacket and dropped it into the spring.

"Don't do that," Charlie told her.

"What's wrong?"

"Don't you know a horsehair left in a spring turns into a snake?"

"It what?"

"It turns into a snake."

Ellen considered that seriously. "Does it turn into a hoop snake?"

"Aw, you're too smart for me."

Charlie grew serious when he told Ellen about the wildlife that roamed the prairie. The antelope were her favorite. They were curious and would come close if Charlie tied his bandana to a stick and held it up. Then they'd get spooked and would turn and run, their white rumps flashing. Charlie pointed out a rare trumpeter swan that flew over and bald eagles that swooped down from the sky to catch mice or jackrabbits. He named the flowers and shrubs that grew on the flat land or in the arroyos.

When they stopped for lunches that Ellen packed, Charlie spoke of events he'd read about in the newspaper or told Ellen about local politics. There were rumors that Mr. Gurley would run for governor, but Charlie knew his boss wasn't interested. Ellen wondered if she would ever know as much about Wyoming as Charlie did.

ONE SUNDAY, CHARLIE rode into town with the Gurleys, and Ellen was delighted that he would attend church with her. He refused to go inside, however, and waited with his horse until the services were over.

"Why won't you come in?" she asked.

"I'm not much acquainted with the Lord," he replied.

Ellen didn't understand. "Why not?"

Charlie shrugged. "Reasons."

He didn't elaborate and Ellen didn't push, but later she asked Mrs. Gurley about it. "I couldn't say," Mrs. Gurley replied, then thought a minute. "Well, maybe I could. He never told you?"

Ellen shook her head.

Mrs. Gurley sighed. "I'm not one to pass on tales, but you ought to know, you being so special to him. It's a long story. Charlie's brother told me—"

"His brother?" Ellen interrupted. "He never said he had a brother."

Mrs. Gurley held up her hand. "His name was William. He's the one told me about their folks. It happened a few years back, when they were all living in Montana. They raised horses and ran a few cattle. Charlie was in a wagon with his folks. He was driving. The horses got spooked. It might have been a snake, or it could have been anything. Who knows what spooks a horse? Anyway, the horses took off running, and Charlie couldn't stop them. They were heading right toward a drop-off. Charlie tried to turn them, but he couldn't do that either.

"He yelled at his folks to jump. Jumping was dangerous, of course, but if they went over that cliff they'd have been dead for sure. Charlie jumped, and his folks did, too. Nobody knows exactly what happened, even Charlie, but near as he could figure his ma's skirt got caught in the wheel and his pa tried to grab her loose. They got trapped under the wagon and went over the drop and were killed. Charlie went and got William, and the two of them climbed down to bring up the bodies. William said they were so banged up from the fall that you couldn't hardly recognize them. Charlie blamed himself, said it was his fault for driving fast like he did. He was so broke up that he and William left Montana and came here to Wyoming. That's when we hired them."

How awful, Ellen thought. She had lost her own parents, but they had died in bed. She wondered if Charlie still carried the grief, but of course he did. "Where is William?"

Mrs. Gurley looked off across the prairie, then turned back to Ellen. "William got gored by a bull. He and Charlie were working the cattle, and William got off his horse to check its foot, thought maybe the horse had got something under his shoe. Charlie was watching William, and neither one of them saw the bull until it was too late. That bull came charging out of nowhere. It went after William and ripped open his stomach. I saw the body. William's guts were spilled out. Charlie wanted to go for a wagon to take his brother to the house, but William knew there was no use. He told Charlie he didn't want to die alone. He wanted his brother beside him. So Charlie stayed with him till he passed on. It wasn't more than a few minutes. Charlie loaded William's body on his horse, and then he took out his gun and shot that bull dead. It was a prize bull. We'd paid a lot of money for it, but Mr. Gurley never said a word about it to Charlie. He told me he'd have done the same thing. Saddest thing that ever was." Mrs. Gurley stopped, remembering. Then she said, "That's why Charlie Bacon doesn't have truck with the Lord."

Ellen closed her eyes when Mrs. Gurley was finished. Charlie had seemed so easygoing, so good-natured, that she couldn't imagine he had endured such tragedy. Ellen had told him about her parents' deaths, but he had never talked about his family, had told her only that they were gone and hadn't wanted to elaborate, so she'd never questioned him. "I'm so sorry," she said, thinking those words were inadequate.

"We all are. It wasn't my place to tell you, Ellen. It's personal. So don't let on to Charlie I did. But I thought you ought to know. I can see he thinks highly of you. He's kind of opened up to you. Charlie hasn't cared about anybody since William died, and I wouldn't like to see him get hurt again."

"No."

Charlie came toward them then, and Ellen did her best to smile. "I was thinking it was a mighty pretty day for a ride," he said.

"You take my horse for her, Charlie. I'll ride home in the wagon with Pike and Margaret."

"Yes, ma'am," he said, tipping his hat at her. Charlie untied Mrs. Gurley's horse and moved to help Ellen mount, but she said she had to go home and change into her riding clothes. Leading the horses, the two of them walked toward the boardinghouse. After a time, Ellen reached out and took Charlie's hand.

THOSE WERE THE best days, the days between winter's cold and summer's heat, when the air was mild and the prairie was in bloom. Charlie came for her at unexpected moments, sometimes with a horse for her to ride. Other times they went for walks through Wallace and out onto the plains. Charlie pointed out badger holes and trails left by rodents, showed her a coyote den. Coyotes were called God's dogs, Charlie told her. "When the Lord made coyotes, He had a reason," Charlie said. "But I surely couldn't tell you what that reason was."

On a sunny Saturday in May, not long before school was to close for the summer, Charlie took Ellen for a ride out on the prairie. He had invited her the week before, and Ellen had prepared a picnic. That day, they followed a stream for miles until they came to a grove of cottonwood trees.

"Don't get too close to the bank," Charlie warned. "Spring runoff makes the water so fast it can pull you right in." He stripped a branch off a cottonwood and dropped it into the stream, where it swirled around in the churning water and disappeared.

"Everything's so different here," Ellen told him. "The Mississippi is a mile wide and has as much water as an ocean and is filled with sandbars and snags. Back there, this would be only a slippery little creek."

"Wyoming's different, all right. You think you could come to like it right well?"

"I already do. I'm thinking of staying on another year."

Charlie didn't say anything. He went to his horse and removed the lunch sack that Ellen had prepared. He spread a blanket on the ground under the cottonwoods, and Ellen set out the picnic.

"This is as pretty a place as I've ever seen in Wyoming," Ellen said, handing Charlie a jar of pickles to open. She had helped Ruth bottle them in the fall.

"I know another just as nice. There's a homesteader giving up over past the Gurleys'. Fellow said I could buy him out cheap."

"You'd be a farmer?" she asked, surprised. She couldn't imagine him giving up ranching.

"A rancher. I've got ambition. I want to do more than eat, drink, and ride a pony all day. I've been thinking I ought to buy a place. I could grow hay and potatoes, maybe other crops, build up a herd. Mr. Gurley said if I was to help him when he needs me, he'd let me run a few cows on his land. It's a real generous offer."

"Why, that's wonderful. How far away is it?" She wondered if she'd see much of Charlie if he went to ranching. Maybe she wouldn't see him at all; maybe this was his way of ending their friendship. Ellen felt a weight on her heart as she stared at him, thinking, as she had that first day, how handsome he was. But he was so much more than that—kind, intelligent, generous. She was fond of him.

"Up north, just past where Gladys and Morris live. I got money saved up. My folks left . . ." He stopped and studied Ellen. "Mrs. Gurley said she told you about them."

"She did. I'm so sorry, Charlie—"

He waved his hand. "Nothing to talk about."

"No." She wished he'd open up, but she'd learned that cowboys kept things bottled up. Perhaps he'd be more forthcoming in time.

They ate in silence for a few minutes.

Charlie started to say something, then closed his mouth and thought for a minute before he spoke. He looked away and said, "They might have to find another teacher."

Ellen looked at him in surprise. She'd never inquired if the school board wanted her to continue teaching but had just assumed she'd be asked to remain. Mrs. Gurley was a member of the board. Had she told Charlie they were dissatisfied with her? Where would she go if she had to leave? "I don't understand. Don't they want me?"

"Oh, I reckon they do. It's just I want you more."

"What?"

Charlie looked back at her, then turned red with embarrassment. "Well, you see, I was thinking that it would be lonely on that ranch all by myself, and me and you get along pretty good, and I think you like me as much as I do you, and oh heck, Miss Ellen, this wasn't the way I planned it at all."

Ellen bit the sides of her cheeks to keep from smiling. "Planned what?"

"Well, you know, the only reason I'd go to ranching in the first place is if you were to marry me. Don't you think that's a fine idea?"

"Charlie Bacon, are you proposing to me?"

"I think I just did. You going to make me wait for an answer?"

"Not on your life. I accept your proposal."

Charlie leaned over to kiss her and said, "Miss Ellen—"

"No more *Miss* Ellen, just Ellen from now on. And you can take off your hat when you kiss me."

"Is that all the change I got to make?"

Ellen shook her head. "I won't have a husband who chews tobacco."

Charlie thought a minute, then reached into his shirt pocket and removed a pouch, flinging it into the creek. "Done," he said. "Now I got to ask a thing of you. Don't you ever serve me vinegar pie. I don't ever want us to think we're so broke we have to eat vinegar pie. Why, it would mean I couldn't provide for you."

"Done," Ellen agreed.

Charlie took off his hat.

Eight

The wedding did not take place until June, after Charlie had built a house for Ellen.

Not long after they became engaged, Charlie borrowed the Gurley buggy and took Ellen to see the homestead. It was indeed a pretty place—pretty for the windblown High Plains, that is. Ellen was used to Wyoming now and she loved the far view with not a thing to block it. There was a clump of cottonwoods and an old sod house on the homestead site. Ellen knew soddies—made of strips of prairie grass stacked one on top of another—were warm in winter and cool in summer, and while she didn't much like the idea of living in a dirt house, she thought she could put up with it until they built one of lumber. The house really didn't matter. She could live anywhere with Charlie, she thought.

"The soddy's well built, and I can tack material on the ceiling to keep the dirt from falling down. I'll plaster the walls with clay and water," Charlie told her. He had cleaned up the place earlier, had swept out the clods of dirt that had fallen from the ceiling and repositioned sod that had slipped out of place. He had repaired the broken glass in the window. Charlie had even fashioned a way to keep the door secure on the inside, since there would be times when he would be away and he wanted Ellen to feel safe when she was there alone. As he opened the door for Ellen and saw the way the sun illuminated the room, he was sure she would like it

Ellen stepped inside. She had been in sod houses before and was aware that this one was nicer than most, was larger and snug. She didn't mind living in one, at least for a year or two. She thought it would do nicely. Then suddenly she screamed and put her hand over her mouth. She backed into Charlie, who was standing in the doorway. "What?" he asked.

"There!" Ellen sucked in her breath as she pointed at the sod wall. A snake was making its way into the room between two layers of sod. It dropped to the floor and slithered toward them, its tongue flicking back and forth. Ellen turned and ran outside. "Kill it! Kill it!"

"It's just a snake. I'll get you a hoe so's you can kill them when they come around."

Ellen had backed away and climbed into a corner of the buggy, her arms wrapped around herself.

Charlie frowned. He didn't like snakes either, but they were a fact on the prairie. He'd never thought of Ellen as being squeamish. The snake hadn't coiled, and Charlie smashed its head with his boot. "Best not to touch it. A serpent's tail doesn't die till sundown." He smiled at another of his snake jokes.

Ellen didn't smile. Instead, she whispered, "It's a rattlesnake! I hate them. I hate them more than anything in the world." As she looked at the dead snake, Ellen knew she shouldn't be hysterical, but when she saw it squeezing between the sod layers she couldn't help it. Her mind had gone back to when she was a little girl and a boy had handed her a wriggling sack, claiming there was a kitten inside. When

Ellen took it into the schoolhouse and opened it, a rattlesnake fell out and bit her. She remembered the teacher screaming and a boy killing the snake. The teacher picked her up and ran almost a mile with Ellen in her arms until they reached a doctor's office. Ellen developed a fever and was in bed a long time. She had been terrified of snakes ever since and sometimes had nightmares of them crawling over her while she slept. McGinty had killed a rattler in the barn and held it up to show her, and Ellen had felt faint. Her hands and forehead had grown wet with perspiration. With great difficulty she had acted unafraid, because she sensed that if he knew how snakes terrified her he would torment her with them.

"I'm sorry, Charlie," Ellen said as he climbed into the buggy beside her and took her hands, soothing her as he might a frightened colt. "Something happened a long time ago." She told him the story, then added, "I am so afraid of them. I could never live in a soddy where I'd always be watching the walls to see if one was coming in. I couldn't sleep at night for fear a rattlesnake would fall on top of us. Couldn't we build a house now, before we're married?"

Because Charlie loved her and wanted to please her, because he knew that life was hard on a Wyoming ranch and broke many women, he agreed. "It'll have to be a small place. I can't spend much time on it, what with crops to be planted, but we can do it. I'll get Pike to help me, and maybe Mr. Gurley will loan me one of the hands."

"Small is all right with me. It means less housekeeping." She put her arms around Charlie's neck and drew him to her, and he knew he would build her a mansion if she asked him to.

Ellen was ashamed at her fecklessness. She vowed that no matter how much she had to grit her teeth or calm her churning stomach, she would overcome her fear of rattlesnakes and learn to kill any that she encountered. She'd never let Charlie down like that again.

THE HOUSE WAITED until Charlie had finished the planting, and then it went up quickly. It was small, made of batten-and-board construction with a sheet metal roof. There was just one room with a door and two widows and no insulation. Charlie had built a bed in the corner, a sort of scaffold attached to the wall and supported by one leg, and there were cupboards made from boxes and a pie safe with hearts and their initials in the punched tin inserts. A cowboy at the Gurley ranch made it for him. Charlie had constructed a bench so that the two of them could sit outside in the evenings and watch the sunset. Ellen ordered kitchen chairs from Montgomery Ward and hung yellow curtains in the windows. She'd sewn them by hand, because she did not have a sewing machine. The centerpiece of the house was a fine cookstove that Ellen paid for out of her teacher's salary. At first, she had wanted to order a six-burner model with a warming closet and hot water reservoir, but Charlie pointed out that a stove that size would take up half the space in the house. So she had purchased a Dandy Windsor four-hole model and had it shipped from Buffalo, New York.

After Charlie installed the stove, Ellen and Ruth rode out to the homestead in the McGinty buggy so that Ellen could show it off. "Oh my!" Ruth exclaimed. "Brand-new! Look how the nickel gleams against that black."

"I'll have to work to keep it looking new," Ellen said.

"Well, I'd scrub mine all day long if it would look like that. I expect I ought to give you a can of stove black for a wedding present."

"I don't want you to give me anything. After all the help you've been to me, that is enough." She touched Ruth's arm. "You'll come and visit, won't you?"

"'Course I will. I'll miss you, Ellen." Ruth brushed her eyes with her arm. "I never enjoyed a person as much as I do you."

"You'll have the new teacher boarding with you next year." Ellen knew the school board had already advertised for her replacement.

Ruth shook her head. "McGinty's already found us a boarder, a fellow he knows from someplace."

"A cowboy?" But a ranch hand wouldn't board in town, Ellen thought. He probably was a clerk. Or maybe he was the new minister. Ruth would like that.

Ruth shook her head. "He does odd jobs."

"Is he a nice fellow?"

"I don't like him much. You know him. Name's Wade Snyder."

Ellen did indeed know him—McGinty brought Snyder home sometimes, and the way the man stared at her made Ellen uncomfortable. "Maybe he could give you a hand around the place so you wouldn't have to chop wood and care for the horse. He might even shame your husband into doing more of the work." Perhaps she shouldn't have said that, but she and Ruth had grown close and Ellen spoke her mind more often now.

"Maybe." Ruth said. "It's for sure he won't be sitting at the table of an evening, keeping me company."

THE WEDDING WAS a simple one, but then most country weddings were. The church wasn't finished, so Mrs. Gurley offered the ranch for the ceremony. Ellen wanted it in the schoolhouse, however. Under the direction of Ellen's favorite student, Hattie, the children decorated it with crepe paper streamers and flowers from their mothers' gardens. They cut out hearts and colored them and hung them around the room, while Hattie used chalk to draw a big heart pierced by an arrow on the blackboard. Ruth pushed the tables used for desks together and spread a cloth over them for the cakes and lemonade that she and others would bring. Mr. Gurley contributed a half-dozen bottles of whiskey. At first Ellen objected to the liquor, but Charlie insisted the men expected it, and she decided that after all, it was Charlie's wedding, too.

The Gurleys stood up with them, and the new minister performed the ceremony in front of the blackboard. With Ruth's help, Ellen had made a wedding dress of creamy white Japanese silk she'd ordered from Ward's. It wasn't practical—where in Wyoming could she ever wear it again?—but this was a special day. Hattie made her a wreath of daisies for her head, and Ellen carried a daisy bouquet, tied with white ribbons. When he saw her coming through the schoolhouse door on Mr. Gurley's arm, her dress shimmering like dew on the early morning sage, Charlie couldn't help but sigh. His eyes shone, and he bit his lip to hide his grin. He thought she was as fresh and pretty as dawn.

Ellen walked toward Charlie, who was standing in front of the big heart, and she smiled, and for a moment he was the only one in the room.

After the ceremony was over and Charlie had kissed his new wife, guests came up to congratulate them and write "Best wishes" and other comments on the blackboard. Some were coarse, and Ellen blushed when she read them.

She hadn't expected so many guests, but the entire community was there. The schoolchildren attended, of course, along with their families. But childless couples and those whose offspring were grown came out, along with the Gurley cowboys and the merchants. Johnny Dare brought his fiddle so that people could dance. Gladys came with her husband and infant son, Bailey, and Ellen glimpsed Frieda, dressed in what must have been her schoolteacher's outfit. Ellen didn't mind that Frieda attended—nobody else did either. In fact, Ellen thought it was nice that folks didn't turn up their noses at the prostitutes, just considered them part of the town.

"I'm sorry we haven't gotten to know each other. We had a lot in common," Frieda said after she congratulated the bride. She laughed. "I mean, we were both teachers." Frieda waved to Ruth but ignored McGinty, who smirked at her. Ruth looked lovely, Ellen thought. She was dressed in a black silk gown with a train that was years out of date but flattered her nonetheless, and Ellen realized the woman might have been a beauty in her day. Why in the world had she married McGinty?

Ellen didn't dwell on the thought, because this was a day of great happiness, maybe the best day she had ever had—or ever would have. The only disappointment was that her sister was not there. The two had always been close. Lizzie's letters had made Ellen less lonely when she arrived in Wallace, and they helped her through the dreary days of winter. Ellen hoped that Lizzie would make the trip for the wedding, but she understood that her sister could not leave her home because she had just had a baby. She would be there in spirit, Lizzie wrote, and later she would come for a visit, when she could have Ellen all to herself. In the meantime, Lizzie sent a silver teapot with a matching sugar bowl and creamer. Ellen laughed at the gift, because it was far too elegant for a prairie shack—a gray speckled pot would have been more useful—but she treasured it because it had come from Lizzie.

There was dancing into the afternoon and loud singing as more bottles appeared. When it was time for the bride and groom to leave, Pike said he would get the wagon for them. Charlie had purchased the wagon, which was far more practical on a farm than a buggy, a few days before. Pike returned with the vehicle decorated with red bows and a string of tin cans ten feet long. He must have gone through every trash pile in Wallace to find them.

With the wedding gifts piled in the bed of the wagon, the couple rode off to the cheers of their friends. When they were out of sight, Charlie stopped and removed the tin cans, but Ellen told him to leave the bows in place. "We'll decorate the house with them to remind us of this day," she said.

"You think I'd ever forget it?" Charlie asked. With the wagon stopped, he put his arms around her and kissed her with more passion than he had shown at the church. Then he held her with one arm and drove with the reins held in his free hand.

It was close to evening now, and while the trip took well over an hour, neither of them minded. Halfway home, Charlie spotted a herd of antelope and reached in back for his rifle. "That's a bit of luck. We'll have fresh meat," he said.

He aimed the gun, but Ellen told him no. "Don't shoot it. Please, Charlie." When Charlie started to protest, she added, "Today is about life, not death. I don't want to spoil my wedding with a killing. Let it live."

Charlie put the rifle back in the wagon bed. "I wonder if that antelope knows how lucky he is that my new wife is so soft." He liked that about Ellen, that she was kind. The two watched the antelope bound off before Charlie picked up the reins again. "It's just as well. I wouldn't want to get blood all over my new shirt."

Ellen slid over next to him on the wagon seat and put her arm through his. "Thank you, Charlie."

They rode along without talking, into a glorious sunset that was shafts of purple and pink, the clouds edged with gold from the dying sun. Darkness was coming on by the time they reached their place. They unloaded the presents and the food from the reception that Mrs. Gurley had insisted they take with them. Charlie found a match and lit the kerosene lamp on the table. Beside the lamp was a glass jar of flowers. "Gladys asked me if she could put them there," Charlie said. "She wanted you to have something pretty when you arrived." Gladys was their nearest neighbor, and Ellen hoped the two women would become friends.

Ellen had been at the house the week before, had filled the mattress ticking she'd stitched with prairie grass and placed it on the bed, had made up the bed with new sheets and a blanket. She'd brought her mother's painting called *A Yard of Pansies* and hung it on one wall. She'd frame her marriage certificate and hang it, too. Now she noticed a quilt spread over the bed. It was made up of intricate pieces in a pattern of stars. As she ran her hand over the spread, she recognized some of the materials that her sister had sent to her to give her landlady at Christmas. "Ruth must have made this. It's our wedding quilt," Ellen said. She was touched by the bed covering, which must have taken hours of work and been assembled in secret. She realized that Ruth would have had to purchase the batting and binding and thread and how she must have scrimped to do so.

"She wanted to surprise you. She came all the way out here just to put it on the bed," Charlie told her.

He said he would unhitch the horses and feed them, then milk the cow, and he left Ellen alone. She placed the food in the pie safe, then stacked the wedding presents on the floor to be put away later. She stared at the bed for a long time, then put her arms around herself and smiled. She removed her wedding dress and placed it in her trunk.

When Charlie returned, he found his bride wearing a long white nightgown, the shape of her body illuminated by the lamplight behind her. He stood still staring at her. Her hair curled around her shoulders. Charlie had never seen her with her hair down. He had thought she was beautiful when he saw her walking into the schoolroom earlier that day in the silk dress, but now she looked like pictures he'd seen of angels. He opened and closed his fingers, then wiped his hands on his pants, thinking she was so small and delicate that he might break her.

"With all the refreshments at the reception, I didn't know if you'd want any supper," she said, her voice breaking.

"I'm not hungry," he replied, his voice raw. He took a step toward her, and Ellen came forward into his arms.

Nine

Ellen would always remember their first summer together like a talisman, holding on to the memories in hopes those times would come again. She would recall the glistening days when the sky was bluebird blue, when the dew at sunrise sparkled on the grasses, when there was just enough rain to make things grow. There were violent sunsets that mirrored her passion for Charlie and his for her. She would remember how much in love they were, how they could not keep their hands off each other. Sometimes Charlie held on to her for no reason, burying his head in her breast, and she thought of how he had lost his family and vowed she would never hurt him, never make him sorry he had opened his heart to her. He would never lose her.

As the years went on, their affection would deepen, especially as hardships came and they clung to each other. Challenges might drive others apart, but not them. Hard times would only strengthen their love. They had no idea what lay ahead, and maybe it was a good thing. That first summer was one of supreme happiness with no knowledge of what the future held.

They rose at four in the morning, grinned at each other across the table as they ate breakfast, the dawn light shining golden through the yellow curtains. Charlie milked the cow and fed the horses before he left for the fields or the Gurley ranch. Ellen fed the chickens Mrs. Gurley had given her and cleaned the chicken house and tended her garden, glancing up from time to time to see if Charlie had found an excuse to come home for a few minutes. She canned tomatoes and peaches that were shipped to Wallace from Colorado, and a side of beef the Gurleys gave them, because fresh beef did not keep in the hot months. Once a week she heated water in a boiler on the cookstove and used a washboard to scrub their clothes, wringing them out by hand because she didn't have a wringer, then hanging them on a wire stretched between two poles. The next day she ironed everything—aprons, pillow-cases, even sheets. Sometimes she walked out into the field to see where the hay was coming up or rode in the wagon with Charlie to Plug Hat Creek for water, which they brought home in barrels. A well would come later. At the end of the day, they lingered over supper, talking of what they had done and their hopes for the future. They played checkers or Authors, or Ellen read aloud the old news on the newspapers Charlie had nailed up as wallpaper. Charlie taught her cowboy songs. They were in bed by dark and sometimes before.

Ellen reveled in her responsibilities as housekeeper. She knew how to cook and was thrilled to have her own kitchen, simple as it was, in which to experiment. There was much to learn, however. The week before the wedding, Charlie had stocked the larder with huge sacks of flour and sugar and beans. Their meals were made up principally of potatoes, rice, dried beans, dried corn, and bread, with sometimes tomatoes or fruit when Charlie brought them home. Ellen almost cried when she removed her first loaves of bread from the oven to discover they were flat and hard. The yeast from the Wallace store was bad.

Gladys came to the rescue when she called a week later, handing Ellen a container of sourdough starter. "Somebody gave it to me when I was first married. I tried to make my own yeast by boiling cornmeal and hops, but it took forever and stunk like a skunk. This was a lifesaver," she said before she explained to Ellen how to use the starter to make bread. "You add it to your flour and milk, but save you a piece and feed it with a little flour for the next batch of bread. Keep on doing that, and your starter will last forever. 'Course in the winter, you got to keep it warm so it don't freeze; maybe take it to bed with you. There's women here that have starters that's ten years old." She thought a minute, then laughed. "Starter's good for other stuff, too. A fellow came by the house to see Morris last spring. He was driving a Model T motorcar instead of riding a horse, and he ran over a rock that punctured his oil pan. Him and Morris mended it with a plug of my starter, and it held till he got back to Wallace."

As she set the container on the table, Gladys looked around the house and sighed. "My, but you got it nice here. I never saw a pie safe so pretty." Then she pinched the quilt between her fingers and told Ellen, "This material's choice. Ruth didn't get it from no mercantile in Wallace. Wonder where she got the money. Old McGinty didn't give it to her, the skinflint."

"You know him?" Ellen asked.

"Not in the biblical sense, if you know what I mean." She winked at Ellen. "I guess you do know what I mean. I expect you've heard where Morris met me."

Ellen shrugged.

"At the Columbine. That's a fact. I don't mean no embarrassment, but it don't matter to him, so why should it matter to anybody else?"

"It's not my business," Ellen said.

"Right you are." Gladys thought for a moment. "Sorry, I didn't mean to sound like that. It just riles me when women think they're better than we girls. Fact is, we had standards at the Columbine. That's why old McGinty wasn't allowed in the place, the bastard. He liked to hurt the girls. It's a wonder his wife stays with him."

"Where could she go?" Ellen asked.

"That's the shame of it. When you're married to a man like that, there ain't no place you can go except the graveyard."

The two women were silent for a time; then Gladys said, "Well, ain't this a nice conversation for a social call on a bride! I brought you something else." She reached into a sack and removed a stem wrapped in wet burlap. "It's a cutting from my yellow rosebush. I'll show you how to plant it. I don't know how I learned to raise flowers; I just always knowed. You manure it and water it when it's dry, and it'll grow even in Wyoming. The canes are downright cruel with all those thorns, but the roses will bloom half the summer for you. There's nothing so pretty, except maybe hollyhocks. I don't know how I came to forget to bring you hollyhock seeds. I'll fetch them to you next time."

Gladys had brought her baby, of course, and set him on the bed to nap, and the two women went outside and planted the cutting beside the door.

They were sitting at the table drinking leftover breakfast coffee that Ellen had heated and poured into the silver teapot when Charlie came in. "My first caller," Ellen said, nodding at Gladys.

"And one who's almost wore out her welcome by staying too long," Gladys said, getting up.

Ellen and Charlie watched her ride off holding the baby. "She's going to help me plant a flower garden," Ellen said.

"She'll be a good neighbor. Morris is lucky to have her. Those girls can make fine wives." He paused. "You don't mind that she . . . ?"

"Why would I mind? She's a good woman."

"So are you."

THERE WERE OTHER callers, women mostly, because summer was a busy time and men couldn't get away. Ellen was grateful for their company. As a teacher always surrounded by children, she wasn't used to being alone. Hattie came. Ellen had not realized the girl lived close by and was delighted to see her. Hattie was upbeat and never tired of helping Ellen with washing the dishes or hanging up the laundry. Ellen loaned Hattie books, and the two talked about the contents. They read newspapers out loud when they could get them. The two gossiped and laughed, and Ellen confided in her, because their age difference was not so great.

Ruth called a few times, although she never stayed long, fearful that McGinty would come home and find her gone and accuse her of all sorts of things. Ruth was thinner and more harried than she had been in the spring, but she never complained. When Ellen inquired how things were going, Ruth replied only that she missed her.

"How is Mr. Snyder working out?" Ellen asked.

Ruth shrugged. "He's tolerable."

"Is he trouble?"

"I see you planted you a rosebush. I always liked a rose, but I never could grow them."

"Gladys gave it to me. She's been quite neighborly."

"Her husband's a worker. I expect she is, too."

Ellen asked about a bruise on Ruth's face, and Ruth explained she had run into the door. "Don't tell me that," Ellen replied. "I know what goes on. If you ever want to come and stay here, you are welcome."

She told Charlie about that, and he frowned. "I don't know it's right to come between a man and his wife. It's not our business."

"How can you say that? He hurts her. That makes it *my* business."

"I wouldn't feel right," he said, and they left it at that.

Ellen didn't bring up the subject again, but she noticed that at church Charlie studied Ruth, as if searching for signs of abuse. Charlie escorted Ellen to church every Sunday, but he didn't go inside. He waited with the wagon until services were over, then drove Ellen home.

"WHO IS THAT?" Ellen asked one day. She and Charlie had been standing in the yard when a wagon came barreling down the road. The woman driving it was wiry, and her face was tan and wrinkled. She looked straight ahead and didn't return Ellen's wave. "She's come past here before."

"Oh, that's Frances Ferguson." Charlie chuckled. "She drives like she's being chased by Indians."

"She's not very friendly."

"No, I doubt she has a friend in a hundred miles."

Ellen was curious. "Why's that?"

Charlie stared at the dust settling in the road, then turned to Ellen. "I think she's still mad at everybody in Wyoming, and it's been thirty years, forty years, something like that."

"What happened?"

"It's a long story. I wasn't here then, but folks still talk about it." Charlie took off his Stetson and wiped his forehead with a bandana, then replaced the hat. "You ever hear of the Willis family? They moved on quite a while back."

Ellen shook her head.

"No reason you would. They weren't too highly thought of."

"Get on with it," Ellen told him.

Charlie grinned. "It's a pretty fine story, worth waiting for. Ben Willis was a good-looking fellow."

"As good-looking as you?"

Charlie grinned at her. "Not quite. Nobody is."

"I should have known better than to ask." She took Charlie's hand, and the two started walking back toward the house.

"Seems he met Frances when he went to Kansas City with a load of cattle. He got to romancing her and what all. She said he proposed marriage and that he had to go home to Wyoming, but he'd come back for her. He never did. Before he left, he got her in the family way, and when Ben didn't show up, she came to Wyoming to claim him. She hired a man in Wallace to take her and her trunk to the Willis ranch and went up to the door to surprise Ben. He was surprised all right. So was Ben's wife."

"How awful!" Ellen said. "What happened?"

"Way I heard it, both women lit into Ben. The wife says, 'You can have him,' and Frances told her she didn't want him now."

"Didn't Frances go home?"

"Nope. She'd sold her farm—she had a bit of money—and I guess she was afraid of going back to Kansas City in her condition. Instead, she bought a ranch and stayed on here. That's when things got to be a real mess. It seems Ben's wife couldn't have any children, so after Frances's baby was born, Ben and his wife tried to take it away. They were a mean couple. They even went to court, claiming Frances was an unfit mother because she got pregnant when she wasn't married. It was quite a scandal, so I heard, with folks taking sides. The judge said if that was so, then Ben was an unfit father, because he'd had carnal knowledge of a woman who wasn't his wife. He said neither one could raise the baby and was about to send the baby off to an orphanage when Frances said that wasn't right. She'd rather Ben and his wife took him. They did and wouldn't let Frances visit him."

"What became of him?"

"That's the worst part of all. He got trampled by a horse when he was just a tyke and died. After that, the Willises pulled out. Funny thing is some people blamed Frances for the boy's death because she gave him up. They said she was an unnatural mother. She's a bitter old lady and won't have anything to do with her neighbors. I think you can forget about making friends with her."

ELLEN DIDN'T FORGET. When she could get away from her chores, she returned the calls her neighbors had made on her, sometimes taking a jar of relish or a batch of fudge she'd made. When Charlie brought home a bushel of Colorado peaches he bought at the mercantile in Wallace, she bottled most of them, but some were left over and one morning Ellen made a peach pie for supper and a second one to take to Frances Ferguson. She didn't know why. For all she knew, the woman would refuse it.

Ellen told Charlie what she had done, and he said to forget it. Other people—even Mrs. Gurley—had tried to make friends with the old woman, and she'd slammed the door in their faces. "I wouldn't want you to get your feelings hurt, honey. Your heart's too tender. There's some folks you just can't turn, and she's one."

"I have to try," Ellen said as she climbed onto the wagon seat. The pie was wrapped in a towel and placed in the wagon bed behind her.

Ellen had been past the Ferguson ranch. It was one of the best in the area. The frame house was painted and the outbuildings in good shape. A windmill flapped near the barn. Miss Ferguson lived alone, except for the cowboys who worked for her. The road leading to the house was graded, and Ellen saw curtains fluttering in the windows. They appeared to have been starched and ironed. There was no sign of the owner, and Ellen thought she might be out with the cattle, but when she reached the porch, the door opened and Miss Ferguson stepped outside. She didn't say anything, just stared at Ellen.

Ellen wondered then if she'd come on a fool's errand. The woman probably didn't want a pie any more than she wanted a visit from a nosy neighbor. Ellen cleared her throat and said, "I'm Ellen Bacon. We—that is, my husband Charlie and I—live down the road. We're new."

Miss Ferguson looked at her for a long time, then said, "You think I don't know who you are?"

"Oh." The two stared at each other for a minute; then Ellen said, "Charlie brought home a bushel of peaches from Wallace, and I had some left over after I finished canning, so I made peach pies. I brought you one." She held out the pie, wondering if Miss Ferguson would tell her she didn't want it. Maybe she wouldn't even do that. She might just close the door.

"Why'd you do that?"

"I thought you might like peaches."

"You didn't come to see if I was dead?"

That was so preposterous that Ellen grinned. "If I had, I wouldn't have brought a pie."

Miss Ferguson chuckled. "It's been a long time since I tasted a peach." She didn't invite Ellen inside. Instead, she took the pie and went into the house, then came back with the empty pie tin. "Thank you," she said, handing it to Ellen. The woman seemed to struggle with the words, and Ellen knew they were hard to come by. Before Ellen could reply, Frances closed the door.

Miss Ferguson didn't return the call, but the next time she drove by the Bacon place she waved.

Ten

By late fall, Ellen knew she was pregnant. That wasn't something you announced. You just waited until folks noted a woman's change in shape, and then it was appropriate for women to comment. (But not men.) Mrs. Gurley was the first. "When your time comes," she told Ellen, "you move in here with us. You don't want to be out there by yourself with Charlie maybe working a mile away. We can keep an eye on you. We're closer to town and the doctor, too." She added, "Margaret would be so pleased."

Ellen felt a brief moment of shame. She had decided not to invite Margaret to attend school, fearing that the school might have bad memories for the girl. But was that really the reason? Perhaps she simply hadn't wanted to deal with the girl's problems. What if her own baby turned out to be like Margaret? How would she feel if the teacher didn't want the child in school?

Charlie was thrilled at the idea of a baby, of course. He treated Ellen as if she were as fragile as an apronful of eggs. Ellen felt like she had passed some kind of test. After all, it was a woman's job to produce children. Still, she was ambivalent since she hadn't planned on starting a family so soon.

And apprehensive because she didn't know a thing about pregnancy and childbirth. She could have asked Mrs. Gurley, but she felt self-conscious about doing so. Instead, she turned to Gladys.

"Having a baby smarts some. I have to say that," Gladys told her. "But not no more than maybe breaking your leg, not that I've ever broke my leg. It's kind of messy, too." She considered what else to reveal. "I have to say I'd rather buy a baby at the mercantile than go through that again. It sure makes you know God ain't no woman." She chuckled. "Having a baby just takes a day or so, and the best part is when it's over, you're not pregnant no more. It's being pregnant that's no fun. I threw up for three months; then I got big as a sack of potatoes. My back hurt. I couldn't bend over, and when I turned on my stomach at night, it felt like I'd fell on a water barrel. Other than that, it's not so bad." Gladys arched her back. "Of course, when you're all done, you have the sweetest, cutest baby in the world, and that makes it all worth it."

"I've never taken care of a baby. What do you do with it?" Ellen asked. She was embarrassed at her ignorance.

"I didn't know nothing either, but that don't matter. You just pick it up. Feeding's easy, and any fool can change a diaper. You got to keep it warm in the winter and cool in the summer. Most important thing is make your husband help out, 'cause you'll be tired all the time. Morris hung up the wash for me." She leaned close to Ellen as if telling a secret. "He said he didn't see no reason to iron, and I ain't picked up an iron since except for his shirts and my best dress. And I'll tell you something else. You accept all the sympathy and help you can get this time, because they say you don't get it with the second one."

She told Ellen about the shirts and dresses and bands she'd

need for the baby, the little flannel blankets and caps and sweaters and booties. "I'd loan you mine, but I'm in the family way again. I didn't plan on another this soon, but there's nothing you can do to stop it."

"Well, that's wonderful, Gladys. But I thought—" Ellen clamped her hand over her mouth.

"That the girls at the Columbine knew a way to keep from getting pregnant? Some of them claim you can soak a sponge in vinegar . . ." Gladys wouldn't look Ellen in the eye. "I don't think that worked too well, because there was always girls going to Cheyenne."

Ellen looked confused, and Gladys said "There's ways to get rid of a baby that you don't want."

"Oh." Ellen was shocked. "I wouldn't care to do that."

"Well, who does, but sometimes . . ." She let the thought trail off. "I'm glad for you. Charlie, too. He thinks the sun rises and sets on you. I seen it. Me and Morris, we have a good thing going, but it ain't nothing like you and Charlie. If something happened to me, well, Morris would go into town and find himself another woman. Charlie . . ." She shook her head. "Anything happened to you, it'd kill him."

"Morris adores you," Ellen protested.

"Morris thinks one woman's about the same as the next. I'm not complaining. There's not every man that would marry a girl out of the Columbine."

ELLEN DID NOT pamper herself, although that might have been because she couldn't. There was too much work to do. Charlie hired a crew to help him with the haying, and Ellen had to cook for them. She and Charlie dug potatoes and put them into the cellar that Charlie had excavated. There was canning and jelly making. Charlie bought a bushel of apples that Ellen peeled and sliced and dried. The house was not as warm as a soddy, and Ellen pieced quilts for the cold weather. She made baby quilts, too, and lined a wooden box with fabric for a baby bed. Charlie promised to make a cradle when he could get around to it. Ellen flattened tin cans to cover knotholes in the side of the house to keep out the snow, and holes in the floor that had let mice into the house.

That time of year was busy for Charlie. He not only had the crops to deal with, but he was working part-time for the Gurleys. Sometimes he left before dawn and didn't return until after dark.

When he could get away, Charlie drove west toward the mountains to search for wood for fuel. He was gone three days. Ellen didn't mind being by herself during the daytime, but the nights frightened her, especially when she heard the coyotes howling. They made her realize she was a woman alone on the prairie. What if she fell or something went wrong with the baby? Ellen felt lonelier than she had since arriving in Wyoming. She barely slept and left the kerosene lamp burning all night to keep her company.

One day, Charlie asked Ellen to drive the wagon into town to take a broken piece of equipment to the blacksmith to be welded. He hitched the horses to the wagon for her and warned her to be careful on a rough section of the road halfway to town. Ellen had never driven the wagon that far by herself.

At first, she was apprehensive. Charlie was, too. He had bought two horses for farmwork, because he thought being hitched to a plow was a comedown for Huckleberry. Now he sat on Huckleberry and watched until his wife disappeared. The road was smooth, and the horses moved along steadily.

After a time, Ellen was able to relax and enjoy the ride.

She had been in Wyoming just a year, she realized. When she arrived, she'd thought Wyoming was endless brown land, but now she saw how the sun turned the grasses golden in the early morning light. The sage perfumed the prairie. It was the smell of Wyoming. Ellen heard the calls of birds and searched the prairie for antelope. A group of them suddenly bounded across the plains, and Ellen wondered if one of them was the animal that she had kept Charlie from shooting on their wedding day.

She wore a sunbonnet but after a time took it off so that she could feel the breeze on her face. As she turned to throw the bonnet into the wagon bed, she felt the round lump of the baby and was overcome with joy. So much had happened in such a short time. She had expected to teach school in Wyoming, but she had never dreamed that in just a year she would be a married woman, living on a ranch, and expecting a baby. She cupped one hand around her belly, just the way Charlie did when he came up behind her and marveled at the way her body was changing. The thought of Charlie touching her that way made her blush, although there was no one within a mile to see her. She had been naïve when she married. She hadn't realized the desire that would take hold of Charlie—and her.

She stopped the wagon in front of the blacksmith's and climbed down. In Illinois, Ellen thought, someone would have rushed to help a pregnant woman, but in Wyoming women weren't pampered. The land was too new for such niceties. Women were expected to do their part, and Ellen liked that. After all, Wyoming was the first territory to give women the vote, and with that came some responsibilities. Still, not everything was equal. She might help Charlie with the plowing and the haying, but she alone was having a baby. Wyoming law couldn't change that.

While the blacksmith made the repairs, Ellen drove to the general store with her shopping list. She looked at the supply of jams and cheeses and other delicacies, things she might have bought the year before when she was single, but now she knew better than to waste her money on them. As she pointed to the sack of coffee, she saw containers of tea and had a sudden thought. Ruth loved tea. Ellen would buy a tin of it and stop by the McGinty house on her way home. They would catch up over the tea. She had not called since she married, and it had been a long time since Ruth had visited her.

"Here you go, Miz Bacon," the storekeeper told her. "I'll carry out this box for you."

"I can manage," she said. She was embarrassed that he thought she needed help.

He insisted, however, and as he set the box in the wagon he lowered his voice. "I wouldn't want anybody inside to hear, but I was hoping you'd consider coming back to teach."

"You don't like the new teacher?"

"She isn't you. That's for sure. She keeps a switch by her desk, and she used it on one of my girls, switched her till she broke the skin. You'd never do that. She's a sour old thing. You ever want to come back, you'd be welcome."

"I'm married," Ellen said, as if that settled it.

He nodded. "I don't suppose Charlie would let you work."

"No." They had never discussed it, but if she returned to teaching, Ellen knew, people might think Charlie couldn't support her or that she was sorry she'd married him. She'd never do that to him.

"I didn't figure you would, but I had to ask."

"Maybe she'll leave after a year. You haven't had much luck with teachers staying on." She smiled.

"That's the truth."

As she flicked the reins over the horses, Ellen saw Frieda and another girl emerge from the Silver Dollar, and she waved. The girl looked startled, but Frieda waved back. A few seconds later Morris came out of the saloon, and Ellen pretended not to see him.

THE MCGINTY PLACE looked shabbier than ever. The wind and dirt had scoured the last of the paint off the outside of the house, and the building listed. Ruth's flowers, now brown, clung to dead stalks. Old shirts and pants hung on a clothesline strung between two poles, the wind covering them with leaves.

Ellen climbed down from the wagon and tied the horses to a fence post. Before she could knock on the door, McGinty opened it. "I knew I heard somebody out here. What you want?"

"I came to see Ruth."

"Well, she's feeling poorly. She can't see nobody. Best you go on your way."

Ellen didn't believe him. She peered into the house and saw Ruth sitting in her rocking chair near the stove. "Ruth? Are you ill? It's Ellen. I came to see you." She pushed McGinty aside and stepped indoors.

"Ellen?" The rocking chair creaked, and Ruth stood up.

"Are you ill?"

"Oh no. I fell is all." She gripped the edge of the cookstove to steady herself, then brushed her hand along the wall as she made her way to the door. "Come in."

The house smelled stale, and Ellen wondered if it had when she lived there. No, Ruth was a good housekeeper and put out bits of sage to keep the room fresh. The smell came from McGinty—and from a man who was seated at the table.

He didn't rise when Ellen entered, only stared at her, and she recognized Wade Snyder. When he saw Ellen looking at him, he pulled in his head like a turtle.

"Have I come at a bad time?" Ellen asked. She didn't care to sit in the house with the two men.

"No. Let's go outside," Ruth said.

Ellen saw McGinty staring at her belly, and she turned away from him, but not before the man smirked and said, "Old Fatback poked you good, did he?" He chuckled and glanced at Snyder, who grinned.

Ellen flushed with embarrassment, and Ruth closed her eyes in shame. She led Ellen outside to a log, and the two of them sat down. "He didn't mean nothing by that. You know how he is. Him and Mr. Snyder, well, they worsen each other. Just chalk it up to bad manners."

"It's hard for you here, isn't it?"

"Oh no. I just get lonesome sometimes. Wyoming's a lonesome place for a woman. Ain't you learned that yet?"

"Sometimes."

"Wyoming's a man's land."

"I suppose it is, but still, I like it."

"Maybe that's because you come here by choice."

"Didn't you?"

"I was married. There wasn't no choice. I was married and had a little girl. What else could I have did?"

"You could have stayed behind."

"And did what, teach school?" Ruth snorted. "I can barely read. Onliest thing for a woman like me would be domestic. Folks work you like a slave, and then they maybe pay you a quarter or an old dress. McGinty wasn't so bad back then. He used to be a pretty good man, or at least I thought so when we was courting."

Ruth looked away, and Ellen knew better than to pursue the conversation. "Have you heard from Laura?" she asked, knowing that talking about her daughter gave Ruth pleasure.

"No, but I think she's wrote to me. I saw part of an envelope burned up in the cookstove."

"He still doesn't let you read her letters?"

Ruth shook her head. "But there's some pleasure in knowing she's thinking about me."

"Why don't you visit her?"

"Oh, he wouldn't let me. He don't even let me visit you these days. I used to wait till I knowed he was off somewheres, but now Mr. Snyder tells him if I take the buggy. I got to be careful."

"He hits you?"

Ruth didn't answer. "Now tell me when's the baby due."

Ellen smiled and took her friend's hand. "I wish you could be with me. I'm afraid to be alone with it." She had a sudden thought. "Would your husband let you stay with me after the baby comes, just for a few days?"

Ruth smiled at the idea, then shook her head.

"Even if I paid you."

"Oh, I wouldn't charge."

"No, but Mr. McGinty might be more willing to agree if I did."

Ruth thought it over. "No, he'd be angry I wasn't here to do for him." She stood. "I better go inside. He'll be wanting his dinner. I'd ask you to stay, but Mr. Snyder's not much company."

"I have to get home," Ellen said. She remembered the tea and went to the wagon and took out the tin, handing it to Ruth.

"He'll like it," Ruth said.

"No!" Ellen told her sharply. "It's for you, for when you're alone. Or for when I come to visit."

Ruth smiled at that. "I wish you would. I don't have much company."

Ellen started for the wagon, then stopped. "I have an idea. What if your daughter sent her letters to me? I could keep them for you until you came to visit or I stopped by. That way Mr. McGinty would never know about them."

Ruth closed her eyes, thinking. "You wouldn't mind?"

"It would be our secret. And Charlie's. He'd have to know, of course."

"Well, I believe I could trust him." Ruth gave a mischievous smile. "Wouldn't that be a good trick to pay on McGinty!"

Eleven

Before dawn one morning, a wagon came down the road and pulled into the yard. Charlie and Ellen were lingering over breakfast coffee. They were used to neighbors stopping or chuck-line riders—itinerant cowboys looking for a free meal and a place to stay for a night or two. But nobody came by in a wagon that early unless it was for a reason.

"I'll see to it," Charlie said, rising from the breakfast table. "Might be a puncher from Gurley's or maybe somebody needs help. You stay." As Ellen's pregnancy advanced, Charlie was more and more solicitous of her. He knew even less about babies than Ellen did and was in awe of his wife and the changes that pregnancy brought. He loved touching her growing belly and was overcome with emotion the first time he felt the baby kick. It made him wonder about God.

A minister told him about the wages of sin being death after his parents died and that ended his churchgoing. Still, he believed there was something up there that was bigger than he was, some force or spirit. Maybe even God, although he wasn't quite willing to go that far. He felt that presence on a spring day as he rode across the range on Huckleberry, when he saw the sun's rays move over the prairie at first light, or when he looked at his wife sleeping, her hair spread around her like a cloud. On occasion, he was so moved watching Ellen perform some ordinary chore—washing dishes or feeding the chickens—that he thought she had been a gift from an unknown force. He had to pinch himself to know she was real and that she was his. He had fallen in love with her the first time he saw her standing in the schoolyard, but that was nothing compared to the depth of his love for her now.

"You wait," Charlie said now, putting out a hand as if to protect her from whoever was outside.

Before Charlie could reach the door, they heard a voice call, "Hello, the house!" The two exchanged a glance, curious, because the voice was that of a woman.

"Someone needs us," Ellen said. She thought the person might be Gladys and that maybe Morris had been hurt. She crowded behind Charlie as he yanked open the door. A woman sat hunched over on the wagon seat. "Miss Ferguson?" Ellen said. The old woman had never stopped before, and Ellen couldn't imagine why she was there. Perhaps she was ill. "Come in."

"I brought you some things," Miss Ferguson said, jumping off the wagon. She was spry for her age, which was what? Seventy? Maybe more?

"What things?" Charlie asked. He held the door open for her.

"For the baby. I saw Mrs. Bacon was expecting." She went to the back of the wagon and removed a box with hands that were coarse and rough. She handed it to Charlie. Then she lifted out a cradle. "I figured maybe you didn't have one of these."

Charlie gave the box to Ellen, then took the cradle from Miss Ferguson, who started to get back into the wagon.

"Stop!" Ellen said. "Come inside." The woman hesitated. "Please," said Ellen, and Miss Ferguson nodded.

Inside, Ellen took out a good china cup and saucer and poured coffee for Miss Ferguson. She filled the two tin cups she and Charlie used, then set a can of milk on the table. She had been amused when she first lived in Wyoming that with all the cows, people preferred canned milk. "Take off your wraps. We were just at breakfast. I'll fix you ham and eggs."

"I already ate." Miss Ferguson seemed ill at ease, as if she was not used to visiting, but she took the coffee and sat down at the table, shrugging out of a man's coat. "I thought maybe you could use those things. They aren't doing anybody any good in the barn." She reached over and wiped cobwebs from the cradle. "I should have cleaned it first."

Ellen used her apron to remove a smudge of dirt, then sat back and admired the baby bed. It was walnut and old. The headboard was carved, and the rockers were finely wrought. "It's beautiful," she said. She started to ask where the old woman had gotten it, then realized Miss Ferguson must have acquired it for her own child forty or fifty years earlier. "I will keep it in good condition and return it to you."

Miss Ferguson waved her hands. "What do I want it back for? You think I'll ever have a need for it? I'm glad to get rid of it." She leaned over and touched the carving and let out an involuntary sigh. "A little beeswax, if you can find it, ought to clean it up nice. It never got used except for a little while."

Ellen was uneasy thinking of the baby who had been taken from the woman. She didn't know what to say.

"There's baby clothes, too," Miss Ferguson said.

Charlie brought the box to the table and opened it. The garments were wrapped in tissue. Ellen removed several of them, examining them one by one. There was a long white dress with crochet and lace inserts, a knit sweater and matching booties, a cotton dress embroidered with birds and ducks. Three flannel blankets were decorated with elaborate cross-stitching. The fashions were decades old, and none of the items appeared to have been worn. "Why, they're beautiful!" Ellen exclaimed, running her hand over the intricate stitching. "I wonder who was responsible for the exquisite needlework."

"I was," Miss Ferguson said. For a second, she looked proud, then embarrassed, and dropped her head.

"You did it?"

"I went to finishing school when I was young. Girls back then learned to embroider and tat and make samplers and such—useless skills for a ranch. Still, I always liked to do them. It eased my mind." She took a deep breath, as if she wasn't used to talking so much. She picked up her coffee cup, holding it by the handle, not the bowl—holding it like a lady.

As Ellen continued to remove the clothing, she realized not everything was for a baby. There were clothes for a larger child, including a sailor suit that would have fit an older boy. Hiding her surprise, Ellen returned them to the box. Miss Ferguson must have continued to make clothes for her son even after he was taken from her. Perhaps the woman had expected to get him back. Or maybe she pretended he was hers all along. Ellen's heart went out to the poor mother. No wonder Miss Ferguson was withdrawn and harsh. Ellen glanced at Charlie, but he wouldn't have known a newborn's swaddling clothes from a boy's suit and hadn't seen anything unusual. "These are beautiful, too," Ellen said.

Miss Ferguson looked her in the eye, almost challenging her. "I guess you know I made them for my son. You know I had a son, do you?"

Ellen was tempted to demur, but the old woman would have known she was lying. "Yes."

"I guess everybody knows, even after all these years."

"I'm sorry."

"It wasn't your fault," Miss Ferguson said matter-of-factly.

"Just the same—"

"No use to talk about it." She stood. "I got work to do before the weather turns."

"You think it's going to snow?" Ellen asked.

Miss Ferguson gave a sharp laugh. "Fools and tenderfoots predict the weather." Before Ellen could rise, the woman was out the door. In a minute, the wagon was headed toward the road, Miss Ferguson driving the horses a little too fast.

"What do you make of that?" Charlie asked. "I never heard her say half a dozen words before. Everybody thinks she's an old crow."

"Well, I say she's lovely."

"Nobody'll believe she gave you all those baby things."

"I don't think she'd want us to tell." Ellen had taken the box of baby clothes to the bed and spread them out, thinking they should be washed. Some were yellowed and had rust spots.

Charlie considered that, then nodded. "But my guess is she likes you. Maybe nobody ever called on her with a peach pie before. She's too proud to say so, but I think she wants to be your friend."

WINTER HAD COME, and Ellen did not get out much. She didn't mind. She fed the chickens and scraped away the snow from around the chicken coop because the chickens went crazy when they couldn't see the dirt. She cooked and kept house, but she had no desire to go visiting. She was building a nest for her family. When the days were warm, she put on a heavy coat and sat outside on the bench Charlie had made.

She shaded her eyes to keep out the glare as she stared at the endless white, thinking how pure and fresh the snow was. Sometimes in the early evening, as Charlie worked on the room he was adding onto the house, Ellen stood in the doorway or looked out the window as the sky turned dark. The sunsets that swept the prairie with their streaks of crimson and pink, orange and gold, never failed to surprise her with their overpowering color. They seemed primitive and a little frightening—like the land itself.

After she was sure she was pregnant, Ellen wrote the news to her sister, whose letter came by return mail, saying that she was so happy for Ellen that she would have placed a long-distance telephone call to tell her in person—if either of them had had a phone.

Like Gladys, Lizzie said that childbirth was no fun but that it passed quickly. She sent suggestions for ways to keep the baby warm and safe, remedies for childhood ailments. She told Ellen to care for herself after the baby came, to rest and let Charlie do her chores. She even warned that as joyful as Ellen would be with the birth of the baby, she might also feel overwhelmed and sad. There were days after her own children were born, Lizzie admitted, when she was so depressed that she could hardly care for them. She had thought there was something wrong with her, but she had talked to other mothers and found that she was not alone. It was natural, Lizzie wrote. Ellen did not know how that could be, but Lizzie was older and wiser than she, and Lizzie knew more about childbirth and babies than she did.

Lizzie sent Ellen *The Ladies' New Medical Guide* that told all about babies. It was filled with information about women's bodies, lovemaking, and child care and warned about "self-pollution." (Ellen had never heard of such a thing.) It also contained instructions on childbirth that Ellen thought would be useful if the doctor did not make it in time. Ellen had decided to have the baby at home and had already talked to the new physician in Wallace about delivering it. When the time came, Charlie would ride to the Gurley ranch and Pike would go for the doctor. Mrs. Gurley would return with Charlie and care for Ellen until the doctor arrived. The baby was due in the spring, but spring blizzards were the worst, and there was always a chance he could not make it.

At first, Charlie had suggested that when the baby was due Ellen should stay with the McGintys in Wallace, where the doctor would be close, but Ellen said no. Not for the world would she want old McGinty and his surly friend in the house when she gave birth.

Although Charlie was apprehensive, Ellen was not worried. She read the book Lizzie had sent until she had almost memorized the steps for childbirth. She read the section on marital relations, too, showing it to Charlie, who laughed when he read the chapter that said men should not tax their wives with overindulgence. The book recommended that men take cold showers when they were aroused. "Good thing we don't have a shower," he said. They didn't have a bathtub either but bathed in a galvanized washtub.

"A good thing," Ellen agreed.

THERE WAS PLENTY of snow now, and cold. Sometimes the thermometer dropped to forty below. The hens froze their combs and stopped laying. Ellen covered up her geranium with a blanket at night. Water in the teakettle froze. Frost stars dotted the window, and the glass was cold when she removed the rime. Icicles hung from the sides of the cows that

Charlie had acquired from Mr. Gurley. Charlie's pants froze so hard they rattled like boards. Most of the time, Ellen stayed in the house, sewing or reading *The Saturday Evening Post*—Lizzie had sent her a subscription—or the books she had brought from Iowa. Even if she had wanted to get out, she would have had a hard time of it. Driving a wagon was slow, cold work, even when she wrapped herself in a heavy coat and quilts and put hot rocks under her feet. So she rarely went anywhere, even with Charlie.

Sometimes when he went to Wallace for supplies, Charlie asked Ellen to go with him. He said the fresh air would do her good, although Ellen knew he just wanted her company. One morning, he insisted she go along when he went to town on an errand.

"I don't want to get a chill," Ellen told him, hoping he would agree it was best for her to remain at home.

"It's not so cold. Besides, you can stop and see your friend Ruth while I take care of business. You haven't visited her for a long time."

"Maybe we could make it to church on Sunday. I'll see her then." With the cold weather and the road snow-packed, she had not been to church in a month.

"Aw, come on, Ellen. Don't make me go to town by myself."

Of course she agreed to go then. She heated hot rocks in the cookstove for their feet and wrapped the metal coffeepot in a blanket to keep the coffee warm for the trip. Then, enveloped in her coat and a layer of shawls and scarves, she climbed into the wagon with Charlie. The baby made her feel listless and heavy. She was more than five months along, and she couldn't help but wonder how awkward the remaining time would be.

With the ice on the road, the ride took longer than usual,

and Ellen was shaking with cold by the time they reached the mercantile and went inside for the mail. She stood shivering beside the stove in the store, sorting through the mail, looking for a letter from Ruth's daughter. So far, there had been three, and Ellen had been glad that McGinty and his friend were not home when she'd stopped to deliver them to Ruth. There was no letter from Laura this time. Ellen considered waiting in the warmth of the store while Charlie finished his business, but she knew Ruth would want to know that no letter had arrived. Both Ellen and Ruth worried that if the letter sat for a long time the storekeeper might recognize Laura's handwriting or her return address and give the letter to McGinty by mistake.

So Charlie dropped Ellen at the McGinty house to wait for him. Since McGinty and his friend were playing cards at the table, the women could not have a private conversation. Ellen shook her head at Ruth to let her know there was no letter, and Ruth nodded her understanding. Then Ruth made tea, and she and Ellen sat beside the cookstove while they drank it, chatting about everyday things. The house was gloomy, and Ellen wondered how she could have lived there all those months with McGinty lurking about. She was glad when Charlie returned and said they should be on their way since a storm was coming.

"Have a drink. It'll keep you warm," McGinty said, pointing to a bottle on the table.

Charlie shook his head. "That rotgut would have likely killed me," he told Ellen as they started for home. He hurried the horses, because the storm was beginning. Big flakes of snow swirled about in the wind. By the time they were out of Wallace, the snow was so thick they could hardly see. Ellen snuggled next to Charlie on the wagon seat, wishing he would put his arm around her to keep her warm, but he needed both hands for the reins. He slapped them on the horses' backs, urging them to go faster, but the animals merely plodded along.

There had been enough sun that morning to melt a little of the snow on the road. Now that melt was frozen, so a layer of ice lay beneath the falling snow, and from time to time the wagon slid. Charlie steadied it, but Ellen worried that the horses might slip on the ice and fall, maybe breaking a leg. She asked Charlie if they should stop at Gladys's house to wait out the storm.

"No," he said, turning to her. There was ice on his eyebrows. "I have to feed the cattle, and there's the cow to milk. We'll make it fine!" He had to yell above the wind. "Storm like this isn't much when I think of what I had to put up with at Gurley's, riding out to make sure the cattle didn't freeze. It'll stop before long!" Then he asked, "You afraid?"

"Oh no," Ellen replied quickly. Her words were caught in the wind and Charlie had to tilt his head toward her when she repeated them.

Her toes were numb, and her ears were frosted, and she wound a scarf around her head, then put her hands between her knees, because although she wore mittens, her fingers tingled. "How far?" she yelled. In the blizzard, she could not recognize landmarks.

"Almost there. That's the Gurley place up ahead."

Ellen looked, but she could not make it out.

"There." Charlie raised his hands to point, jerking the reins as he did so. The horses slowed suddenly, and the wagon slid on a patch of ice. Charlie tried to keep it steady, but the horses, confused, reared, then bolted. Charlie pulled back on the reins, but the wagon careened off the road, and as it turned over he yelled, "Jump!"

Terrified, Ellen did as Charlie ordered. She jumped off the side of the wagon, landing in the snow, then watched, horrified, as the wagon overturned, one wheel crushing her leg. "Charlie!" she yelled, hoping he heard her over the wind. Had he gotten free of the wagon? Was he hurt? Ellen tried to crawl out from under the wheel, but she was pinned. What if Charlie was hurt and she couldn't get out to go for help? They would freeze to death, both of them. "Charlie!" she screamed again. "Charlie, are you there?"

"Ellen?" In a few seconds, Charlie was beside her. "I jumped clear. Are you all right?"

"I don't know. I can't get up. I'm caught."

Charlie tried to lift the wheel, but he couldn't.

"You'll have to go for someone," Ellen told him.

"I can't. You'll freeze before I get back."

He tried the wheel again and lifted it an inch or so. "Can you help?" he asked. "Together maybe we can move it."

Ellen was on her back, and she struggled to sit up.

"If we can lift the wheel at the same time, you can pull your leg out. Do you think you can do that?"

"I have to," she said. She steadied herself, praying a little. Then she said, "I'm ready."

The two of them struggled. Ellen dropped the wheel, and it pressed into her leg, and she screamed.

"Try!" Charlie said. Despite the cold, he was sweating. He wondered if he could unhitch the horses and get them to pull the wagon but the effort could break her leg—if it wasn't already broken.

Ellen gritted her teeth. She gripped the rim of the wheel with her hand and said, "On three."

Charlie counted, and at three they both strained to lift the wheel, raising it just enough for Ellen to move her leg.

Charlie helped her up, but she winced when she stepped on the injured leg. "Can you walk?" Charlie asked. She groaned in pain, and Charlie knew she would never make it through the snowdrifts. "Go get help. I can move enough so I won't freeze. I'll be all right." Ellen wasn't at all sure of that, but there was nothing else to be done. She put her arms around her belly as if to protect the baby against the cold. It would die, too, if she froze.

"No," Charlie said. He glanced in the direction of the ranch.

"How far?" Ellen asked.

"Not far." He took a deep breath and picked up his wife. He headed into the storm with Ellen in his arms, stumbling, and once dropping Ellen in the snow. If he faltered, they would die together, he knew, and that thought kept him going. At last, he reached the ranch house, too numb to even knock.

Gurley heard the muffled sound of the two outside the house. "Good lord!" he said. "Come in. Put her by the stove." He called to his wife, "Come quick. It's Charlie and Mrs. Bacon. She's hurt and almost froze!"

Mrs. Gurley grabbed a linsey-woolsey blanket and warmed it a moment by the stove, as Charlie and Gurley unwrapped the coat and shawls Ellen wore.

"The horses," Charlie said. "I should have turned them loose, but I wasn't thinking."

"Me and Pike will go with you." Gurley said and ordered Pike to hitch the sleigh.

Ellen reached her hand to Charlie. "You have to warm up."

"I'm all right. I can't let the horses freeze." He wanted to stay with his wife, but he had no choice. Pike and Gurley might not be able to find the horses on their own. The wagon had to be righted and the horses brought in. Within minutes, Charlie and Pike and Gurley left the house and headed back toward the wagon. It took them a long time to unhitch the horses and right the wagon, then drive it to the ranch. As soon as the three reached the barn, Gurley told Charlie to check on Ellen. Charlie rushed into the house and found Mrs. Gurley sitting beside the fireplace. Tears ran down her face, and she wrung her hands.

"Ellen?" he asked. His fingers curled into fists, and he held his breath.

"Her leg's broke, but I set it. I know something about doctoring. She's sleeping." Mrs. Gurley took a breath. "Ellen's all right. It's the baby. She's lost it."

Twelve

When spring came, Ellen saw the cottonwoods sprouting and the grasses springing up. The cows calved. There were chicks in the henhouse, tiny yellow puffballs. Baby antelope and jackrabbits roamed the prairie. Piglets and foals were born on nearby farms and ranches. It seemed to Ellen that she was the only creature not giving birth. She felt unconnected, disoriented. She wandered about the house, starting chores that she forgot to finish, and when she talked to Charlie she stopped in midsentence, not remembering what she had been about to say. She spent hours staring out at the prairie, mourning the baby she had lost—a girl. She would have been named Elizabeth, for Ellen's sister. The body was buried in the graveyard near Wallace, beside Charlie's brother. Charlie and Pike used dynamite to blast out a grave, then buried the tiny body on a wet, cold day. There was no service. Ellen had been too ill to attend the interment and later refused to visit the spot. She did not want to think of her daughter spending eternity where the coyotes howled.

Ellen had stayed on at the Gurley house until she could be about. The break in her leg had been clean, and when the snow ended and Charlie brought the new doctor to examine her, the man said Mrs. Gurley had treated the leg as well as he could. The limp would go away, he said, but it never did, not completely.

Charlie took Ellen home in the wagon. The snow was gone, but the yard was muddy and Charlie lifted her and carried her into the house. Gladys had left their supper in the pie safe. She had placed a jar of green branches that had begun to bud on the table. As a surprise for his wife, Charlie had purchased a linoleum carpet and placed it on the floor. Gladys had helped him pick out the pattern of big pink roses. "I know you like flowers," Charlie said, anxious for Ellen's approval. She was touched, although she was appalled at the gaudy design. She told him it was perfect and that she was pleased by his thoughtfulness. After all, what other cowboy would think to give his wife a linoleum floor?

It was considered poor manners to speak of a baby who was born dead—bad taste to mention a pregnancy that had gone wrong. People thought that bringing up the loss would just make a woman remember—as if she would forget. Still, Ellen was not anxious to talk about the baby. The miscarriage was too personal. Charlie said it didn't matter. All he cared about was that she was safe, and she knew he meant it. There would be other children, he said. But he hadn't carried that growing body inside him as Ellen had. He didn't know that that life was a real person who could never be replaced, no matter how many other children they might have.

Gladys stopped by a few days after Ellen returned home. She didn't know it was improper to talk about the miscarriage, or else she didn't care. "I'm sorry," she said. "You can't live with that little thing inside you and not love it. Even if it never took a breath, it was still your baby." She set down her little boy, who was almost a year old. "I don't know how the

Lord works. He takes away your baby and gives me another I'm not ready for. I ain't complaining, but at this rate, I could have a kid every year for the next twenty years. I'll be just like Julia Brownell." She laughed, and Ellen smiled.

The Brownells had a farm farther up the road. Ellen had met Julia only a few times. Her five children were young, so they had not attended the school when Ellen taught there. Julia had been a beautiful woman and cultured, raised in refinement and married to a man who believed in the romance of being an agrarian. They had moved to Wyoming to farm and raise racehorses. Richard Brownell knew nothing of agriculture, however. The horses died, and the farm was thin living. The only thing the Brownells seemed able to raise successfully were children. Ellen had called on Julia once, but the woman was so harried, the children unruly, and the house so filthy that she had felt like an intruder. She had noticed that while Julia fluttered about, overwhelmed with chores, her husband sat by the stove, chewing tobacco and reading a book. Julia had tried to make Ellen feel welcome, but Richard only scowled at her.

Now Gladys sat at the table while Ellen built up the fire in the cookstove and heated coffee. "They say there's a reason you lose a baby, like maybe there was something wrong with it. If that's the case, maybe that's a good thing. How'd you like to have a baby like the Gurley girl?" Gladys asked.

"Margaret?"

Gladys nodded.

"I thought about that. I believe it would have been all right. Look at Mrs. Gurley. She loves Margaret as much as Pike."

"Yeah, but what happens when the Gurleys are gone? What would she do if Pike didn't take care of his sister?"

"There are homes."

"Yeah, like orphanages. I know all about them."

"You were an orphan?" Ellen poured coffee into tin mugs. She should have taken out the good cups, but that was too much effort. The silver teapot had been stored away because Ellen hadn't wanted her neighbors to think she was putting on airs.

"Yeah. Why do you think I ended up at the Columbine?"

"I don't know."

Gladys laughed. "It was a step up."

God didn't reward the righteous, Ellen thought. Gladys, a fallen woman, had a healthy child and another on the way, while she, a schoolteacher and churchgoing woman, had lost her baby. Ellen brooded over that until Gladys said, "Hey, did you go to sleep?"

"I'm not much company today," Ellen said.

"Oh, you'll get over it. After all, you got Charlie. I never saw a man so concerned. Morris, now he'd have just shrugged and asked where his supper was. But Charlie, he thought you was going to die. He blamed himself for taking you to Wallace that day. I think if he'd lost you, he'd just give up. He's trying to make it up to you, you know. He wanted to buy you a hat, but what man can pick out a hat for his wife! That's why I told him to buy you that linoleum carpet. It's not romantic like a box of chocolates or a ring or nothing, but believe me, you'll appreciate it more than a piece of jewelry. I wouldn't trade mine for a ruby necklace."

Ellen wondered if the hat might have been a better choice.

CHARLIE TRIED TO get Ellen to go into Wallace with him one day. "It will do you good to get out," he told her. Ellen shook her head. "Maybe there's a letter for Mrs. McGinty," he said, trying to persuade her.

"I'm not up to it."

"Aw, come on."

"I have work to do. I have to clean the house."

"It can wait."

Still, Ellen refused. She was barely aware of Charlie leaving, didn't notice that he had taken care with his appearance and worn a clean shirt. She sulked for a time, then felt ashamed of herself, and since she had told Charlie she was going to clean, she got out the mop and the bucket and the soap and for a few minutes she worked with a fury, as if scrubbing would take away her sorrow. After a while, however, she was tired and lay down on the bed. When she awoke, she left the cleaning supplies where they were and started on supper. She had made no desserts since she returned from the Gurleys' and decided to try a cake. The oven was too hot, however, and the cake was burned so badly that Ellen cried. She'd forgotten to make a try cake to see if the temperature was right. By the time she heard the wagon come down the road, she had given up on supper, thinking she would fix sowbelly and beans. The cake could be fed to the chickens.

She heard Charlie talking to someone as he pulled the wagon to a stop. Ellen sighed. He'd picked up a neighbor or a grub-line rider who would want supper. She didn't want to feed a stranger, but she would have to. It was what was expected. Men never thought about what a nuisance it was for a woman to face an uninvited guest. She was sitting at the table and got up and glanced out the window but could not make out who was with Charlie. She limped to the door, but before she could open it Charlie came in, his face beaming. "I brought you a surprise."

Ellen said nothing. A supper guest wasn't much of a surprise.

Charlie pushed the door open to reveal a woman standing behind him. She was small, not much larger than Ellen, with light brown hair in a fashionable pompadour. Ellen stared, her mouth open, and for a moment she couldn't believe her eyes. Before she could move, the woman rushed forward and embraced her. "Ellen!"

"Lizzie!" Ellen cried, putting her arms around her sister. "Lizzie! Is it really you?"

"In the flesh."

"What are you doing here?"

"I came to see you. Are you surprised? Did you even suspect it?"

Ellen was dumbfounded. "How? Why?"

"Charlie and I arranged it. He said a visit might cheer you up. My neighbor is looking after Arthur and the children, and I can stay a whole week."

Lizzie took off her hat and looked for a place to set it down. She glanced around the house, taking in the mean little structure as well as Ellen, dressed in dingy calico and wearing great heavy farm shoes. Ellen saw the look of dismay on her sister's face. Ellen had written about the house, about how lucky she was that it was made of lumber, not sod or tarpaper. She'd told about the room Charlie had added and how he was going to paint the outside. Now, through her sister's eyes, Ellen realized how dirty and shabby the house was. Despite the new room, the place was small and cramped. The walls were papered with newspaper. The windows did not open. The door had no lock. Even worse was the state of the little house. The mop and bucket were in the middle of the room where Ellen had left them. The windows were dirty, and the curtains needed to be washed and ironed. The stove she had been so proud of had not been blackened since the accident. The prairie grass in the mattress tick needed to be replaced. Lizzie must have been shocked and disappointed at Ellen's slovenliness. Charlie should have told her Lizzie was coming so that she could have cleaned the house. But a man didn't see such things. The fault was hers, and Ellen was embarrassed.

"What a cozy little house," Lizzie said, a smile pasted on her face. "Why, Charlie, I can't believe you built it yourself. You are quite the carpenter."

Charlie grinned. "I guess I'll leave you girls alone. I got work to do."

When Charlie was gone, Lizzie took Ellen's hands. "You poor, sweet thing, are you hurting?"

"Only inside. I lost her, Lizzie. If I'd had just a few more weeks . . . If I'd only stayed home that day."

"Do you blame Charlie?" Before Ellen could reply, Lizzie said, "Of course you do. He blames himself."

"How do you know?"

"He told me. He wrote about it."

"He wrote to you?"

"Of course. Why do you think I'm here? Your poor husband was so concerned that he wrote and invited me to visit. He said it was the only thing he could think of that would pull you out of your funk."

"It's more than funk, Lizzie. My baby's dead."

"I know, dearie. And it's awful. But it happened, and you have to get over it. If you don't, it will spoil your marriage. Remember I wrote to you about how depressed I was after each of the children was born? I don't know what it is, but I think it's something that goes along with childbirth. It isn't fair, of course, but what's fair? I nearly drove Arthur away by my feeling sorry for myself. He started eating dinner at his club and staying out late rather than dealing with me."

"But I don't complain."

Lizzie smiled. She had set her hat on the dresser, and now she took off her gloves and straightened their fingers. "I know you. You don't complain, but you're moody and sullen when you get upset. That's even worse." She dusted off the seat of a chair and sat down. "Do you realize how extraordinary it is that Charlie wrote to me? We didn't even know each other. Don't lose him, Ellen."

Ellen stared at her sister. "You just got here and you're telling me what to do?"

"Somebody has to." Lizzie clapped her hands. "What do you say the two of us finish mopping the floor? We always did make a good team."

Ellen smiled. "Dressed like that?"

Lizzie looked down at her traveling suit. She went to the small trunk that Charlie had brought in. She removed a simple dress and went into the adjoining room and changed her clothes. Then she took over the cleaning. After a time, Ellen, annoyed that her sister was ordering her around, rebelled, saying this was her house and she was in charge.

Lizzie hid a smile and said, "Then you must take over." Under Ellen's direction, the sisters mopped and scrubbed and dusted. They took down the curtains and washed the windows, blackened the stove and polished its nickel trim. They hung the braided rug on the clothesline and beat out the dirt. Ellen got out the silver teapot that Lizzie had given her as a wedding present. It was black with tarnish. Lizzie saw the teapot and said, "What a foolish present that was."

"I have not used it for fear of seeming uppity, but I love to know it is here. Times will be better." Ellen polished it, while Lizzie looked around for something else to do. She saw the newspapers tacked to the walls and said, "What in the world?" She ripped one down before Ellen stopped her.

"That's our wallpaper," Ellen said.

"Your what?" Lizzie began to laugh, but when she saw Ellen's defiant look she said, "Why, that's the cleverest thing in the world, so much more interesting than the awful yellow roses in the wallpaper Arthur insisted on at home. And how delightful to use the funny papers, too."

Ellen softened a little. "I suppose you noticed the linoleum."

"As soon as I came in."

"Well, how could you miss it? Charlie picked it out—instead of a hat."

Lizzie stared at her sister, trying not laugh, but she couldn't help it, and horrified, she began to giggle. Ellen smiled. "Surely, you didn't think I chose it, did you, Lizzie?"

"When I saw it, I was afraid your mind had been affected. I'm glad it's only Charlie's."

When the cleaning was finished, Ellen removed the old prairie grass from the mattress tick and the two women went outside and gathered fresh grass for stuffing. "It's not feathers, but it's not so bad. You won't notice it after a while," Ellen said.

"I won't take your bed. I'll sleep . . ." Lizzie looked around.

Ellen put her hand to her mouth. "Charlie never thought about a thing like where the three of us will sleep. You'll have the bed of course."

"*We* will have the bed," Lizzie said. "Charlie will have to sleep on the floor. He's a cowboy. Isn't he used to sleeping on the ground?" The two burst out laughing, the first time since she lost the baby that Ellen had laughed out loud.

She started to sit down, then remembered supper. "Oh, Lizzie, all we have to eat tonight is sowbelly and beans."

"And cake," Lizzie said.

"It's burned."

"Then I'll make a bread pudding." She looked at her sister and added, "While you comb your hair and wash your face."

"Do I look that bad?"

"It's just from the cleaning we did. We're both dirty."

Ellen knew that wasn't it. When was the last time she had unbraided her hair and brushed it out? Or done more than swished a washcloth over her body? Her hands were red, the fingernails broken, and when she'd put on her shoes that morning she'd seen that the skin on her heels was cracked and bleeding. What must Lizzie have thought when she saw her? And how could Charlie have stood her?

That evening was the best one Ellen had since before the trip to Wallace. Lizzie had made a custard sauce for the pudding that disguised the burnt taste of the cake. Charlie pronounced it first-rate. The three of them talked until late. Then Ellen spread quilts and blankets on the floor for Charlie's bed and the two women went into the bedroom. As Ellen closed the door, Charlie sent her a look of longing. Lizzie saw it and smiled to herself.

Thirteen

Charlie had to work for the Gurleys the following day. Late in the morning, he returned to the house leading two horses. "I told Mrs. Gurley your sister was here, and she wants you to come to supper. She said to take Red Girl and Little Betty for you to ride. You can see the country better on a horse than in a wagon." He added, "Do you know how to ride, Lizzie?"

Lizzie nodded. "Yes, but I didn't bring any riding clothes."

"You can wear my skirt," Ellen said. "I'll put on a pair of Charlie's pants." While Lizzie changed into Ellen's divided skirt, Ellen tried on an old pair of Charlie's pants. They were big, so she rolled up the pant legs, then tied a rope around her waist to keep them from falling down. Lizzie laughed when she saw the effect and asked, "Do women really dress like that here?"

"We make do."

The horses were saddled, and the two women mounted. First, Ellen showed Lizzie the ranch. Lizzie's face was solemn as she viewed the brown earth and the sparse vegetation. "How can you raise anything here?" she asked.

"It's called dryland farming. It's what we do." Ellen was defensive. "We don't think of it as a farm. We call it a ranch.

Charlie's raising cattle. He worked out an agreement with Mr. Gurley to get a start. Of course, it will take time, but we can get more land and have a real ranch one day, maybe as big as the Gurleys'." That was unlikely, Ellen knew, but she didn't want Lizzie's disdain.

Lizzie gave a thin smile.

Ellen saw it and thought of Lizzie's fine house and well-tended garden and added, "I know ranching wouldn't suit you, but it does me. I like the lack of convention and the open space. It's what Charlie and I want."

"He doesn't talk much, does he, your husband?"

"Not so much around other people." Ellen sounded defensive.

"I didn't mean anything by it. I suppose he's more used to being around cows than his wife's relatives."

"Let's ride up the road. There's a woman there, Julia Brownell, who went to college, and we can call on her. She's overworked, what with so many children, but I don't think she'd mind a visit." Ellen hoped Julia's husband wasn't home.

The day was nice. Ellen had given Lizzie her big western hat to wear, so she herself had gone bareheaded. She might wear Charlie's pants, but not for the world would she let Lizzie see her in a sunbonnet while riding a horse. The sun would turn her face red, but the heat felt good after so many days of being cooped up in the house. She hadn't left the place since she lost the baby, and the fresh air was nice, too. There was the smell of newly turned earth, and of sage. She saw how the hay was coming up in the fields and watched the mother cows with their calves. She pointed out antelope in the distance. Birds flew overhead, and Ellen recognized them now—a hawk and a blue-winged teal. She glanced at Lizzie to gauge her reaction to the scene, but her sister looked ahead, her mouth a straight line. Ellen knew Lizzie was wondering how anyone could live in such a place. Well, Ellen had wondered that, once, too.

At last, Lizzie laughed and said, "I believe you can see farther out here and see less of anything but dirt and sky than any place in the country." She shook her head. "It must be the loneliest thing in the world riding across these plains. How small one must feel."

"But I feel like the wind that blows so free. There is nothing to hold me in," Ellen told her.

"I suppose that's true."

When she saw the Brownell house, Lizzie's eyes grew big. "What in the world?"

"It's called a soddy. You strip layers of sod off the prairie and pile them on top of each other. The grass from one layer grips the next one. Sod's as tight as bricks and warmer than a frame house. Of course, it's old. Not many people build soddies anymore."

"But there's grass growing on the roof."

Ellen nodded. "Wildflowers, too. They bloom in the summer. Soddies are pretty then. There are all sorts of stories about them. They say Indians couldn't pierce them with arrows." Ellen started to tell her that snakes sometimes came through the lawyers of sod but stopped. Lizzie hated snakes, too, and she probably wouldn't go inside if she thought a snake might fall out of the wall. "Lumber's scarce around here, so people improvise. Don't you think a soddy is clever?"

"I suppose." Lizzie did not sound enthusiastic.

Several small children, their faces and clothing dirty, ran out of the house as the two women reined in their horses. The children jumped up and down on bare feet, their faces showing their excitement. "Ma, we got company!" one called.

Richard Brownell sat on a stump, whittling, and didn't
get up. There was mud and manure on his boot soles, which
he probably tracked into the house. "Who is that?" he asked,
pointing at Lizzie.

"That is my sister."

"Well, she looks old enough to be your mother." He
laughed at the mean joke. "What do you want?"

"We are being neighborly," Ellen told him stiffly. "My sister is from Illinois, and since your wife is, too, we thought
we'd call on her."

"The missus is busy."

The missus? Lizzie mouthed at Ellen, who shrugged.

Julia came outside then, holding a baby wearing a diaper
made out of a flour sack. She was pregnant. *That makes five
children, all under the age of six*, Ellen thought, *six when the baby's born.* "We were out for a ride and thought we would say
hello, since we are all from Illinois," Ellen said. She and Lizzie
dismounted.

"My sister and I grew up in Chicago," Lizzie told her.

"Galena," Julia replied.

"Mrs. Brownell went to college," Ellen told her sister again.

If Lizzie was surprised that the slatternly woman standing
in front of her was educated, she didn't show it.

"Not that Shakespeare milks the cows or washes diapers,"
Julia said and smiled a little. "Will you come in?"

"Don't you have work to do?" her husband asked.

"I always have work to do," Julia told him.

Ellen had been inside the soddy before and wasn't sure what
Lizzie would think as the two followed Julia through the door.
"I haven't had time to clean it, what with all the children . . . ,"
Julia said. The little ones went inside, too, crowding the

women. Julia looked at them and then at her house as if seeing it through a visitor's eyes. She bit her lip.

"There is never time to do it all," Lizzie told her. "I'm a mother, too. Sometimes I think I would sell my soul for one hour of peace." She looked around the soddy taking in the crumbling walls, the muslin stretched across the ceiling to keep clods of dirt from falling onto the floor, the dirty dishes on the table, and the filthy bedcovers. She spied a small walnut chest of drawers with a marble top. "Look, Ellen. Isn't that cunning. It's like mine, but ever so much nicer. Mine doesn't have that pretty marble."

"I suppose it will go next. I had a whole bedroom set that matched it when we moved here, but . . . well . . . times are hard."

"We make sacrifices," Ellen said. "We all know the farm comes first."

There was an awkward silence before Julia said, "There's nothing in this house fit for a dog to eat, but I believe there is tea."

"Ah, tea." Lizzie took off her gloves and looked around for a chair.

"That would be lovely, but we can't stay," Ellen said quickly. "We promised Charlie we wouldn't be gone long, and I'm afraid he will worry. We were riding past, and we just wanted to say hello."

"Perhaps another time before I leave," Lizzie added.

Julia gave them such a longing look that Ellen almost wished she hadn't spoken up. She and Lizzie likely were Julia's only visitors in weeks, and the woman must go crazy cooped up in the dirt house with just the children and her surly husband for company. Men could get out. They went to town or to a neighbor's to borrow a piece of equipment or ask for advice on crops. Women like Julia had no escape, however. Ellen vowed she would return to visit Julia after Lizzie left.

Outside, she saw that Richard had not moved. He was smoking and looked them up and down, saying, "I don't hold with women wearing pants and riding straddle." He spat tobacco juice on the ground.

"Then it is fortunate we are not married to you, for I could not abide a husband who chewed tobacco," Lizzie told him.

Richard glared at her. "I wouldn't allow my wife to speak such impertinence."

And if I were your wife, I would kill myself, Ellen thought but was too polite to say so.

Richard called to his wife, "Be at getting my dinner!"

Ellen and Lizzie mounted and waved to Julia and the children, then rode until they were almost out of sight of the soddy. Lizzie pulled up and looked back toward the house. "What an odious man. And his poor wife. Why doesn't she leave him?"

"And go where? She has more children than the old lady in the shoe."

"Poor thing. I suppose you were afraid of her tea. God knows whether we'd dare drink it."

Ellen shook her head. "Oh no, I'm sure it's fine, but it is likely rare and her only luxury. I would feel awful knowing we had deprived her of even a cup of it."

"I hadn't thought of that. Oh, Ellen, are people here really so poor?"

"Some of them. The women have it the worst. Too much to do and too little time for it, no rest and no money."

"But that man has money for tobacco. I saw him smoking."

"The men always have money for tobacco. But a farm

woman like Julia won't spend so much as a penny on something to make her own life easier. Some of these women are so beaten down. They have no hope."

"But you are not one of them."

"Of course not," Ellen said quickly. "I shall always have hope."

THE EVENING AT the Gurley ranch was as different from the visit to the soddy as wheat from chaff. They rode there in a wagon that was rocked by the wind. The women held on to their hats and covered their faces to keep out the dirt.

"Does the wind always blow this way?" Lizzie asked Charlie.

"Hell no. Half the time it blows the other way," Charlie told her.

Lizzie laughed and told Ellen, "I like your husband."

The Gurleys gathered at the door to welcome them, even Margaret, who said shyly, "Hi, Teacher."

"What a darling girl. I am Teacher's sister," Lizzie told Margaret, taking the girl's hand. She went inside and looked around at the Persian rug, the fine furniture, and the big, stone fireplace where a small fire burned to take away the evening chill. "What a splendid house you have."

"We are comfortable. We started out with a place just like Charlie's. We grew with the country," Mrs. Gurley said.

Lizzie asked if Mrs. Gurley called it a farm or a ranch. "We raise hay and a few other things, but it is a ranch, never a farm. Out here, anything with more than one cow is considered a ranch. Mr. Gurley believes God made the earth this side up and it's wrong to turn it over."

The men sat down by the fire to talk of ranching, while the women went into the kitchen. "We stopped to see Julia

Brownell," Ellen said as she used the lid of a baking powder can to chop cabbage.

"Her husband's another who doesn't want to turn over the earth, but that's because he's lazy. I wonder how much longer they will be here," Mrs. Gurley said.

"All those children." Lizzie looked around for something to do, and Ellen nodded at the boiled potatoes. Lizzie peeled them and began to smash them with a wooden masher.

"And another on the way," Ellen added.

"I didn't know. They never should have come here." Mrs. Gurley removed a roast from the oven. She turned to Lizzie. "There are folks here like your sister and Fatback—"

"Fatback?"

"Well, yes, that's what he's called on account of his name is Bacon."

Lizzie laughed. "Of course. How clever." She glanced at Ellen, who wouldn't catch her eye. Ellen had never liked the nickname.

"As I was saying, folks like the Bacons understand what they're getting into. Fatback grew up in the country, so he and Ellen know about the sacrifices it takes to make a go of it. Then there's the dreamers like Mr. Brownell. He's dumb enough to try to rope a jackrabbit. All he knows about farming comes from his fine books. He told Mr. Gurley that Thomas Jefferson said the farmer is the future of the nation. That was why he came out here. He brought those fancy horses that couldn't take the heat and the cold and got snakebit, and now he sits around thinking crops will spring out of the ground on their own. Meanwhile, Mrs. Brownell is worked to death. If he doesn't do something soon, they'll all starve. Those kids are already as thin as sticks." Mrs. Gurley looked around. "Margaret, you can call the men to the table now."

The evening was a fine one. Mr. Gurley explained ranching to Lizzie, and his wife, who was from Virginia and was schooled, talked of books and refinements. Supper was the best meal Ellen had eaten since the Christmas Eve she had spent with the Gurleys. Dinner consisted of roast beef with potatoes and beans, cabbage, rice, and bread. For dessert, there was cake with slices of canned pineapple.

"Fresh vegetables are hard to get," Ellen explained on the way home.

"Nobody eats them anyway," Charlie said. Like other cowboys, he could live on a diet of potatoes and bread and meat.

"Well, I was surprised to find pineapple," Lizzie said.

"Pineapple is considered a real luxury. It's a great favorite out here," Ellen told her.

"A great favorite anywhere," Lizzie agreed.

THE TWO WOMEN were sore from riding and stayed at home for the next few days. Lizzie had left in such a hurry that there was not time to find a suitable house gift for her sister, but she had brought lengths of fabric with her. She and Ellen cut out two calico dresses and stitched them by hand. Lizzie, who owned a sewing machine, said she had forgotten how much time it took to make a dress on her fingers. Ellen ought to have a sewing machine, she said.

"It will come. After electric lights and an indoor bathroom," Ellen said, laughing. She had laughed a great deal since Lizzie arrived. "You must think we are barbarians, but honestly, Lizzie, I don't mind being without such things."

"I understand. You are building a future for your family."

"For Charlie anyway."

"Stop that, Ellen. You know there will be children."

"I know." Ellen put down her stitching and stared at the big tomato can that held her geranium. It had made it through the winter and begun to bloom, the red flowers bright against the drab wall. The chickens squawked outside, and Ellen thought the little one that was so self-important must be fighting with her sisters. Ellen would have put her into the cooking pot long ago if she hadn't been such a dependable layer. "Oh, Lizzie, I feel so much better since you came. Sitting around this house all day was bad for me. I didn't think about Charlie at all, only about how sorry I was for myself."

"You just needed another woman to talk to."

"I suppose that's so." She picked up her needle and took a few stitches. "I must remember that and call on Mrs. Brownell more often, even if her husband is a stinker. And Gladys. She's come by, but I was such poor company that she must have given up on me. I ought to be a better friend to her."

"You have mentioned Gladys."

"She's our nearest neighbor and my closest friend. I'll take you to meet her tomorrow."

"Has she gone to college, too?"

Ellen smiled over her sewing. "Oh no. She was an orphan."

"I'm sure she is a perfectly delightful woman. I admire someone who can rise above circumstances."

"Gladys certainly has done that."

"WE'RE GOING TO see Gladys today," Ellen told Charlie as she watched him milk the cow. It was time for her to learn to milk, and she would ask Charlie to show her how after Lizzie was gone.

"Does your sister know about her?" Charlie raised an eyebrow.

"Whatever do you mean?"

"You know exactly what I mean."

"No, I'm not sure I'll tell her." Ellen liked sharing that bit of sly deceit with her husband as the two smiled at each other. They hadn't done that much lately.

The two women took the wagon, and after a time Lizzie said, "You're awfully good at driving this. I can barely manage a buggy."

Ellen felt a surge of pride. Lizzie had always been the accomplished one, the clever one, who had married well and managed a large home as if it was no bother. There didn't seem to be anything she couldn't do. Ellen had always been a little in awe of her sister and was pleased at her approval. "It's drive a wagon or go by shank's mare," she said.

"Or horseback, riding like a man for all the world to see. That pompous Mr. Brownell. He lets his wife work herself to death without lifting a finger, but God forbid she should insult his sense of decorum by riding astride a horse. I hope your friend Gladys is not so concerned with propriety."

"Oh no," Ellen said. "I would not think Gladys is concerned with propriety at all."

"Good. I think I shall like her." And she did, Lizzie confided after the visit.

It had gone well. Gladys kept a better house than Julia. It was tidy and clean, the curtains starched, the floor scrubbed, and the coal-oil lamp washed, then dried with newspaper to make it shine. Gladys was outside feeding the chickens. "Oh, what an honor," she said as the two women came into the yard. "I'm starved for company." She ushered them into the house, then added kindling to the banked fire in her little two-burner stove and made coffee. She removed a pie from the cupboard. "Dried apple," she explained. "Every time I make it Morris recites that poem, 'I hate and despise dried apple pies.' Still, it's his favorite."

"Charlie made me promise when he proposed to me that I'd never serve vinegar pie," Ellen said. "He told me that would mean we were as poor as . . . well, as the Brownells."

"What's vinegar pie?" Lizzie asked.

"You use vinegar instead of lemon. It's really not so bad. Mrs. McGinty used to make it."

"I can't tell the difference," Gladys said. She cut the pie and placed the slices on tin plates. Then she handed around spoons. "We've got only two forks, and I broke the tines on mine. I guess I ought to order some from the Montgomery Ward's."

"Spoons work just as well. I won't drop crumbs on my shirtwaist," Lizzie said.

"Gladys chose the linoleum in our house," Ellen told Lizzie as they sat down at the table, which was covered by a clean tablecloth. She and Charlie had been eating on bare wood, and Ellen decided to get one of the tablecloths out of her trunk.

"Such a nice, bright pattern on your floor. It will cheer you in the winter."

"Winter here is hell's hip pocket. That's for sure," Gladys said. She glanced at her own linoleum floor, which was even gaudier than Ellen's. "I'd have told Charlie to get this one, but they don't sell it anymore."

"Such a pity," Lizzie replied. "But Ellen's linoleum is quite as nice." She avoided Ellen's glance.

Gladys's little boy sat down on the floor and began to play with a rag ball that his mother had made for him. Lizzie smiled at him and asked, "How in the world do you keep him so clean?"

"I give him a bath in the washtub this morning. He'll be filthy by suppertime, but I don't mind. We're used to dirt.

We're not as prissy as city folks." She glanced at Lizzie, then covered her mouth. "I didn't mean that."

"I take no offense. It's ever so easy to be critical when you have running water and a bathtub."

Gladys finished her pie and licked the spoon. "A bathtub. I never had one, except . . ." She glanced at Ellen and didn't finish."

"We saw Julia Brownell," Ellen said, changing the subject.

"Poor woman." Lizzie licked her spoon, too, winking at Ellen as she did so. "She seems unprepared for this life. You know she went to college."

"Fairy tales don't milk no cows, not that they have milk cows," Gladys said.

"I'm sure that is true," Lizzie replied.

The three talked about housekeeping and children and sewing. Gladys got out her quilt blocks and showed them to her guests, explaining that Mrs. McGinty had given her the pattern. "She says I have a natural eye," Gladys told them, then looked embarrassed at her bragging.

"I never could quilt, but I'd like to. Mrs. McGinty said working with the colors cheered her," Ellen told them.

"She sure needs cheering," Gladys said. "I can show you how to piece. It's the easiest thing in the world. If I can do it, any fool can. I used to do it at the Columbine when I was waiting—" She stopped and cleared her throat.

The women talked for two hours, before Ellen realized how much time had passed and said they had to get home to start supper. As they rode away, Lizzie said, "What a perfectly delightful woman. How do you know her?"

"Charlie introduced us."

"Was she married when she came here?"

"No. She worked in Wallace."

"She wasn't a teacher, was she?"

Ellen shook her head.

"A domestic? She said she lived at the Columbine. I assume that was a boardinghouse."

"Not exactly."

Lizzie cocked her head. "What did she do? I don't imagine there are many jobs for women here."

"There aren't."

Lizzie waited.

"The Columbine is a brothel," Ellen said. Then as Lizzie frowned, not sure she'd heard right, Ellen said, "Lizzie, Gladys was a prostitute."

THE DAYS WENT too quickly. Ellen begged her sister to stay longer, but Lizzie insisted she had to return to her family. As she and Ellen and Charlie stood in the depot waiting for the train, Lizzie said, "Why don't you come to me?" She turned to Charlie. "When is your slack time?"

"Winter," he replied.

"That would be perfect. You could both come and spend Christmas with us. The children would be thrilled to meet a real cowboy, and you and Arthur would have so much to talk about, Charlie. He's quite taken with the idea of the West."

Ellen glanced at her husband, who shrugged. She knew he hadn't the least desire to go to Chicago. He disliked cities and didn't even own a suit. "If you couldn't do it, maybe I could go by myself," Ellen said.

"Sure," Charlie told her, relieved.

"Next winter then," Lizzie said. "Promise, Ellen."

"I promise," Ellen replied, not knowing it was a promise she would not keep.

Charlie wandered off so that the sisters could have their last few minutes alone. Ellen looked at Lizzie a moment, then said, "I know you must think it's an awful life out here."

"I think no such thing, although I admit I was shocked at first. Wyoming seems so . . . so brown, and I could never live in one of those wretched soddies. It's a good thing you made Charlie build you a house before you married. Even so, I could never put up with a lack of, well, refinements. I am not cut out to be a pioneer, Ellen. But I can see that it suits you. Charlie suits you."

Ellen smiled at her. "Yes, he does. You understand."

"I do. But, Ellen, promise me you will tell me if you need anything. Arthur is very successful, and I would not want you to do without if I can help."

Ellen nodded, but she knew she would never ask Lizzie for anything.

Her sister must have known it, too. Several weeks after Lizzie left, Charlie returned from Wallace with a huge box in the back of the wagon. Inside was a sewing machine that Lizzie had ordered for Ellen from Montgomery Ward.

Fourteen

That first summer on the ranch had been a honeymoon for Ellen. She had fussed over the house, experimenting with cooking, stitching curtains and quilts, bleaching flour sacks and embroidering red birds on them for dish towels, sewing carpet rags, learning to care for chickens, and sometimes just sitting in the sun, dreaming and watching the clouds that were like a canopy over the prairie. She had been settling in.

Now she had been married a year, and it was time she acted like a ranchwoman, not a bride. Charlie showed her how to milk. From now on, she would be in charge of milking and storing the crocks of milk in the storm cellar and skimming off the cream. She churned enough butter to sell the surplus to the mercantile in Wallace. It brought fifteen cents a pound. That wasn't a schoolteacher's salary, but Ellen was still proud that she was contributing to the family purse.

She planted a vegetable garden, fertilizing it with rotted cow manure and watering it from the barrels of water they hauled from Plug Hat Creek. Because water was precious, she used only an inch or two of it to wash dishes, then emptied even that onto the plants. The rabbits ate the first crop, and Ellen convinced Charlie to build a chicken-wire fence around the garden. Charlie didn't care much about lettuce and radishes and green beans, but Ellen was grateful for a change from potatoes and dried beans. Gladys gave her hollyhock seeds, and Lizzie sent iris bulbs for her to set out near the house. Ellen took cuttings from her geranium and planted them in big tin cans that she placed on the rock that served as a doorstep. She helped Charlie with the hay crop and aided him when the cows they had acquired from the Gurleys dropped their calves in late winter.

Ellen deepened friendships with her neighbors, too. At least once a month, she called on Julia and on Gladys. She made it a point to visit new people who were homesteading near Wallace. Hattie hoped to go to college, and Ellen worked with the girl, drilling her in English and arithmetic. Hattie feared there would be no money for schooling, and Ellen told her about scholarships. When Ellen heard of illness, she took custard and soup to the bedridden.

She even learned to kill rattlesnakes, although she still feared them more than anything except coyotes, whose yip-yipping kept her awake at night. It was the loneliest sound she'd ever heard on the prairie. One morning, she and Charlie spotted an enormous snake and Ellen begged Charlie to kill it. "It's a black snake. It won't do you any harm," he said.

"Kill it anyway!"

"No, Ellen. Black snakes eat rattlers."

"They do?"

Charlie nodded.

They also ate chicken eggs, Ellen discovered when she went to gather them one morning and found the eggs gone. At first, she thought a skunk or a coyote had gotten into the henhouse, but it would have eaten the chickens, not just the eggs. Then she saw the slithering trail and followed it to where the black snake was stretched out in the sun. She tried to keep the snake from the nests, but nothing she did worked. "I don't understand. There aren't any broken shells," she said.

"They swallow the eggs whole," Charlie told her.

Ellen thought that over, and on her next trip to Wallace she bought a nickel's worth of plaster of paris. She cut off the end of an eggshell and sucked out the egg. Then she mixed up the plaster of Paris and carefully spooned it into the shell, returning the egg to a nest. The next day it was gone, along with the rest of the eggs. That was the last time she saw the snake. Charlie said it was a shame that it had gone off, but Ellen didn't care. She'd never liked it. She hadn't seen a decrease in rattlesnakes and thought the idea the black snake ate them was one of Charlie's snake stories. Even if the black snake had kept down the number of rattlers, the increased supply of eggs that she now had was worth the snake's demise.

AT SUPPER ONE evening, Charlie told her that Margaret Gurley was ailing. "They had the doctor out today, but he doesn't know what to do with her."

"I'll call on them and see if I can help," Ellen said.

In the morning, she hitched the horses to the wagon— hitching the horses when she took the wagon was another chore she had taken on—and drove to the Gurley ranch. She took one of her schoolbooks along to read to Margaret in case the girl was confined to bed.

"Margaret cries if I'm not with her every minute, and I can't seem to get the work done. If you'd sit with her for even an hour, I'd be so grateful," Mrs. Gurley said. For once, she looked overwhelmed.

Ellen went into Margaret's room, where she was propped

up in bed. "Hi, Teacher," she said. Ellen did not know if the girl actually knew her name. Still, Margaret remembered when Ellen had stayed there one Christmas, because she said, "You can sleep with me."

Ellen read to Margaret until the girl fell asleep, then went outside to where Mrs. Gurley was hanging up the wash. "I've got behind. It's a blessing you came here. Hattie stops when she can and helps me out. Otherwise, it's just me."

"Hattie stops to see me, too. She seems to know when you're longing for someone to talk to. She's a lovely girl."

"That she is."

Ellen put a couple of clothespins into her mouth, then picked up one end of a sheet, and the two women hung it on the line. "What's wrong with Margaret?" she asked.

Mrs. Gurley gave her a look of annoyance. "There's nothing wrong with her. She's just slow."

Ellen colored. "I know that. I mean what's wrong with her now? Why is she ill?"

"Oh, I take your meaning. I'm sorry. It's just that I get tired of people asking me that. It makes me want to reply, 'What's wrong with your daughter that she's such a nasty, mean girl?'" She reached for a handful of clothespins. "Margaret's weak, and she catches colds or the influenza or anything else that goes around. It isn't enough that the Lord made her slow and gave her those looks. He had to make her sickly, too. After she was born, we took her to a doctor in Cheyenne who said she wouldn't live long. '*Those* children never do,' he told me. I wanted to ask what he meant by 'those,' but I knew. Thing is, we never think of her as one of *those*. She's just Margaret to us. I wish she was to everybody else, too."

Ellen wondered if *she* was one of the people Mrs. Gurley described. Now she wished she had encouraged the girl to go to school. "I was thinking," she said suddenly, "that maybe I could come over once a week and work with Margaret, maybe teach her the alphabet. Can she write her name?"

Mrs. Gurley took a clothespin from her mouth. "No. Do you think she could learn? That would be such an achievement."

"We could try," Ellen said.

The two women finished hanging up the laundry. "I'll come back on Wednesday," Ellen said, as she started for the wagon.

"Wait," Mrs. Gurley said. "Just wait here." She went into the barn and came out a few minutes later, leading a saddled horse. "You take Little Betty with you. Margaret used to ride her, but she's too weak now, and I'm afraid she might fall out of the saddle. The horse needs exercise. It would be a favor to me if you'd ride her for us. A horse is so much more comfortable than a wagon, and besides, Charlie needs your horses for plowing and such. You know how to saddle a horse, do you?"

Ellen stared at the woman, aware what a gift the horse was, even if only as a loan. "Are you sure?"

"Of course I am." She smiled at Ellen, then grew serious as she looked beyond her. Margaret had awakened and was standing on the porch.

"Little Betty," the girl said.

"Miss Ellen's going to ride her," Mrs. Gurley said. "She'll take good care of her until you're strong enough to ride her again. Don't you think that's a good idea, Margaret?"

Margaret's face lit up. "Teacher can ride my horse."

FOR THE NEXT few weeks, Ellen rode to the Gurley ranch whenever she could get away. Margaret's health did not improve. She spent most of her time in bed. Sometimes she sat outside on the porch, wrapped in quilts because she always seemed to be chilled. The doctor came by, but he didn't know what was wrong with her. Maybe her heart, he said. Margaret was a sweet girl, and she was happy when she saw Ellen ride up. So was Mrs. Gurley, who knew that she would have an afternoon to catch up on chores.

One morning, Ellen brought a first-grade reader and pointed out the letters in the book. "That's M for 'Margaret,'" she said. Can you sound it out? Mmmm."

Margaret made the sound.

"Now let's see if you can write it." Ellen took out a slate and a piece of chalk, and she wrote an M. Margaret tried to copy the letter, but she pressed so hard with the chalk that it broke. She glanced up at Ellen, tears in her eyes. "I'm sorry," she said.

"It's all right," Ellen told her. "Now we have two pieces of chalk. One for you, and one for me." She handed the longer piece to Margaret, who worked for a long time copying the letter M. Ellen could see the strain on the girl's face, and after a while she said, "That's enough lesson for today. Next time we'll work on more letters."

Margaret wouldn't give up the chalk, however. She erased her attempts at writing until the slate was smudged. Then she tried again and held up the slate to show an M that looked like a bunch of sticks leaning against one another. "There!" she said.

Pike came into the room and asked, "Whatcha doing?"

"I can write my name," Margaret said. "Look." She showed him the slate. "M for 'Margaret.' It's my name."

"Well, hey, that's good, Margaret. Maybe Miss Ellen will teach you to write P for 'Pike.'"

"I'm learning," Margaret said. She snuggled down in the quilts. "I'm tired." She closed her eyes, and Ellen and Pike left the room.

"You're a good brother," Ellen said.

Pike shrugged.

"You'll have the care of her one day, won't you?"

"I don't mind. She's my sister."

MARGARET DID NOT improve but instead grew weaker. She rallied when she saw Ellen, and sometimes when the two sat on the porch step Margaret picked up a stick and wrote an *M* in the dirt. Then she and Ellen smiled at each other. Ellen tried to teach her to print *P* for "Pike," but Margaret was no longer interested in learning the rest of the alphabet.

While Margaret rested, Ellen helped Mrs. Gurley catch up on chores. "She enjoys your visits," Mrs. Gurley said, as the two washed dishes.

"Sometimes I wonder if she even knows I'm here," Ellen said. That afternoon Margaret had drifted off to sleep shortly after Ellen arrived.

"Oh yes. I can see her face light up when she spots you coming down the road. You cheer her in these last days."

"Last days?" Ellen turned to Mrs. Gurley and saw how the woman had aged in just a few weeks.

"The doctor said it won't be long. He says he's sure it's her heart. It never was too good, but it's gotten real bad."

"Oh, Mrs. Gurley." Ellen put her hand on the older woman's arm, not sure what to say.

"We're lucky we've had her this long." Tears ran down the woman's face, and Ellen realized how much she loved her daughter. She never viewed Margaret as a trial but rather as a gift. "Mr. Gurley and I have always known she wasn't strong, that she might never live to grow up, but Pike . . ." She shook her head. "He's never accepted that."

"Pike?"

"He's always been protective of his sister. He's even talked to us about how he'll take care of her after we're gone. I don't know what he'll do when she dies."

"When," not "if." Ellen caught the word. The two worked together without talking, until it was time for Ellen to leave. She went into the barn and saddled Little Betty. When she rode out into the sunlight, Margaret was awake. The girl waved and Ellen called, "I'll be back soon!"

NOT SOON ENOUGH, however. A few days later, Pike came into the yard where Ellen was hanging up the washing. He didn't dismount but sat on his horse until Ellen finished pinning a shirt to the line and went to him. His face was red from crying, and Ellen knew. "It's Margaret," she said.

Pike nodded. He tried to talk but only blubbered. Then he took a deep breath and said, "This morning. She didn't wake up from her nap. Ma sent me. She wants you to come."

"I'll be right there. Pike, I'm so sorry."

ELLEN FINISHED HANGING up the washing, then put on one of her schoolteacher white blouses and dark skirts, which would make it awkward riding Little Betty astride, but she thought her divided skirt might not be proper. She saddled Little Betty and went to find Charlie. "Margaret's gone," she told him, letting out a sob. "I'm leaving for the Gurleys' to see what I can do."

Charlie bowed his head a little. "I'm real sorry, honey. They'll be broken up. They sure set store by that girl. I'll be along pretty quick."

Ellen left, and halfway to the Gurley place she spotted Hattie walking down the road and stopped. "You know?" she asked.

"Pike came and told me."

"Get up behind me," Ellen said.

The two rode Little Betty into the Gurley barnyard, where several men stood awkwardly, not knowing what to do. Mr. Gurley was leaning against the corral, the doctor next to him. A cowboy helped the two women dismount. The doctor came up to them then and said, "There was nothing I could do. Nothing. Maybe it's for the best."

Ellen and Hattie looked at each other. Both of them knew the Gurleys didn't believe Margaret's death was for the best.

"I'm told she lived longer than she was supposed to," the doctor said as if that were some consolation.

"But not as long as she should have," Hattie said.

"Maybe not," he replied. "Maybe not." He started for his buggy. "I'll leave it to you women."

Ellen and Hattie went into Margaret's bedroom, where Mrs. Gurley sat next to her daughter's body. She looked up at the two and shook her head. "I can't believe it. She looks just like she's sleeping. I ought to wash her and put on her best dress, but I'm afraid if I do, I'll have to accept she's dead. I want to sit here for a time and hope she'll wake up."

Ellen and Hattie sat quietly beside Margaret's mother for a few minutes. Then Mrs. Gurley sighed, and Hattie took her hand and helped her rise. "Folks will be coming by. Would you make the coffee?"

Once she'd led Mrs. Gurley into the kitchen, Hattie came back to the bedroom and she and Ellen removed Margaret's nightgown and gently washed her body. They slipped the girl's good dress over her head, carefully pulling her arms through the sleeves. It wasn't easy because the body was dead weight, Ellen thought, understanding now what that phrase meant. They brushed Margaret's hair and arranged it like a halo on the pillow. Then they straightened the bedcovers.

When Mrs. Gurley came back into the room, she gasped. "Why, isn't she pretty! Isn't Margaret pretty! I'd thought we'd lay her out in the dining room, but her bedroom seems so much more appropriate."

THE NEWS OF Margaret's death spread quickly, and neighbors began to arrive. Death was common in the Wyoming ranch country, and people knew what to do. The women gathered around the body and exclaimed that Margaret looked like she was resting. Why, they expected her to wake up any minute now. They brought cookies and fried chicken and beef stew, enough to feed the family for a week. The men gathered outside with Mr. Gurley. They passed around pint bottles and kicked at the dirt with their boots, not knowing what to say. Charlie stayed with them for a time, then went into the barn and helped two cowboys build a coffin.

People didn't linger. There were chores to do. Ellen remained until it was time to milk the cows. By then, almost everyone was gone. Charlie had waited for her, and they rode down the road side by side, not hurrying.

"Folks are saying it's for the best," he said.

"It's never for the best."

"That's what I was thinking."

THE SERVICE WAS held the next morning at the cemetery where Ellen's baby was buried. It was past the season for flowers, so the only bouquets were of goldenrod and late-blooming wild asters. Ellen went to the ranch early that morning, and she and Hattie wrapped Margaret in a pretty quilt, because Mrs. Gurley was too distraught to do so. Pike lifted his sister into the coffin. Then Pike and Charlie and two cowboys carried the coffin outside and placed it in a wagon that Pike drove to the grave site.

The Gurleys were well liked, and people came from all over to attend the service. Ellen had attended funerals back home and dreaded this one. She braced herself to hear the new minister tell of Margaret being born in sin. If anyone had sinned, it had been God for creating a child whose mind was simple, then taking her away from the family who loved her. The minister eschewed such talk, however, and instead, he spoke of Margaret being a gift to the family. She had been a loan from God, who now needed her for Himself, he said. Ellen didn't know if that made the family feel better, but she liked the sermon. When the preacher was finished, people sang Margaret's favorite songs, some of them hymns but mostly cowboy ballads.

The service was brief, because families had brought their children, who didn't understand what was going on. Ellen was surprised to see the Brownells—all of them. "Did you know Margaret?" Ellen asked Julia after the service.

Julia shook her head. "No, but I know Mrs. Gurley. She

gave us a milk cow when one of the babies was born." Ellen hadn't known that, but she was not surprised. Ranch people helped their neighbors, and because they were better off than most, the Gurleys were known for their generosity.

Mr. Brownell joined them, and they watched as men lowered the coffin into the grave, then shoveled dirt over it. "I don't understand. Gurleys had only two kids, and now they got just one. The Lord should have taken one of ours."

He turned away, chuckling a little at his joke, and did not see the look of disgust on his wife's face.

Fifteen

Ellen was pregnant again. She told no one, not Lizzie, not even Charlie. If she miscarried, she would face the tragedy on her own. If that happened, she vowed to fight the depression by herself and not repeat the lassitude that had caused her husband and sister to worry so. Ellen had chosen the hard life of a ranchwoman, and she would deal with disappointment and loss on her own.

She could keep the pregnancy a secret only so long, of course. After the first three months passed, she told Charlie. "I know," he said. "Did you think I didn't notice? Were you going to keep it a secret till the baby came?"

Ellen laughed at that. "I should have known if you can see a cow's with calf, you'd realize your own wife was expecting." He had known for a while, Ellen realized. For the last few weeks, Charlie had been solicitous of her. He had carried the pails of milk from the barn to the cellar for her and hadn't asked her to accompany him to Plug Hat Creek when he filled the water barrels. He'd helped her hitch the wagon and voiced concern about her riding Little Betty, who now belonged to her, thanks to Mrs. Gurley's generosity following Margaret's death.

After a time, her state was obvious to everyone. "I'm happy for you," Gladys said. "There's nothing in the world better than a baby. Still, I wouldn't mind giving you Ellis. Morris would kill me, though. Sometimes I think he cares more about Bailey and Ellis than he does about me." Ellis, her second son, had been born in early summer. When Gladys went into labor, Morris had fetched Ellen to stay with her while he went for the doctor. The man had arrived with little time to spare, so Ellen hadn't been required to deliver the baby. She'd stayed to help, however. She had been almost unconscious during her miscarriage, and now she knew all about childbirth—and caring for a new baby, since she had come every day for more than a week to help Gladys with the newborn.

"So much easier with the second one," the doctor had said, although Ellen hadn't thought it looked easy at all. She began to dread her own confinement.

"Two boys is three times the work," Gladys said as she sat in a chair, holding the baby in one arm. "You want coffee?"

"Too hot," Ellen said.

"Hot enough to fry eggs."

The summer was hot even at night. Despite the wind, the house was so stifling from the metal roof that Charlie and Ellen slept on blankets spread outside on the ground.

Gladys nodded. "I'll just pour us a glass of water. It ain't giving birth I mind so much as being tired all the time. Look at this house."

Ellen glanced around the soddy, which seemed as clean and tidy as ever. Gladys was, too, although there were sweat rings under her arms and perspiration on her face.

"Morris says he hopes we have ten." Gladys fanned her face with her hand. "I told him he was as bad as Mr. Brownell. Poor Julia. I remember when she first come here to Wyoming.

She had the most beautiful gold hair you ever seen. Glorious it was. The girls at the Columbine was all jealous."

Julia's hair had been a solid, dingy mat that last time Ellen had seen her, and she wondered when the woman had the time—or the water—to wash it. The Brownells lived even farther from Plug Hat Creek than Ellen.

"You seen Julia lately? That shiftless Mr. Brownell knocked her up again, the bastard. Couldn't have waited a week after the last one was born till he was at her again. At least Morris . . ." Gladys gave a wry smile. "Here I'm talking to you like I was still at the Columbine. Excuse it, will you?"

Ellen was amused at Gladys's talk. She'd never seen a prostitute before she came to Wallace, and now her best friend had been one. "Julia's last baby—a girl, I think, but how can you keep track?—was number five. So the next one will make six," Ellen said. "I visited her not long ago, and she was just sitting in a chair with all those poor, dirty little children gathered around her. It was like she had so much to do that she didn't know where to start. Or maybe she was thinking it didn't matter because whatever she did would have to be done again the next day. I'd baked bread and taken her a loaf, and the little ones just picked at it till it was gone. I wonder when she has time to bake." Ellen remembered one of the children looking up at her after the bread was eaten and saying, "I'm hungry, lady. I'm awful hungry." It was a terrible thing for a child not to have enough to eat, but what could Ellen do about it, except to take bread or cookies when she called?

"You know her husband won't do a thing to help her," Gladys said. "He come to Morris and asked for the borrow of his seeder, only Morris wouldn't loan it. Mr. Brownell borrowed the last one and broke it. He claimed there was something wrong with it and it wasn't his fault. Morris felt bad about saying no. It ain't neighborly, and those poor Brownells are about to starve to death, but we can't afford to buy another. We just ain't got the money." She poured water into two jelly jars and handed one to Ellen.

Ellis began to cry, and Gladys sat down and rocked him back and forth. The look on her face as she gazed at her son was pure rapture, and Ellen thought of pictures she'd seen of the Madonna. Despite Gladys's complaints, she loved her babies. "You ever taken you a good look at those Brownell kids?" Gladys asked.

"They're a little wild, but they seem like nice children."

"They are. I love every one of them. But did you see the oldest girl? Maybe she's not the oldest, but she's the biggest. There's something wrong with her. She puts me in mind of Margaret Gurley."

Ellen remembered that one of the girls had been sitting on the floor the last time she was there and seemed to babble. "How do you know?"

"Take a look at her face. Besides, Julia told me. She said her husband calls her the runt of the litter and makes fun of her. I think he treats her bad."

"You mean he beats her?"

Gladys nodded. She had unbuttoned her dress so that Ellis could nurse. Bailey was jealous of his brother and began to fuss. Ellen picked him up and set him in her lap, then played pat-a-cake with him.

"He beats all of them. They all got bruises."

"But they're children. Children fall down and get bruises all the time."

"You think Julia falls down, too?"

Ellen put her hand to her mouth. "He beats his wife? How dare he! I know Mr. McGinty hurts Ruth, but he is a cruel man, and I thought he was an exception."

Gladys stood, the baby still at her breast, and went to the cupboard and took out a cracker, handing it to Bailey. "You don't know much about men—that kind of men anyway—and I hope you never do, Ellen. I bet your Charlie would cut off his hand before he'd hit you. I told Morris when I married him, I'd leave if he ever whipped me, and he never has. But me and you are the lucky ones. Most men think they got the right. And their women do, too. Some of the men that's went to the Columbine liked to hurt the girls. One got paid extra to put up with it, but I never would." She shook her head. "Old McGinty was the worst, until they wouldn't let him go there no more. My guess is Brownell beats those kids one after the other for no reason. He'll blame his hard luck, but if he was rich as Mr. Gurley, he'd still do it."

"But he's educated. He graduated from college."

"Ha! You think that makes a difference?"

"What a horrid man. No wonder Julia is in such a state. I wish we could do something."

"Drown him, I say." Gladys gave a little laugh. "I guess we can't do that seeing as they don't have no well."

Ellis had finished nursing, and Gladys put him down in the makeshift cradle. Bailey had fallen asleep in Ellen's lap, and Gladys placed him in a trundle bed that she pulled out from under her own bed. "Morris made that when Bailey was born. He sure sets store by those boys. He's never once spanked Bailey."

"I wish Julia's husband was as good."

Gladys nodded. "You mark my words. Those kids'll leave

home the minute they can and never come back. The boys'll run off, and the girls'll get married, maybe as young as twelve or thirteen. And likely they'll pick men just as bad as their father, because they don't know no better."

"What do you suppose will happen to Julia?" Ellen finished her water and set down the jar.

"Oh, she'll work herself to death." Gladys thought that over. "Or kill herself."

ALTHOUGH CHARLIE TRIED to keep Ellen from performing the hardest chores, she still had plenty of work. When the hay crew came, she and Hattie cooked for them. She scrubbed the dirty clothes on a washboard and starched them with starch she made herself. She milked and made butter to sell and cared for the chickens. She kept up her garden, hauling water from the barrel and fertilizing the radishes and lettuce, the tomatoes and carrots and beets, with rotted horse manure. She cared for her flowers, too, and was delighted with the bright colors of the iris and hollyhocks against the drab house. She planted a lilac bush beside the door, although she knew it would be years before it bloomed.

She made hollyhock dolls and took them to the Brownell girls next time she called. To Ellen's relief, Mr. Brownell was out when she arrived. "I've brought us a treat," she told Julia, who was sitting on a bench inside the dark soddy, a baby in her lap, staring into space. "My sister sent me her favorite tea and said I was to take it to you since she never had a chance to come back for a visit. If you have the time, I'll just add a little fuel to the fire in the stove and heat the water." The stove was a cheap two-burner, and Ellen wondered how the woman could cook for all the Brownells on it. She went outside to the woodpile. There was no kindling, no wood, in fact, only a pile of cow chips, so Ellen picked up several for the stove. "I hope you have time to sit just a minute," she said when the water in the teakettle was steaming.

"Time?" Julia repeated, with a hard little laugh. Then she added, "Of course. I am grateful for a chance to do so, Mrs. Bacon."

"Oh, let's just use first names, shall we? After all, we're friends."

"I should like that."

Ellen took note of the proper language and said, "You must have been raised in refinement and aren't used to this life."

"Who is? Are you?" When Ellen didn't answer, Julia said, "Sometimes I wonder what I have brought my children to. It is not the life I planned when Richard and I were married. I did not want to come here—in fact, I was bitterly opposed— but what choice did I have? I had a child and another was expected, and a woman cannot deny her husband. 'Whither thou goest . . .'" She laughed again. "Besides, there were no options, no way I could have supported myself on my own."

"You had no family?"

"Yes, but they were so opposed to my marriage that they said I was dead to them. They warned me, but I was too taken with Richard. He was my teacher, and he read his beautiful poetry to me. I was so young I thought such things mattered. My parents were gone. I had inherited a bit of money, but Richard took it." She looked away embarrassed. "It is unseemly to talk so. I should not say such things, but there is no one to talk to here, and sometimes I am desperate."

The tea had steeped and Ellen wiped out two dirty cups,

poured the tea into them, and handed one to Julia. "It's lonely here, especially for a woman."

"When I hear the coyotes cry at night, I cry, too. It is the saddest sound in Christendom. I fear I will spend eternity in a grave on the prairie, attended only by those dreadful beasts."

"I would not like that either." Ellen sipped her tea and glanced around at the children, looking for the girl Gladys had told her about. She spotted her sitting on the floor cooing to a hollyhock doll.

"That is Lucy, my second-oldest child. She loves babies and will treasure the little dolly you brought her long after the flower has withered." Julia smiled at the girl. "As you can see, she is simple. Richard blames me, but I think she is the Lord's doing, for she is the dearest and most helpful of all of them. I should not say so, but I believe I love her above the others." A dark look came over her face, and she leaned forward and whispered, "Richard says we should have drowned her."

"Oh," Ellen said.

Julia nodded. Her eyes grew dark, and for a moment she stared into space as if she had forgotten Ellen was there. Then she caught herself and said, "Of course he was joking."

"Of course." Ellen finished her tea and said she must be going. "Keep the tea, since my sister sent some to me, too," she said, but that was untrue.

Julia didn't seem to hear her and started humming to the baby she was holding. She didn't notice that Ellen stood and made ready to leave. Lucy did, however, and whispered, "Thank you." Gladys was wrong. The girl could talk, although she lisped and the words were hard come by.

"You're welcome," Ellen said, but Lucy had turned away

and was patting her hollyhock doll. Both she and her mother seemed to be in another world then, and neither paid attention as Ellen left.

ELLEN WASN'T SURE when her baby would arrive but thought it would be early in the new year. She was ready. The cradle was waxed and the baby's blankets and clothes washed and set aside, along with the cloths and other things she would need for childbirth. The day before Christmas, she baked eight loaves of bread and prepared a ham that would not only serve as Christmas dinner but last for several days. She had jars of canned tomatoes and peaches and beans in the cellar and crocks of onions and potatoes, along with sacks of dried beans. She would not have to cook for a week after the baby came.

Charlie offered to take her to the Christmas Eve service at the church in Wallace, but a storm was brewing and both of them remembered the blizzard in which Ellen had lost the first baby. Charlie was relieved when Ellen told him she'd rather stay home.

Money was tight. Still, Ellen had ordered a watch for Charlie from the Montgomery Ward catalogue for Christmas. His other watch had been smashed when he was bucked off a horse. He bought her a hand mirror. Ellen had not seen her reflection in a long time, and she stared into the glass. There were wrinkles around her eyes and a streak of white in her hair. The Wyoming sun and wind had aged her.

Because there were no pines on the prairie to serve as Christmas trees, Ellen collected tumbleweeds and covered them with starch to form what she called a Christmas bush. Then she popped corn, and she and Charlie strung the kernels together to make strands for the tree.

The two of them dressed up for Christmas Eve dinner, Charlie in a clean shirt and Ellen in the better of her two Mother Hubbard dresses, with the horseshoe brooch that Charlie had given her that Christmas on the Gurley ranch, pinned to the neck. Instead of the kerosene lamp, Ellen lit candles. She bowed her head as she said grace. Charlie never gave thanks, but that evening, after Ellen finished the prayer, he said, "You keep my wife safe." It was more an order than a request.

The baby felt heavy that night, and Ellen ate only a little. The ham tasted dry to her, and the cake she had made with custard between the layers and whipped cream on top turned her stomach.

"You okay?" Charlie asked.

"Indigestion. I'll be glad when the baby comes."

"You think it'll be a boy or a girl?"

He'd asked that question dozens of times, and Ellen replied, "I don't know, but my guess it will be one or the other."

"You sure are smart, schoolteacher." Charlie grinned at her. Then he asked, "You still don't want to go to the Gurley place when the time comes?"

They had talked about that before, and Ellen had been adamant. She had lost her baby girl at the Gurley ranch. She didn't want to give birth there again. "I'll be fine," she assured him with more confidence than she felt. They had agreed that when she went into labor Charlie would fetch Mrs. Gurley, while Pike rode for the doctor. Ellen got up from the table, her hands holding her belly, and took the supper dishes to the basin.

"I'll wash them," Charlie said. He'd never offered to do that before. "You go on to bed."

Doing dishes was her job and Ellen was about to object,

but she was tired and smiled at her husband. "That's real nice, Charlie." She put on her nightgown and lay down while Charlie finished cleaning up, then went to check on the animals.

He expected Ellen to be asleep when he returned, but she was shifting around on the bed, trying to get comfortable. He slid in beside her and reached for her hand, then fell asleep.

Close to midnight, Ellen woke him. "The baby's coming."

"Now?"

"Now."

"But it's Christmas."

"I forgot to tell it that." Ellen started to laugh, but a pain hit her.

"I'll get Mrs. Gurley," he said, rolling out of bed and grabbing his pants.

"I don't think there's time."

"What?" Charlie stared at his wife in the dark. "I'll hurry."

Ellen reached for his arm. "It's too late. The baby's coming fast. You'll have to deliver it."

Charlie stammered, "I don't know how."

"I do," Ellen said, hoping he didn't know how frightened she was. "You've delivered calves. It's not much different, only you don't lick the baby clean." She tried to joke because she realized Charlie was even more frightened of his delivering the baby than she was. "I'll tell you what to do."

Charlie lit the kerosene lamp and then built a fire in the stove and heated water. By the time her husband was finished, Ellen was twisting on the bed as the delivery pains came on. "Help me, Charlie," she whispered.

For a few seconds, he stared at her. He had faced wild horses and blizzards, but nothing frightened him so much. Still, this was his wife, and he realized that without his help she might die. The thought actually calmed him. He went to the bed and said, "Easy now," just the way he did to a cow in labor.

When the tiny boy slid into his hands, Charlie began to cry. Ellen had never heard him cry and was alarmed. Was there something wrong? "Is it all right?"

The infant cried, too, and Charlie said, "Better than all right, honey. Perfect. You gave us a son."

Later, as she rested in bed, the baby in her arms and Charlie at her side, beaming at the infant, Ellen whispered, "I was thinking we ought to name him William, after your brother."

Charlie felt a lump in his throat. "I'd like that. You want to give him a middle name, too?"

Ellen glanced at the tumbleweed bush and realized that it was morning and that her son had been born on Christmas Day. He was their gift. She thought for a moment, then said, "Joseph. William Joseph."

"Joseph? Are you partial to it?"

Ellen shook her head. "Joseph, because I don't know the names of the shepherds or the three wise men."

Sixteen

Winter was the slack time on a ranch. It was too early for calves to be born and branded and castrated, for steers to be rounded up and sold. So there was not much work for Charlie at the Gurley ranch. But that didn't mean there wasn't plenty to do on his own place. He still had to take care of his cattle and repair equipment. The small barn, which was really just the remains of the old soddy, needed to be expanded, and he wanted to add a porch to the house. Still, he made time to take over some of Ellen's chores until she recovered. He did the milking and fed the chickens and gathered eggs. He tried to cook, but he was hopeless. It was a good thing Ellen had baked a ham and made bread before the baby arrived, although between them, Gladys and Mrs. Gurley brought enough food for days.

Pike rode by and peered at the infant, then handed Ellen a silver dollar. "For baby Fatback," he said, then grinned. "Or maybe we should call him Sausage. Or Hambone."

"We'll call him Billy. His name's Billy," she told him, adding, "Or I'll start calling you mud."

Miss Ferguson came, too. Gladys was there at the time, and her jaw dropped when the old woman entered the room.

She'd never spoken to Miss Ferguson, had never even seen her up close, and she wasn't aware that Ellen knew her. But in fact, after she took Miss Ferguson the pie that summer day, Ellen made it a habit to call on the old woman when she baked pies or cookies or bottled tomatoes or beans. Miss Ferguson told her once that while she enjoyed housekeeping and did a man's job with the cattle, she never got the hang of cooking. One of the cowboys prepared the grub that she and the ranch hands ate, and it was beef and beans or sowbelly, cornbread, and more beans. So she was grateful for what Ellen brought. In return, in her brisk way, Miss Ferguson taught Ellen ranch chores—how to doctor the milk cow and what to do about the chickens when they stopped laying. From time to time, she presented her with odd presents such as arrowheads and bones that were polished by the wind and snow until they looked like ivory. Once she brought a buffalo skull to hang on the barn, and another time she gave Ellen a scrap of Indian beadwork that she found lying in the field.

Miss Ferguson seemed just as surprised to spot Gladys when she walked into the room. Ellen was afraid the woman would bolt. "Gladys brought a cake. We were just having a piece. I'll cut one for you," Ellen said before the old woman could turn around.

Perhaps it was the cake, not Ellen's gesture of kindness, that kept Miss Ferguson there. She gave a single nod and pulled out a chair and sat down at the table. Ellen worried that she would leave the minute she finished eating, so she was slow in cutting the cake and finding a fork. "This is Gladys. Her place is just to the south."

"I know about her."

Gladys bristled. "I'm perfectly respectable now."

"I wasn't talking about that. You think I got the right

to be high-and-mighty? I just said I know who you are. You keep a neat house. Nice flowers." She finished the cake and stood up. "I brought you something." She'd left a gunnysack beside the door, and now she retrieved it. She opened it and pulled out a wooden frame.

Ellen stared. She couldn't imagine what it was.

"I got it somewhere. It's Indian, for a papoose, called a cradleboard. You wrap up a baby and put it in here, then fasten it to your back. Let's you walk around with both hands free. You can even ride a horse with it. Of course, people around here will stick up their noses at anything Indian, but I was partial to it. It's never been used since, well . . ."

Gladys examined the carrier. "Why, it's the cleverest thing I ever seen. Too bad it don't work for two boys."

Miss Ferguson gave a brittle laugh at that. "Now there's some that'll say you've gone Indian if you wear a cradleboard, but it'll help you get your work done."

"I never seen a thing wrong with Indians," Gladys said.

Miss Ferguson narrowed her eyes. "Me neither. They never did anything to me. But there are folks here that rate them right about the same as coyotes."

"You mean the old-time settlers?" Ellen asked. She had heard an old man at the mercantile talk about Indians as if they ought to be stamped out.

"Them and others. That Mr. Brownell hates them as much as anybody."

Ellen knew Miss Ferguson didn't gossip and wondered how she knew the Brownells.

"He came out here thinking the Indian was the noble redskin," the woman continued. "Something he read in books, I expect. He offered two Cheyenne a day's work in the field and said he'd pay them fifty cents. When the Indians finished up, Mr. Brownell said he'd meant fifty cents for the two of them, not for each. One of them pulled out a skinning knife and made him pay up. Now Brownell goes around spouting they're savages."

"Don't that beat all," Gladys said.

"His wife offered them a pan of biscuits, but he grabbed it out of her hand and threw the biscuits on the ground. Then he told her to pick them up and feed them to the kids for supper."

Ellen said, "I don't think I've ever heard anybody say a nice thing about Mr. Brownell. I'm partial to Julia Brownell, however."

"She won't last. I've seen it before. Won't be long till she goes crazy. Or maybe they'll get starved out."

Ellen stared at Miss Ferguson a moment, wondering how the woman knew all about the Brownells, then realized she must have taken food to them—not cookies and pie but maybe a sack of beans or flour or even a side of beef.

"I've said too much. My mouth's dry from it." Miss Ferguson stood. "I'll be on my way. You use that carrier or not. It's up to you." She left before Ellen could thank her.

"I always thought she was a nutty old lady. Wait till I tell Morris about her."

"She might not want you to do that," Ellen said.

Gladys thought that over, then nodded. "She wants people to think she's a tough old bird. Are you going to use the cradleboard?"

Ellen wasn't sure. She and Charlie had never talked about Indians. He might be embarrassed if she carried Billy on her back. "Maybe around the ranch. It'd sure be easier than carrying him."

"Well, I think it's a swell idea. Maybe I can make one just like it for Ellis."

"What would Morris say about that?"

Gladys thought a moment. "I don't know. We never talked about Indians neither."

The two babies had been sleeping on the bed. Now Ellis began to cry and woke Billy, who cried, too. Bailey, playing on the floor, felt left out and joined them. Gladys looked at the three bawling children and asked, "How does Julia Brownell put up with this?"

Ellen remembered Julia staring off into space and replied, "I think she goes off into her own world."

"What do you think will happen to them Brownells?"

"Miss Ferguson's probably right. They're already as thin as cornstalks. They could starve. Or move away."

"You think maybe she'll turn crazy?"

That was an awful idea, and Ellen thought it over. "I think maybe she is a little bit crazy already. But with all those children and no food and both the wind and the coyotes howling, who wouldn't be?"

HATTIE HAD COME each day for the first couple of weeks after Billy was born, but now she was back in school. The baby and the snow had kept Ellen cooped up inside, but the weather had turned sunny. In fact, the bottom half of Charlie's face was already sunburned, although his forehead, shaded by his hat, was a white as ever. One morning, he asked Ellen to go into Wallace with him to pick up supplies and stop at the blacksmith's. "It'd do you good," he said.

She hadn't taken the baby anywhere, not to the Gurley ranch or to Gladys's place, and she said the drive to Wallace might be too much for Billy's first outing.

"We could stay at the hotel if the weather turns or at the McGintys' place," he suggested.

"It's a long trip."

"I could drop you off to see your friend Ruth. She hasn't come by to see the baby."

In fact, Ellen hadn't seen Ruth since long before Billy was born. She had hoped the woman might call because she had two of Laura's letters for her but figured McGinty wouldn't let her go out. Charlie had offered to drop off the letters, but Ellen knew that would make McGinty suspicious. Now Charlie said he could leave her and the baby at Ruth's house while he went on to the blacksmith's. If Gurley was there, he probably wouldn't want to be around a baby and would leave.

Ellen decided that was a fine idea, and she began placing food in a sack to take along for their dinner. Charlie told her a restaurant had opened in Wallace, however, and they'd eat there. Ellen smiled to herself then, realizing now that the real reason Charlie wanted her to go with him was to show off the baby. She wrapped Billy in quilts and put a knit cap on his head, while Charlie found a wooden box and placed an Indian saddle blanket in it for a baby bed. He helped Ellen onto the wagon seat, which was covered by a buffalo robe, then handed up Billy. The sun was bright, and she put a scarf over the baby's face.

"I'll buy him a Stetson at the mercantile," Charlie said.

"He'll outgrow it before we get home."

Despite the snow that had drifted along the fence lines, the sky was clear, and Ellen was glad she'd agreed to the outing. The snow was clean, and the white stretched so far that it made her eyes hurt. Charlie pointed out tracks of deer and antelope—and coyotes. "What's that?" Ellen asked, indicating huge paw prints.

"Maybe a bear." When Ellen shivered, he added, "We don't get too many of them out here on the prairie." He turned so that he could look at Billy. "Don't worry, Son. I'll teach you to shoot." He glanced at Ellen. "He'll keep you safe when I'm not around, Mom."

She liked that he called her Mom. It made them seem like a family. And that was just what they were. Billy was a fine, healthy infant, and Ellen had experienced none of the depression following childbirth that Lizzie had warned her about. Ranch life was hard and things were tight, but Ellen and Charlie had each other—and enough money for dinner in a restaurant. Life was swell, Ellen thought as they reached Wallace.

They stopped first at the mercantile, where the men sitting around the stove winked at Charlie and told him he'd done all right. They peered at the baby, not sure what to say. One said, "He's only a button," and another let Billy curl his tiny fingers against the man's dirty thumb. Ellen thought to pull the baby away, then decided it didn't matter. Billy would get used to dirt.

After they left the mercantile, they had dinner at the restaurant. Then Charlie drove to the McGinty house, which looked even more forlorn. Its unpainted boards were silvery in the snow, and Ellen tried to remember moments when she'd enjoyed living there. She thought of going over lessons in the evening while Ruth sat beside her, mending or piecing, the two of them venturing outside on icy nights to look at the millions of stars that shone against an immense black sky. Ruth had made it easier for Ellen to last through that winter, and she was grateful.

The door was shut against the cold and there was no light shining through the windows, but a wisp of smoke rose from the chimney. Ellen hoped Ruth was home. It would be a shame to miss giving her the letters. Ellen stayed in the wagon while Charlie knocked on the door. In a minute it opened, and Ruth answered it, a grim look on her face when she recognized Charlie. Then she saw Ellen, and her face lit up. "Come," she said.

Ellen handed Charlie the baby and climbed off the wagon seat. "We brought our boy," she said. Charlie handed back the baby, saying he would return after he finished with the blacksmith.

The two women went inside, and Ruth said, "Oh, do let me hold him. I heard he was a boy. What is he called?"

"Billy," Ellen said, handing her the baby.

"A noble name. Did you know it was my father's name?"

Ellen shook her head, and Ruth added, "He was a fine man, dead these many years. I suppose that's why I married McGinty. It's why he married me anyway, because Father left me a good farm." Ellen wondered what had happened to it but was too polite to ask. Ruth must have sensed that, because she added, "McGinty borrowed money against it, and we couldn't pay it back. We came out here to start over." She gave a little laugh. "It didn't turn out the way we thought."

"Where is Mr. McGinty?"

"He said he was going to collect buffalo bones, him and Mr. Snyder. But there haven't been bones to collect in years, and if there was, you couldn't do it with five feet of snow on the ground. I expect they're at the saloon. Or somewhere."

Ellen had heard McGinty was suspected of rustling, although nobody had caught him. Not yet anyway. She wondered if Ruth knew that.

"I've brought you something." Ellen reached into the quilt wrapped around Billy and removed the letters. "Two of them! I wanted you to have them earlier, but with the baby, I couldn't get to town, and I was afraid your husband would know something was up if Charlie came by. I'll wait if you want to read them now, before Mr. McGinty gets back."

Ruth studied the letters. "Two. What a treat. He won't return for a long time. Let's have a nice chat, and I'll read them after you're gone." She hid the letters in a cupboard drawer under her dish towels, then dipped water out of a pail into a teakettle. "I've got chamomile tea. I dried the flowers last summer."

Ellen glimpsed her friend's face in the lamplight, then looked at the woman's arms. They were covered with long scratches, some red, others scabbed over. There was even one on her neck. "Ruth!" she gasped.

Ruth raised her head, confused. When she realized that Ellen was looking at her scratches, she turned down the lamp. "It was an accident."

"An accident? What happened."

"Oh . . ." Tears came into Ruth's eyes, and she sniffed to hold them back. "I fell."

"No, Ruth."

"You know how clumsy I am."

"You aren't. It was your husband, wasn't it?"

Ruth didn't reply. Billy fussed, and Ruth held out her arms, smiling at the infant. "I was always sorry I didn't have more babies." She took Billy from Ellen and rocked him in her arms, humming tonelessly. "He will grow up to be a good man."

Ellen sipped the tea Ruth had made, then said, "Tell me what he did."

"What does it matter, Ellen? Once I thought I could change him, but I can't. It got worse after Mr. Snyder came.

Sometimes Mr. Snyder slaps me and McGinty doesn't do anything about it."

"Mr. Snyder did this to you?"

"Oh no. It was McGinty. He whipped me with a thornbush."

"He what?" Ellen was incensed.

Ruth wouldn't look at her. "Maybe it's my fault. I should have stopped him from coming to Wyoming. That's when it started. Nothing's worked out for him here. It seems to make him feel better to hit me." She sank lower in her chair.

Ellen was sick at how degraded Ruth must feel. "It is never your fault." Ellen was holding Billy now and looked down at the little face, wondering how an innocent child like her son could turn into a cruel and violent man. "Why don't you leave him, Ruth?"

"Oh, I couldn't. Where would I go?"

"To your daughter's."

"I'd be shamed, Ellen. I never told nobody but you how he does me. What would Laura think of me?"

"She doesn't know?"

Ruth shook her head. "I wouldn't burden her."

"But she's your daughter. If you won't tell her, I'll write to her."

"No!" Ruth raised her head, defiant. "She's never to know. It's not your business."

The woman was agitated, and Ellen sought to calm her. "If you don't want me to, I won't."

Ruth sighed. "I know you mean well, but I couldn't stand it if she thought I was a beaten-down old woman. Her respect is all I have left. Don't take that from me."

Ellen put her hand on Ruth's arm and said, "Of course I won't." The two sat quietly until Ruth jumped up suddenly.

"I almost forgot. I have something for you." She went to the cupboard and pulled out a quilt and handed it to Ellen. "I made it for the baby. I'm glad you stopped before he's too big for it." She unfolded a baby quilt with a pattern of stars. "I made it to remind you of the nights we went outside to see the stars." As Ruth ran her hand over the little quilt, she said, "Those was the happiest times I had since Laura left us."

Ellen wondered why the girl had gone away, but she was afraid to ask.

CHARLIE ARRIVED A few minutes later. Ellen hadn't heard the wagon and for good reason. Charlie had left it at the blacksmith's. The front axle was cracked and they would have to spend the night in Wallace, since it couldn't be repaired until morning. Ellen pointed out that the cow would have to be milked and that she had left supper on the stove, ready to be heated, but Charlie told her it would be dangerous driving the wagon home and back. What if it broke down? They didn't have any choice but to stay overnight.

Ruth invited them to spend the night with her, but Charlie replied he'd already booked a room at the hotel. He hadn't, but he knew Ellen would not want to sleep in the house with old McGinty, even if there had been room for them. So he and Ellen walked back to the hotel and engaged a room. It wasn't much, but Ellen had never stayed in a hotel in Wyoming and she looked on the evening an adventure.

THE WAGON REPAIRED, they were on their way by the next afternoon. As soon as they arrived home, Charlie milked the cow, while Ellen went inside to feed Billy, then see to dinner. When Charlie came in with the milk pails, he found Ellen ripping the sheets off their bed. As she flung them onto the floor, she told Charlie, "While we were gone, some grub rider helped himself to our supper and slept in our bed."

Seventeen

Ellen was now responsible for the chores that Charlie had done for her after Billy was born, and added to the care of the baby, her work seemed to have doubled. She began to look for shortcuts, such as baking four loaves of bread at a time instead of two and setting a braided rug inside the door to keep the floor from being muddied. She cut back on ironing and ordered soap from Montgomery Ward instead of making her own. One afternoon, she wrapped Billy in a quilt and placed him in the cradleboard and strapped him to her back, then went out to milk the cow. She wouldn't have to worry about him when she milked or when she gathered eggs either. After she returned, Charlie stared at her and said, "What the hell?"

"Isn't it clever? Miss Ferguson gave it to me. It's called a cradleboard, and it's for an Indian papoose."

"Billy's not an Indian."

"Of course not, but it's a good idea, don't you think? Putting him in the cradleboard lets me carry him around but keeps my hands free."

"I don't like it, Ellen. That thing's Indian. You're new to Wyoming. You don't know feelings about Indians are still pretty raw round here. There's folks that's survived Indian fights, and what are they going to think?"

Ellen wondered when Charlie had ever worried about what people thought, but perhaps he was like the old settlers and didn't care for Indians. He'd never said. "Don't you like Indians?" she asked.

Charlie shrugged. "I never minded them. It's just that there's folks that would think poorly of you."

"Don't you want me to use it?"

"I don't reckon I do."

Ellen was disappointed, but she removed the baby and the quilt from the cradleboard and set it aside.

She offered the cradleboard to Gladys, but Gladys told her Morris didn't want her to use it either. "He says if I use it, people'll think I'm Indian." She shook her head in exasperation. "Indians ride horses, too, but nobody thinks a white man on horseback's an Indian. I guess it's what men wants and women wants that makes the difference." The women laughed at that, but neither thought to go against her husband's wishes.

Winter lingered, and Ellen was reminded of what Gladys had said once, that Wyoming seemed to have three seasons: this winter, last winter, and July. But now spring had come, and she no longer had to stay cooped up inside. She got out more, especially on the days Charlie worked at the Gurley ranch, since he didn't come home for dinner. He was grateful for the work. Coyotes had killed one of Charlie's calves, and a steer they had planned to sell in the fall had disappeared, maybe taken down by wolves. A skunk had gotten into the henhouse and eaten many of the chicks, which made Ellen wish the black snake was still around. Charlie worried about a

drought and feared Plug Hat Creek might go dry. Money was
scarce, and he told Ellen they might have to live on potatoes
next winter if things didn't get better. The potatoes they had
dug in the fall were already a big part of their diet, although
many of them had rotted in the cellar and she had to peel two
for every one she used.

Ellen was no spendthrift, but still, she chided herself for
a dress she had bought from the catalogue that winter and
hair combs that she had thought were essential. At least she
had not had to buy calico because Lizzie sent remnants to her.
Gladys was teaching Ellen to piece, and working with the
colorful scraps of material brought her pleasure on the dark
days of winter. She and Gladys met nearly every week to stitch
on quilt pieces.

One afternoon, the two sat on chairs Gladys had dragged
from the house so they could sew in the sunshine. The babies
slept inside on the bed, while Bailey played in the dirt with a
rag dog that his mother had made for him. "I miss porches,"
Ellen said. "When I was a girl, we had one that went across
the front of the house and down the side. There was a trumpet
vine for shade, and it was so lovely to sit there in the heat of
the summer. I haven't seen a real porch since I came to Wyoming."

"Do you miss it?" Gladys asked.

"My life back there?" Ellen paused for a moment while she
thought that over. Of course, she missed it. Who wouldn't?
She'd have to be crazy not to think it would be nice to have a
proper house with a porch, to have a washing machine instead
of a scrub board, trees instead of tumbleweeds. But if she had
all those things, she wouldn't have Charlie. "Yes, I suppose,"
she said. "I was never lonely when I was a girl. But I chose this
life, and I wouldn't have any other. I can't imagine Charlie

wearing a suit and a high collar and going to work in an office every day. If I want to be married to him, this is my life."

"I like it, too," Gladys said. "You think if you was back where you come from you'd be friends with a woman worked in a hook house?"

Ellen laughed and didn't reply. The answer was obvious.

"I like it here because nobody cares much what you was," Gladys said. "They just care what you are now. That's not just true with women either. It's true with men. You ever hear what Morris done?"

"Morris?" Ellen shook her head as she took a small stitch in two scraps of material that had been cut into triangles. Morris struck her as nice enough but rather stodgy. Sometimes he was even moralizing. She couldn't imagine he'd ever done anything improper except maybe drink too much at the Silver Dollar.

"He held up a train and got sent to the prison in Laramie. He was there three years."

Ellen stopped with her needle in the air, dumbfounded. "Morris? Robbed a train?"

"Good thing he's a better farmer than a robber. He was with two pals, and they told him to take the valuables off the passengers. Morris was young then, maybe only fifteen, and he said that was a mean thing to do. He wouldn't rob a woman. So them two others took the money from the mail coach and rode off with Morris's horse. He was the only one got caught, and even though his partners left him behind, he wouldn't rat on them. Down at the Silver Dollar they call him the dumbest train robber in Wyoming history. Sometimes I think Morris is a little proud of that."

"Why, Morris is as honest as the day is long."

"He sure is. He told me he learned his lesson. He said if

our boys ever stole as much as a nickel, he'd whip them. Morris has a real sense of honor, not like some I know."

Ellen looked up from her stitching. "Who?"

"Oh, you know. There's talk of rustlers around here."

"Mr. McGinty?"

Gladys paused with her needle in the air. "He's a good guess, but there's others. Morris thinks Mr. Brownell might have butchered a cow."

"He doesn't own any cows."

"That's what I'm saying: It weren't his."

Ellen set her sewing in her lap. "We had a steer that we thought was eaten by wolves."

Gladys nodded. "Maybe it was."

"Do you really think it could have been stolen by Mr. Brownell?"

"He's got to feed his family."

"But he knows we're not rich. Why would he steal from his neighbors who aren't much better off than he is? What kind of man does that?"

"A lazy, sneaky son of a bitch who's got no morals."

Ellen was a little shocked by Gladys's words, but she had to agree Mr. Brownell was not an honorable man.

THAT NIGHT AT supper, Ellen repeated her conversation with Gladys to Charlie. "Do you think Mr. Brownell could have butchered our steer?" she asked.

"I'm sure of it," Charlie replied.

Ellen looked at him in surprise. "And you didn't tell me?"

"Mrs. Brownell's your friend. Besides, I don't have any proof. I guess I felt kind of sorry for the wife and kids. Maybe that steer kept them from starving to death." Charlie leaned back until he was balancing his chair on two legs. "Thing that bothers me is he stole it. Hell, I'd have given it to him if he'd asked."

"What if he takes another?"

"I don't think he will." Charlie glanced up at the ceiling, then looked at Ellen. "I told him I'd kill him if another of my animals went missing."

"Charlie, you wouldn't!" Ellen said, shocked. Then she asked "Would you?"

Charlie thought that over. "Once upon a time, you got hanged for rustling in Wyoming."

"But you wouldn't kill him."

Charlie shrugged. "It's not likely to come to that. The man may be as sneaky as a coyote, but he's as cowardly as one, too. We won't have to worry about losing any more steers."

"How will the Brownells eat?"

"Maybe he'll learn how to farm." Charlie shrugged. "Mr. Gurley told me Brownell asked him for a job. Mr. Gurley didn't need any more hands, but he said he'd try him for a week. He didn't show up until eight o'clock and told Mr. Gurley that any fool who got up before daylight should poison himself. Brownell can barely ride a horse. He fell off and nearly broke his backside. Then Mr. Gurley put him to shoveling manure, but Brownell said that was no work for a man who'd gone to college. So Mr. Gurley paid him two days' wages and told him he wasn't needed. Brownell whined and cussed and said he ought to get at least a week's pay. Mr. Gurley said he wasn't worth the two days' wages he gave him, but he did it because he felt sorry for the man's wife and kids. And he told Brownell if any of his cattle went missing, he'd know where to look for them, made sure he knew rustlers aren't looked on too kindly around here."

"I wish there was some way we could at least help Julia."

"She got any kinfolk?"

"They disowned her when she married Mr. Brownell." Ellen was holding Billy, and she shifted him from one hip to the other, smiling at him. She wondered if Julia loved each of her children as much as she loved Billy. "Maybe we could help out."

"You already do that, honey. I've seen the things you take to them, things maybe you didn't want me to know about. You think I didn't notice one of our chickens wriggling around in a flour sack?"

"I wasn't sure you'd approve."

"You'd have got your way even if I didn't. You have a kind heart. It's your nature. I guess that's one of the reasons I love you." Words of affection didn't come easily to Charlie, and he cleared his throat. "Everybody else helps out the Brownells, too, but there's only so much you can do for folks that won't help themselves."

"He's the one who's lazy. What in the world can Julia do?"

"She could stop having babies."

Ellen frowned. "There's only one way she could do that. Are you saying she should . . . deny him?"

"It's the only way I know about." Charlie's face was red, but maybe that was because it was already sunburned.

"Well, it's something to think about, Charlie," she teased.

"Nah. I'm not worried. We only got one kid."

A DAY LATER, Ellen baked six loaves of bread and put three aside to take to the Brownells. She placed them and a dozen eggs wrapped in newspaper in a flour sack and set them in the back of the wagon. "I guess you know where I'm going," she told Charlie, adjusting the sunbonnet she had put on to keep her face from getting burned. She thought she must look like a hollyhock.

"I expect I do. We got half a ham you might take along. I'm getting tired of ham."

"That's real nice of you."

Charlie brought out the horses, then said, "Why don't you ride Little Betty instead of taking the wagon? You can tie the sack to the saddle."

"What will I do with Billy? I'm afraid if I carry him, I'll drop him."

Charlie thought that over. "Maybe you could use that cradleboard this one time. Nobody'll see you except the Brownells, and if he says anything you tell him he can take it up with me."

Ellen nodded, hiding a smile. She hadn't expected Charlie to give in on the cradleboard and wouldn't gloat. She went inside and put Billy into the carrier while Charlie saddled the horse. At first the cradleboard felt awkward, but after a time she got used to it, and when she turned to look at Billy she found the jogging of the horse had put him to sleep. The day was glorious, with dandelions turning the prairie into a yellow carpet.

The Brownell place was dreary, however. The smallest Brownell children were playing outside in the mud when Ellen arrived, and Julia was bent over a laundry tub. Ellen thought to tell Julia she had baked too many loaves of bread and hoped the Brownells could eat them, but she'd said that before and had run out of excuses for bringing food. Besides, Julia knew why the neighbors took food to her. So Ellen set her sleeping baby in the doorway and went inside and placed the bread and eggs and ham on the table. Mr. Brownell was cleaning his fingernails with a knife and looked over the offerings. "I was hoping for a fryer. I got a taste for chicken right now."

"A skunk got most of my chicks, but I can spare a couple if you want to raise them."

"Talk to Julia about it. That's woman's work."

There was a clatter across the dark room. Lucy, the oldest girl, had dropped something and backed into a corner, cowering. "What'd you do, dummy? You drop my breakfast, I'll smack you good," her father said.

The girl began to cry, and Mr. Brownell raised his hand. Before he could get up, however, Ellen said, "It can't be too bad. I'll help clean it up." She went to the stove where a dish of cornmeal mush had overturned. "Why, it's nothing. Will you help me scrape it up, Lucy?"

The girl stared at her and didn't answer.

"No use to talk to her. She's got the brain of a goose," Mr. Brownell said.

Ellen swallowed a reply and cleaned the stove. Then she scooped thin cornmeal mush from a pot into a bowl and set it in front of Mr. Brownell. She took Lucy's hand and led her outside into the sunshine. The laundry forgotten, Julia was sitting on the ground, nursing the latest baby, ignoring the whining children. Ellen picked up the next-smallest one and began rocking him in her arms. "Lucy's a sweet little girl," Ellen said.

Julia looked up, as if surprised to see Ellen. "She's the best of them," she said.

"What's his name?" Ellen asked, nodding at the baby at Julia's breast.

"My husband wanted to name him Wendell, but he forgot we already have a Wendell." She gave a bark of a laugh. "So he doesn't have a name."

Ellen had brought her piecing with her, hoping Julia would want to sit outside and sew, but she realized that was impossible. If Julia had any leisure time for sewing, she would have been mending the children's clothes, not stitching a quilt. So she kept the sewing in her pocket. "It's a beautiful day. I love spring; don't you?"

"Is it spring?" Julia asked. "Have the apple blossoms bloomed?"

Ellen started to say there weren't any apple trees but stopped, realizing Julia had slipped into another world. Why remind her she was sitting in the mud in Wyoming? Ellen went to the laundry tub and finished scrubbing the clothes, then rinsed them in the second tub, which held cold water, and spread them on the bushes to dry.

By then, Julia had gone inside, and it was obvious she had forgotten Ellen was there. Ellen strapped the cradleboard to her back, mounted Little Betty, and rode home, her kind heart heavy.

Eighteen

Late one morning, Ellen saw a little boy running down the road. He turned in to her yard. He was panting and stopped, doubled over to catch his breath. "Pa says come," he managed to sputter. "Pa says come quick."

"You're the Brownell boy?" Ellen asked.

He nodded. "Chester. I'm the oldest."

"What's wrong?"

"It's Ma! She's acting crazy."

Well, of course she is, Ellen thought. She waited for the boy to gulp more air. He held his side as if he had a stitch in it, then raised a bare foot and pulled out a thorn.

"Is your mother ill?" *Maybe Julia is pregnant again and having a miscarriage.*

"No, lady, she's crazy."

Charlie had been in the barn, and he heard the conversation as he came out. "What's wrong with her, son?"

"She's sitting in the washtub. She ain't got no clothes on."

Ellen and Charlie exchanged a glance; then he said, "Maybe she's taking a bath."

Chester shook his head. "No, sir. She's holding the baby. He's dead. Pa says she drowned him."

"I'll hitch up the wagon; you can take the boy back with you. Then I'll go into town and get the doctor. And the sheriff," Charlie told Ellen.

"Stop and tell Mrs. Gurley. She'll know what to do," Ellen said. She'd started for the house to get Billy.

"Mrs. Gurley went to visit her sister who's ailing. She won't be back for weeks."

"Then tell Gladys to come."

"Sure." Charlie nodded and went back into the barn. He saddled Huckleberry, then brought out the team and hitched it to the wagon.

Chester followed Ellen into the house and glanced around with awe. Ellen caught the look and thought, *Poor little fellow. He's probably never been in a clean house with food on the table.* Chester stared at a dish of apples and the four loaves of bread Ellen had taken from the oven an hour earlier. "I'm awful hungry," he said.

"Help yourself," Ellen told him. She put a quilt in the Arbuckles' box that she used as a bed for Billy in the wagon, then dressed the little fellow in warm clothes, because the weather could turn bad. By the time she had finished, Chester had eaten two apples and half of a loaf of bread. She shoved the rest of the apples and the bread into a flour sack and handed it to Chester; then carrying Billy, she went out to where Charlie was waiting beside the wagon.

"I'll be there as soon as I can," Charlie told her as he mounted Huckleberry. "You think you'll have any trouble with Brownell? You can take my gun."

"No. I'll be all right."

"What do you think happened?"

"She broke. She couldn't handle it anymore." Ellen climbed into the wagon, the boy beside her, and she flicked the reins on the horses' backs. "Giddyup," she urged them. When the team was partway down the road, Ellen turned to Chester. "Tell me what happened."

The boy shrugged. "Ma went crazy and drowned the baby. I was in the house, and when Pa called me, I went out, and she was sitting in the tub singing to him."

"Which baby is it?"

"The new one. He ain't got a name yet." The boy scratched the spot on his foot where the thorn had been. "I guess he won't ever have one now."

"What about the other children?"

"Oh, they're fine. The dummy's looking after them."

"That's not a nice thing to call your sister."

"We all call her that. Can't none of us remember her name."

Ellen hurried the horses, hoping she'd reach the soddy before Julia harmed any of the other children, and at last she pulled into the Brownell yard. Julia was still sitting in the washtub. The baby was on the ground. Ellen checked Billy, but he was sleeping, and she left him in the wagon. She climbed out and went to the baby. The poor little thing was lying naked in the dirt, so she wrapped him in a clean dish towel that she'd brought along and handed him to Mr. Brownell, who was sitting on a broken chair by the door. Ellen walked to the washtub. "Julia?' she said.

Julia was humming to herself and didn't reply. Ellen wasn't sure what to do. She took her friend's arm. "You'll catch cold if you stay in the water too long," she said. "Let me help you out."

Julia didn't respond, but when Ellen pulled her she stood and let Ellen help her step out onto the dirt. There was no towel, no clothes, so Ellen put her arm around the woman and led her into the house. "Where is her dress?" Ellen asked.

"How should I know? Fool woman. What the hell's the

matter with her?" Mr. Brownell replied as he rose and put the dead baby on the chair. It was the first thing he'd said.

"She must be having a breakdown."

"Well, I don't know why."

"Maybe it's having all the babies so close together."

Mr. Brownell sniffed. "It's her own durn fault. She pops them out like hen's eggs."

Ellen stared at him, incredulous.

"What are you looking at me like that for?"

"I am of the understanding it takes both husband and wife to create a child."

Mr. Brownell turned away and told his wife, "You best get dressed. You shame me standing there like that. There's work to do."

"She won't be doing any work for a while." Ellen found the dress and slipped it over Julia's head. She gently pushed the woman so that she was lying on the bed. "She is ill, Mr. Brownell. There is nothing she can do."

"Who's going to take care of all these kids?"

"Perhaps you can."

"Me? Maybe you didn't notice I'm a man."

"You are their father. It is your responsibility."

He didn't reply, and after a time Lucy crept forward and said, "Baby dead."

"I know, sweetheart. I'm so sorry. He drowned."

"Pa. Hit. Him."

Mr. Brownell backhanded the girl, who fell to the floor, then crawled away. "She doesn't know what she's saying."

Ellen turned to Chester and raised an eyebrow. "I don't know nothing," the boy said, not looking Ellen in the face.

"You tell her it was your ma drowned him."

"Yes, sir," the boy muttered.

"But it wasn't, was it?" Ellen asked.

"Ma put him in the washtub. Maybe she thought he'd get better. It was Ma drowned him."

Chester glanced at his father, looking for approval. "Go outside, boy," Mr. Brownell said and followed his son out the door.

Ellen had no more time for the man. She turned to Julia, who was still lying on the bed, shaking now. "Let me help you get under the covers," she said, pulling up a blanket. There were no sheets, only a filthy mattress. She called Lucy over and told her to wet a cloth and wipe her mother's face. The little girl's gentle touch might calm Julia, although the woman seemed to be in a trance. Ellen turned to the other children and asked if they had eaten that day. They stared at her, their dirty faces solemn. "First we'll wash your hands and faces," Ellen said, leading them outside to the tub in which Julia had been sitting. She put their hands in the water and showed the little ones how to rub them together, then splashed water onto their faces, which made the children laugh.

She heard a cry and realized Billy was awake. She lifted him out of the wagon and settled him on her hip. "Here you go, little boy. We'll feed the others, and then you can have your dinner." She went back inside and took out the bread and set it on the table, then found a knife and cut it into slices. The knife was dull and the slices were ragged, but Ellen knew the children would not mind. She told Chester to bring in kindling for the cookstove, then built up the fire and fried half a dozen eggs. Cooking was awkward with Billy on her hip, but the house was so dirty she didn't want to set him down. The children ate the eggs from the frying pan. Ellen didn't know if a year-old baby would eat an egg, but the child got it down.

While the children ate, Ellen nursed Billy. She turned aside when Mr. Brownell entered the shack, but he paid no attention to her as he rummaged through boxes and trunks. Ellen didn't know what he was doing, but she didn't care. He called to Chester and said, "Look to your gatherings." He should have been taking care of his children, but Ellen knew he wouldn't.

A few minutes later, Gladys pulled up. She got down from the wagon, went to where the little body lay on the chair, and crossed herself. Then she picked up her boys and brought them inside. "What happened?" she asked.

"Her husband says she drowned the baby, but Lucy told me he hit the poor thing."

"What do the others say?"

"Chester . . ." Ellen nodded at the boy who had just left the house with his father. "He's so afraid of Mr. Brownell that he just says what he's told. Julia can't talk, so I don't suppose we'll ever know."

Gladys went to Julia, who was lying on the bed staring at the ceiling. "Hello, dear. How are you feeling?"

Julia didn't move, didn't even turn her head to acknowledge Gladys.

"Are you cold? Do you need a quilt?"

Julia kept staring at the ceiling.

"She's been like this since I arrived. I don't know what to do," Ellen said.

The two heard the sound of a wagon and looked out the door. Mr. Brownell and his son were headed for the road.

"Where do you think he's going?" Ellen asked.

"Maybe Julia's got people somewhere. He might be sending them a telegram."

"She told me they disinherited her when she married. Besides, Wallace is south. He's going north."

The two women stared at each other. "You think he's running off?" Glady asked.

"Looks like it."

"Why, that dirty bastard." She glanced at Ellen to see if the words had offended her.

"That's just what he is."

"What are we going to do with all these kids?"

Ellen shrugged. "I don't know." She glanced at Julia, who was still comatose. "Take them home for now, I guess."

"That's what I'm thinking. We better gather up their clothes." The two women began to look around for the rags the children wore. There weren't many and they were dirty. They would have to be washed and mended. The women were trying to sort out which clothes belonged to which child when they heard horses. Charlie had arrived with the sheriff and the doctor.

The three men came into the soddy and glanced around. The sheriff wrinkled his nose at the smell of dirty diapers, then looked at Julia. "She's a little off in the upper story," he said.

The doctor didn't respond but went to Julia. "Mrs. Brownell," he said, but Julia didn't answer. The doctor opened a worn bag and took out a stethoscope and checked Julia. He peered into her eyes and mouth, then turned back to the men. "I've seen it before. Some women can't take it. Gets to be too much for them. Too much dirt and too much work that never gets done. Then all the kids that never stop coming. Funny how men blame their wives for that. And this one's got a worthless husband to boot. Only things we can do is send her to the asylum. She might get better, might not."

"Can she tell us what happened to the baby?" the sheriff asked.

"You can ask, but my guess is she won't. She might not even know," Ellen said.

The sheriff went to Julia and sat down on the edge of the bed. "Mrs. Brownell, there's a dead baby out there. You want to tell me what happened?"

Julia stared at the ceiling.

"I sure would appreciate it."

Julia didn't move.

He got up. "You think any of the kids know?" he asked Ellen.

"Lucy said her father hit the baby. I asked Chester, the oldest, but his father told him Julia drowned the child and Chester's too afraid of his father to speak against him."

"Where's he at?"

"He went off with Mr. Brownell."

"We didn't pass him coming here," Charlie said.

"He went the other way. I think they're running off. The horses are old. You shouldn't have any trouble catching him."

"That is if I want to." The sheriff asked, "Who's Lucy?"

Ellen nodded at the girl, who was cowering in the corner, her thumb in her mouth.

"She's too young to testify." He narrowed his eyes. "Is she simple?"

"Slow," Ellen told him.

The sheriff shook his head. "It ain't worth the county money to go after Brownell when he'll only say his wife done it."

"We could do an autopsy," the doctor said.

The sheriff shook his head. "What'll that prove? If the baby died of a blow to the head, Brownell'll blame his wife, and if the kid drowned, what do you do with the wife? Maybe it was an accident. Looks like she'll be locked up anyway."

"What about the children?" Ellen asked.

The sheriff put his hand over his mouth and thought. "The only thing I can see is put them in the orphanage in Cheyenne."

"No!" Gladys spoke up. "An orphanage ain't no place for children."

"You got a better idea, do you, Gladys?" the sheriff asked.

"Julia told me she has people in Illinois," Ellen said. "They disowned her, but maybe they'll change their minds when they know the situation."

"That a pretty big state."

"Galena. That's where she's from. I don't know Julia's maiden name, however."

Ellen went to the walnut commode and opened the drawers searching for letters or documents—a marriage license for instance—that would give Julia's maiden name, but she found nothing. Then she knelt down beside Lucy and asked the girl if she had any aunts or uncles. Lucy didn't understand and shook her head. "There has to be a record somewhere," Ellen said.

"Might be I could wire the authorities," the sheriff suggested.

Ellen looked around and spotted Mr. Brownell's books and thought Julia's name might be in one of them. Mr. Brownell had written his name inside them but not Julia's. Then Ellen picked up a Bible and opened it. It was Julia's and old, and inside the front page was a list of family members, their births and dates. At the bottom was the name Julia Epperson, the date she was born, and the date she married Richard Brownell. Beneath that Julia had listed the names of her children. "Epperson," Ellen said. She looked at the names above Julia's and added, "She has two brothers, George and Wendell, but I think we should contact one of the sisters. Georgia Markham. It looks like she's the oldest."

"Meantime, me and Ellen will take care of the babies. Don't you send them to no orphanage," Gladys said.

Ellen glanced at Charlie, who looked surprised, then told her, "I reckon we can do that."

Nineteen

Ellen made a bed for Julia in the back of the wagon. Charlie and the doctor would take her to the depot where the doctor agreed to arrange for a cot to be set up in a baggage car for her. He would accompany her to the state asylum in Evanston. Gladys picked up two of the children and Ellen the third and lifted them into their wagons, along with the clothes they had found.

"What about her?" Gladys asked.

"Lucy?" Ellen asked.

"I'll arrange to have her sent to the orphanage," the sheriff volunteered.

"She ain't going there!" Gladys insisted.

"No. I'll take her," Ellen said. She glanced at Charlie for approval. "It's only until Julia's family gets here."

"If they do," he said, but he nodded.

"Come with us, Lucy," Ellen said, and the little girl rushed to the wagon. She tried to climb up the wagon wheel but couldn't do it. Charlie picked her up and set her down in the bed. The girl looked at him half-afraid. Charlie smiled at her, and she smiled back.

Ellen had torn a leaf from one of Mr. Brownell's books and

written out a telegram for the sheriff to send to Julia's sister
when he reached town: "Your sister Julia taken state asylum.
Brownell gone. Four children left behind. Please advise."

"You think she'll reply?" Ellen asked.

The sheriff shrugged. "Would you?"

Ellen didn't know. It was one thing for Julia's family to
take on two children, but four? Still, if it had been Lizzie's
children, Ellen would have done so. She hoped Julia had once
been as close to her sisters as Ellen and Lizzie were and that
they would feel responsible.

Charlie and Ellen stopped at the ranch, and he took Huckleberry into the barn and unsaddled him. Ellen touched Julia's
face, but the woman was sleeping and could not say good-bye
to her children. Ellen lifted the little ones from the wagon
and led them into the house, then went back for Billy. When
she returned, the two children were sitting on the floor. They
had pulled the tablecloth off the table, along with the spooner,
and were beating the spoons against each other. She should
have known better, leaving them there alone. She picked up the
spooner, which was cracked but not broken, and was about to
take away the spoons. But what harm was there in letting the
children play with them?

She set Billy in his cradle, then nodded at the smaller
Brownell child and asked Lucy, "What is its name?"

Lucy thought that over. "Wendell." She grinned at Ellen,
proud of herself, then said, "Lucy."

"How old is Lucy?" Ellen asked, but the little girl didn't
understand the question. Ellen had brought Julia's Bible
with her and would have to consult it as to the children's
ages. She brought out crackers and spread them with jam,
then set the two children on chairs at the table, wondering
if they were used to chairs. They squirmed but stayed seated

until they were finished eating. "Bath time," she told them. She had heated water on the stove and poured it into a washtub. Now she took the children outside and undressed them and discovered that Wendell was a girl. She and Gladys would have to line up the children by height and compare them with the names in the Bible to discover who was who.

She placed Lucy and Wendell in the tub and washed not only their little bodies but their hair, then dried them and went to where she had stored the garments Miss Ferguson had given her and found a nightgown that fit Wendell. Lucy was too large, so Ellen slit the seams in a feed sack and slipped it over the girl's head. Lucy, happy, traced the flowers printed on the sack. While the children napped, Ellen cut apart a feed sack with ducks on it and stitched a proper dress on the sewing machine for the girl.

Charlie came home later and said, "Mrs. Brownell's on her way. The telegram's been sent. What do we do now?"

"I guess we wait."

"What if we don't hear?"

Ellen shrugged. "I don't know. We might have a bigger family."

In fact, they did hear. Not more than two days later. The sheriff rode out to the ranch and gave Ellen the telegram: "Sister Georgia and I arrive Tuesday train." It was signed "Grace Yancy."

The sheriff agreed to meet the women at the depot, then take them to the hotel for the night. He'd drive them to Gladys's place, which was closer to Wallace, the next morning. Ellen would take the children she was caring for to Gladys's, and the two women would wait there for the sisters.

Gladys came by the next day and asked, "What do you think? Will they take the kids?"

"They're coming here, aren't they? That's a good sign. They could have ignored the telegram." The two watched the children play in the yard. "Like trying to line up puppies," Gladys observed as the little ones scattered in all directions. Only Lucy sat quietly, rocking a rag doll in her arms. Ellen had found the doll on the floor of the Brownell soddy and slipped it into the sack with the clothes.

"I suppose we ought to figure out who's who," Ellen said after a while. She clapped her hands. "Everybody line up."

The children stopped what they were doing and stared at her, not understanding. "Come," she said, motioning.

"Crackers?" Lucy asked. The others repeated the word and surrounded Ellen.

"In a minute," Ellen said. "Now stand still." She and Gladys lined up the children so that they formed stairsteps, with Lucy at one end, the year-old baby at the other. Ellen took out the Bible. "We know Chester was the oldest. Next is Lucy. Then Wendell." She pointed to one of the boys Gladys had taken. "Next is Helen. She's mine. Then Elizur." She paused. "Is that a boy's name, do you think? It must be, because the only one left is a boy."

"Ain't it a good thing you found that Bible. Otherwise, we'd have to name them ourselves: Eeny, Meeny, Miny, and Moe," Gladys said.

ELLEN AND GLADYS were waiting with all the children when the two women stepped down from the sheriff's buckboard at the Turnbull place on Wednesday morning. The children were bathed and dressed in Miss Ferguson's creations or their own mended clothes. Despite the baths, most were dirty again.

The sheriff introduced them, and the two women looked around. "I thought you said there were four children," Georgia said.

"Oh, three of them's ours. We'll keep them straight for you," Gladys told her.

The women laughed, and Ellen thought that was a good sign. Gladys had placed a table outside and covered it with a cloth and set out tin cups. Now she brought out tea. The guests were dressed fashionably in narrow traveling suits and smart turbans. Georgia looked at Gladys's bare hands, nodded at her sister, and both women slipped off their gloves.

"The sheriff has told us about our sister. We had hoped to go on to see her, but he said it was best not to, since she does not recognize anyone and we might only agitate her. I suppose at the moment the children are more important," Grace said.

"We have heard that the asylum is a good one," Ellen told her. "We loved Julia, who is a lovely person. She did not deserve what happened to her." The sisters said the sheriff had given them the details.

There was a long silence before Georgia asked if Ellen and Gladys were from Wyoming, and Ellen replied, "Gladys is. I came here from Iowa to teach school and married a cowboy. We have a ranch between here and where your sister lived."

"Did you, like our sister, find it hard to make the transition to living in such a barren place?" Georgia asked Ellen.

"Of course. What I wouldn't give to see flowers and trees. But I love the broad vista and the openness. There is a wonderful sense of freedom here. Why, a person can make it in Wyoming through hard work."

"Which our sister's husband was unwilling to do?"

Ellen didn't know what to reply, but Gladys answered, "Laziest man I ever saw, and the meanest. It's no wonder Julia went loopy."

"She was such a sweet girl, so trusting," Grace said.

"So foolish," her sister added. "We tried to talk her out of marrying him, but she would not listen. He promised her a beautiful home. We should like to see it."

"That's not a good idea," Ellen said.

The sisters exchanged a glance. "Why not?"

"They lived in a soddy. It was not a beautiful home." She explained what a soddy was, then said, "It is in poor shape. There's no reason for you to see it. I believe it would upset you."

"Nonetheless . . . ," Georgia said, and the women rose. Ellen agreed to drive them there in her wagon while Gladys minded the children. The drive took over an hour and the three were hot and dusty by the time they arrived.

"What in the world?" Grace asked. The women went inside the soddy and held their noses at the stench. The room was filled with trash, and Georgia kicked at one of Mr. Brownell's books that was lying on the floor. "Those books were the undoing of Julia," she said. A rat scurried out from behind the stove. Grace jumped, and she and her sister rushed outside. "Our sister was reduced to this? She once lived in refinement, and this is a hovel. Poor darling, she didn't deserve it. Why didn't she tell us?"

"She said you disowned her."

Georgia bowed her head. "She could have come home. She knew that. Maybe she was too proud. She never even wrote us."

"Did you write her?" Ellen asked.

Georgia didn't answer. "I wonder what happened to her clothes, her jewels, her bedroom suite."

"Perhaps Mr. Brownell sold them."

"He would. It's for sure he went through her inheritance."

The women were quiet on the drive back. Then they announced they were taking the train home the following day.

"What about the kids?" Gladys asked, while she and Ellen held their breaths.

"Why, we shall take them of course. Grace will take the smallest one, and I will take the older two. Our husbands will not be pleased, but they will understand."

"Which one of you will take Lucy?"

The two looked at each other. "She is touched, is she not?" Georgia asked.

"She's slow," Ellen replied.

"More than that. She appears to be a nice child, but I cannot take her. My husband would never accept a child who is so flawed."

Ellen bit her lip and looked at Gladys. Then she turned to Grace, who blushed. "I wish I could take her, but I cannot. I have four of my own, and adding another will be a strain. I am afraid I am not up to the challenge of such a child. I'm sorry. I know it does not speak well of me, but you must understand how difficult it will be adding just one more to my family. That girl will be much better off in a home that is prepared to handle such children. We would be glad to pay for her keep? When Julia is better, she may want that one with her."

"*That one*," Ellen said.

THE TWO WOMEN and three children left the next day. Ellen and Gladys, along with Lucy, saw them off. Lucy was more interested in the train than in the departure of her brothers and sister.

"We must be grateful they took three of the children," Ellen said as she watched the train disappear in the distance. Lucy was staring at it and waving.

"I guess you can't blame them. Still, leaving Lucy behind is a mean thing to do. She's their kin. What are we going to do with her?"

"I don't know. Maybe they'll change their minds. Till then, I'll take her home with me," Ellen said.

"You up to it?"

"You already have two."

"Yeah, but one of them's not . . . how did you put it . . . slow."

"What else can we do, send her to an orphanage? You're against that. I suppose I am, too."

"Might be that woman's right and Julia'll get well and come after her."

"Might be."

"You don't think so."

"No, and you don't either."

"There's always Mr. Brownell."

"We'll never see him again, and that's good riddance. I only wish we could have kept him from taking Chester. The boy will grow up to be just like his father."

"The bastard," Gladys said. She glanced at Lucy, who was still waving, although the train had disappeared. "Poor tyke."

"Come along, Lucy," Ellen said, holding out her hand.

"Train," Lucy said.

"Yes, loud train."

"Loud train." Lucy grinned.

"What's Charlie going to say?" Gladys asked.

Twenty

In fact, they had discussed Lucy most of the night before, had sat at the table after it was dark, talking about whether they would take Lucy if the sisters didn't want her.

"You planning on keeping her?" Charlie had asked.

"Not *me*. *Us*. It's *our* decision."

"Would it be for good?"

Ellen thought that over. "I don't know, but I think we'd have to accept that it is. Those sisters aren't going to change their minds, and you saw Julia. It'll be a long time till she's normal, if she ever is."

"What about Brownell?"

"Even if he came back, and I don't suppose he would, I'd never let him take her!"

"No, I don't expect I would either." He paused. "There's homes for kids like that, you know."

Ellen nodded. "Gladys was in one."

"Sounds like we don't have much choice."

"Look at it this way, Charlie. What if it was Billy? What if something happened to us and nobody wanted him? Lucy's a little girl who doesn't have a family. It's not right not to take her in."

Lucy was sleeping on a pad on the floor, and she cried out, then woke and clenched her little body. Ellen went to her and held the girl until she went back to sleep. "I think her father whipped her."

"It won't be easy. Looks like she's damaged." He sat down on the bed and stared at Lucy. "You think it's fair for Billy? He'd have to take care of her when we're gone."

"That's a long time away." Ellen smoothed the quilt over the girl. "No, of course it's not fair for him. It's not fair for us either. Mostly, it's not fair for her." Ellen sat down on the bed beside Charlie. "Could you love her like she was one of our own?"

"Maybe we can try." He took Ellen's hand. "I guess if you want to be her mother, I could try to be her father."

"We can't change our minds later on. We have to decide now. We can't keep her for a year, then put her into an orphanage. It would have to be forever." She couldn't see Charlie, but she knew he nodded in the dark.

WHEN SHE RETURNED home from seeing off the sisters, Ellen discovered that Charlie had made a bed for Lucy and painted it red. "Bed," he told the little girl.

"Bed," Lucy said.

"Red bed."

The girl laughed.

"Lucy's red bed."

"Lucy."

He picked up the child and placed her in the bed, which he had lined with one of Ellen's quilts. In a few minutes, the girl was asleep. Ellen watched her lying there, curled up, the soiled rag doll in her arms, and said, "If only it were all going to be this easy."

"Maybe it will be."

Ellen smiled, remembering that morning when Lucy had tried to help with breakfast and had knocked over the sugar bowl. The bowl had broken, spilling its contents on the floor, and Lucy had looked up at Ellen in terror. Then she'd stared at Charlie, as if waiting for him to strike her. Charlie had picked up the pieces, however, while Ellen swept up the sugar. Later, Lucy had tried to play with Billy, but she was too rough, and Billy cried. Lucy smacked her doll then and said, "Bad girl!" Ellen knew she would have to discipline the child but didn't know how. There was so much she didn't know about a child such as Lucy.

In the next few days, Ellen learned that Lucy was not only full of energy but also strong—and could be willful. When Ellen tried to take Billy's rattle from Lucy, who was hitting it against the wall, the girl held on to it until it broke. One morning, Ellen took Lucy outside to help gather eggs and Lucy smashed the eggs on the ground. "No," Ellen told her. "Do not break them."

"Yes," Lucy said, throwing another and laughing as it spattered.

The girl tried to help with the cooking but knocked things over, and when Ellen hung up the wash, leaving Lucy by herself for a few minutes, Lucy climbed into the washtub with her doll. Ellen gave them both a bath. It was frustrating but funny, too. There were times the girl made her laugh—and Billy and Charlie, too—and when Lucy hugged her legs, Ellen was filled with love. Still, the girl wore her out, and Ellen was exhausted by the end of each day. She wondered how Julia had managed to put up with Lucy, the other children, and an obstinate husband, too. Then she realized that Julia hadn't.

"Are you sure you're up to this?" Charlie asked one evening after the girl fought going to bed.

"Of course," Ellen said. There was no other reply she could make.

PIKE STOPPED ONE afternoon to tell Charlie he was needed at the Gurley ranch to help with castrating and branding the calves. "Who's that?" he asked when he saw Lucy. The girl was hiding behind Ellen's skirt. She had warmed up to Charlie, but other men frightened her, and in the three weeks since she'd been with Ellen and Charlie she'd hidden whenever a man came by. Ellen wondered if the girl was afraid the man might be her father.

"She's Lucy, the Brownell girl," Ellen told Pike, taking the girl's hand, because she understood Lucy's fear. She felt the girl tremble, and her heart went out to the poor little thing. "It's all right," she whispered.

"I heard they taken out."

"I guess you could say that. Mr. Brownell left. Mrs. Brownell was sent to the asylum, and her family came from Illinois to take the other children."

"And let this one get throwed away, it looks like. You going to adopt her?"

Ellen nodded. "There's no one else to take her in, and we love her."

Pike smiled at Lucy and said, "Hi. I'm Pike."

Lucy squeezed Ellen's hand and looked away.

"It's okay. I won't hurt you." He dismounted and reached out a hand, but Lucy buried her head in Ellen's skirt.

Pike studied the girl, then sat down on the bench with his

back to her. He glanced over his shoulder to make sure that Lucy was watching him, then drew out his bandana. Slowly, he straightened it, then rolled it up, carefully tucking in the ends until it was a smooth little mound. He made a couple of folds, then pulled out two corners, shaping them into tiny ears. When he was finished, the handkerchief resembled a mouse.

Lucy let go of Ellen's hand and stepped forward. Pike ignored her, and she took another step.

The boy paid no attention but kept his eyes on the bandana. He laid it on his arm and patted it. He worked slowly, ignoring Lucy, who watched, curious. Pike patted the mouse a few times; then suddenly it jumped up his arm.

Lucy, startled, stepped back.

"There now," Pike said to the bandana. He gave it a few more pats before it jumped up his arm again. Lucy laughed. Pike ignored her and kept on playing with the mouse. Lucy took another step toward Pike, then slowly reached out her hand. The mouse jumped again, and she giggled.

"You be still now," Pike told the mouse as Lucy put out her hand, touching the rolled-up bandana. "Jump," she said, and Pike made the mouse jump from his arm to Lucy's. Lucy laughed so hard that she fell onto the ground at Pike's feet. "Again!" she said, and the mouse jumped onto her leg.

Ellen sat down on the bench. "How do you do that, Pike?"

"Secret." He looked at Lucy. "Our secret."

Lucy giggled, although she didn't understand the word "secret."

After a time, Pike stood and unrolled the bandana, putting it back into his pocket. Lucy was disappointed and said, "No."

"Tomorrow. I'll bring the mouse back tomorrow," he said.

Lucy looked at Ellen, not understanding. Ellen didn't know how to explain what tomorrow was, but she put her

arms around the girl and said, "Pike will come back, honey."
She waved as Pike mounted his horse. "Bye-bye, Pike. Bye-
bye, mouse," she said.

Lucy understood that, and she waved, too. "Bye-bye, mouse."

LATE THE NEXT day, Pike pulled into the yard in a buckboard, his mother beside him.

"Welcome home, Mrs. Gurley," Ellen said. "I didn't know
you were back."

"Two days ago. I sure did miss home. All those trees back
there. Made me feel fenced in. You can't see the horizon."

"How is your sister?"

"Better."

Lucy had gone inside when she saw the buckboard. Now
she peered out the door, and when she spied Pike she yelled,
"Hi, mouse!" She came to the wagon and jumped up and
down yelling, "Mouse! Mouse!"

"What a lot of trouble you are," Pike said to Lucy as he
helped his mother down. He sat on the bench and removed
his bandana. Lucy climbed up beside him.

"I see your family's increased," Mrs. Gurley said as she
went into the house with Ellen.

Ellen smiled, then shook her head. "She's a dear little girl,
although I can barely keep up with her. It's a wonder Julia
lasted as long as she did."

"You're tired?"

Ellen nodded.

"You're sorry you took her in?"

"Oh no," Ellen said quickly. "It couldn't be helped. Lucy
deserves a family, and we can give her a home. She's already so
much happier than when we brought her here."

"A family makes a big difference to a girl like that."

"We hope we can be a good family." Ellen went to the cookstove and threw in kindling. "I could use a cup of coffee. How about you?"

"If it wouldn't rob you."

Ellen poured water into the teakettle and let it boil, then ground coffee beans and placed the grounds in the coffeepot. She poured the water over them and let them steep as she took down two cups. She opened a can of Pet milk and placed it on the table. After the two women had doctored their coffee, Mrs. Gurley said, "You are going to adopt the girl then?"

"Charlie agreed to it." Ellen smiled. "He's exceptional, taking in someone else's child, and a child like Lucy at that. Not every man would."

"Not every woman either. You know what you're doing?"

"No, of course not." Ellen sipped her coffee. "But there isn't any other way."

"Ellen . . ." Mrs. Gurley's voice was tentative, and Ellen looked up. "I don't want to interfere. It's not my place, but Pike told us about Lucy, and Mr. Gurley and I talked about her all night. Pike did, too."

Ellen waited.

"You see, we miss Margaret so. There's an empty place in our lives. And we thought maybe . . ."

Ellen frowned, not sure what the woman wanted.

Mrs. Gurley took a deep breath, then said in a rush, "Well, the truth of the matter is, would you let us have Lucy? I'm sure you would do a wonderful job with her, but we know what it's like to raise such a child, and it would be a gift to us if we could take her."

Ellen stared at her guest. "You want to adopt Lucy?"

"I don't want to take your child away from you. It's just

that you are so young and will have more children of your own. Starting out like you're doing is hard enough without the challenge of Lucy. I know in time you will love her as much as we did Margaret. Perhaps you do already." Mrs. Gurley had raised her cup, but her hand shook so hard that she set it down. "We are so lost without Margaret. Wouldn't you consider letting us raise Lucy?" Tears gathered in Mrs. Gurley's eyes. "Oh, this is awful. I am asking you to give away your child. Please forgive me." She wiped her eyes with her sleeve.

"She's not an easy child. And you're . . . older."

"I know. I don't underestimate what it would be like."

Ellen reached for Mrs. Gurley's hand. "At first, I didn't want to take her, but now that she's been here . . ."

"I know. She's already part of you. That's the way we felt about Margaret the day she was born."

"She *is* part of us." Ellen stood and went to the door. Pike had lifted Lucy onto one of the horses and was holding her there. "What's Pike doing? Lucy's afraid of horses. Charlie tried to put her on one, and she screamed," Ellen said, turning back to Mrs. Gurley.

"Pike taught Margaret to ride Little Betty. He has a way with children like Margaret and Lucy. He would be a brother to Lucy."

"I'd have to talk to Charlie."

"Of course." Mrs. Gurley stood and took Ellen's hands. "If the answer is no, I understand, and I'll never mention it again."

CHARLIE HAD WORKED at the Gurley ranch that day, and Ellen waited until after Lucy and Billy were asleep to tell him about the conversation with Mrs. Gurley. The supper dishes were washed and put away, and Ellen had made a second pot of coffee. She sat down at the table with Charlie. "I have something to tell you."

"This sounds serious."

"It is." Ellen took a spoon from the spooner and stirred her coffee, thinking how to bring up the subject. Finally, she blurted out, "The Gurleys want to adopt Lucy."

"What?"

Ellen nodded. She repeated the conversation with Mrs. Gurley.

"What do you think?"

"I don't know."

"I'm getting kind of used to her."

"Me, too. Today when I gave Billy a bath, she put her doll in the tub with him and washed it. She makes Billy laugh. I'd miss her."

Charlie studied the grounds in his coffee. "It would have been different if they'd offered when we first took her in."

Ellen nodded.

"They'd do a good job with her. Margaret was a happy kid, and I never saw Pike be anything but kind to her."

"They have the money to help her if Lucy needs anything."

Charlie nodded. "I wasn't real crazy about taking her in at first, but now it's like she's our own. What do you want to do?"

Ellen looked over at the red bed where Lucy slept. "I think we ought to consider what's best for Lucy. As you said, the Gurleys can do things for her that we can't, and they want her. I think they'd give her a good home."

"They would at that, but would Lucy feel like we threw her away, that we didn't want her?"

Ellen's coffee was cold, but she sipped it anyway. "I thought about that. Would Lucy even understand what was happening?"

They talked about the girl for a long time. Finally, Ellen asked, "What do you want to do?"

"You say."

"No, it's up to you."

Neither would decide, so at last Ellen said, "We'll write it down. Gurley or Bacon." She ripped two scraps from a newspaper and took out a pencil. Then she turned her back to Charlie while she wrote down a name. Charlie licked the pencil, and he, too, wrote a name. The two placed the slips of paper on the table. Both had written "Gurley."

IN THE MORNING, the two still agreed that letting the Gurleys raise Lucy was the right thing for her. "We better do it pretty quick before we change our minds," Charlie said, adding, "I'm going to miss that little girl."

"Me, too," Ellen said. She went outside while Charlie saddled Huckleberry to ride to the Gurleys with the news. "We can still change our minds," he said.

Ellen shook her head. "They'll give Lucy a good home, and they'll know better than us how to raise her."

She watched Charlie ride off, then went back inside where Lucy was sitting in her bed with her doll. "Wake up," Lucy ordered the doll.

"What's her name?" Ellen asked.

"Doll." Lucy replied. She climbed out of bed and sat down at the table. While Lucy ate breakfast, Ellen gathered the clothes she had made for the girl, along with her nightgown and a wooden horse Charlie had whittled for her. By the time she was finished, she heard the Gurley buckboard pull into the yard. Lucy heard the vehicle, too, and she ran to the door, calling, "Hi, Pike!"

Pike grinned at the little girl as his mother got down from the wagon. "Are you sure?" Mrs. Gurley asked Ellen. "Do you need more time to think about it?"

"If we have more time with her, we'll never let her go." Ellen paused. "Charlie and I believe this is best for her."

"You will still be her family. We'll all be her family," Mrs. Gurley said.

They watched Pike pick up Lucy and set her on the buckboard seat. Charlie had followed the Gurleys home and taken Huckleberry into the barn. Now he came and stood beside Ellen, and she took his hand. "Better go before we change our minds," he said.

Mrs. Gurley hugged Ellen, then reached for Charlie's hands. "You won't be sorry," she said.

"Already am," Charlie told her. He went over to Lucy and patted her cheek. "You be a good girl now."

"Good girl," Lucy repeated.

Charlie helped Mrs. Gurley into the wagon, and she put her arms around Lucy. Pike slapped the reins on the horses.

"Bye-bye, Lucy," Ellen said, then gave a sort of strangled cry. She waved her arm and so did Charlie, but Lucy was busy with the Gurleys and didn't wave back.

Charlie stared after the wagon, then said, "I hope the sun shines on that little girl for the rest of her life."

Twenty-one

Lucy had been with them only a short time, but she had become part of their lives. Ellen smiled when she saw the bent tines on a fork that Lucy had taken to bang on a rock. When she went to milk the cow, she glanced around for Lucy to follow her into the barn. Charlie stared at the bed he had made for Lucy and shook his head. "I guess Billy will use it now," he said. "I sure did get to liking that little girl."

Ellen did, too, and she wondered if they had made the right decision. When she visited the Gurleys, however, she knew they had. She and Charlie waited a month before going to the ranch house. That was to give Lucy time to settle in. They didn't want to confuse her.

When Charlie stopped the wagon at the Gurley place, Lucy came running to greet them. "Mom!" she called, and Ellen held her breath. Did Lucy think of her as her mother and that she had only visited the Gurleys? Then Mrs. Gurley came outside and Lucy turned to her. "Mom! Look!" She pointed at the wagon.

"Why, it's Aunt Ellen and Uncle Charlie," Mrs. Gurley said, and that is what Lucy called them ever after.

On the way home, Charlie asked, "Could we have done as

well with her?" They had been impressed with Lucy's manners, how her speech had improved, and, most of all, how happy she was. She'd been gentle with Billy, whose little face lit up when he saw her.

"I'm not sure," Ellen replied, feeling a pang of jealousy. She added, "Maybe not."

"That's what I'm thinking."

"She has her own room," Ellen said. Lucy had taken Ellen into Margaret's old bedroom and pointed at the bed. The covers had been pulled up but were askew, one side of the quilt nearly on the floor and the sheets under it lumpy. "I did," Lucy said proudly. Later Lucy climbed onto Pike's lap so that he could read her a story and the two of them smiled at each other like brother and sister—which was what they were now.

"We did the right thing," Ellen said.

Charlie nodded. "I still miss her." They drove in silence. Then Charlie said, "Maybe we should have a sister for Billy."

ELLEN THOUGHT ABOUT a second child that summer—her third summer in Wyoming—although she did not get pregnant. When she was with Gladys, she saw how close her two boys were. Ellis was only a few months old, so he couldn't play with his brother, but he laughed when Bailey poked him or handed him a toy. Brother, Bailey called Ellis.

"I hope it's not too long before Billy has a brother or sister," Ellen said.

"You expecting again?" Gladys asked.

"No."

"Well, don't think too hard. Some days I feel like Julia Brownell, and I have only two. Morris would be happy if we had a dozen. He sure does love his boys. The other day, he said

he thought Bailey was smart enough to go to college. I don't
know where that come from. I asked Morris what's a rancher
need with college? He said maybe Bailey don't want to be a
rancher. Maybe he'll be the governor. Imagine that, a governor with a mother right out of the Columbine."

Ellen was helping Gladys with a quilt that day. The two
got together every week or two to sew, although it was difficult
with the chores they had at home. The summer did not hold
out much promise. There had been no rain, and dry winds
parched the land. Ellen's flowers had dried up, and the kitchen
garden looked starved for moisture. She'd hauled barrels of
water from Plug Hat Creek, but the soil was still parched.

Charlie feared it would be another bad year for hay. Only
the potatoes seemed to be doing well, and Ellen dreaded another winter of living on them. She was grateful that Charlie
had plenty of work at the Gurleys'. At first, he'd worked for
Mr. Gurley in exchange for running his cattle with the Gurley herd, but he'd picked up extra days, and Mr. Gurley was
paying him wages. Ellen was grateful because they needed the
money. Once she'd hoped to visit Lizzie in Chicago, but they
didn't have the train fare. Lizzie offered to send a ticket, but
Ellen knew Charlie would be shamed if she accepted it.

She didn't feel deprived, however. She had Charlie, and
she had Billy, and she was content. Besides, they weren't any
worse off than their neighbors. Many had given up. There
were plenty of deserted shacks now. People simply closed the
doors and left, abandoning what they couldn't fit into their
wagons. Ellen missed familiar faces at church, but there were
new ones. Just as some people gave up, others took their
places, many of them easterners who came with high hopes
and little knowledge of dryland farming. Some of them, too,
would be gone in a few years.

"It's the weaklings that don't make it," Charlie said. *Yes,* Ellen thought, *and the visionaries, those who learned of the West through books and thought God had sent them west—dreamers like Mr. Brownell. They failed, too.*

Despite hard times, these were good times, too, with neighbors gathered for church suppers and taffy pulls and dances in the schoolhouse. The women organized a monthly quilting bee, and everyone attended the Fourth of July celebration in Wallace.

The mercantile and the new bank were decorated with colorful bunting. Women wore their best dresses and pinned tiny flags to their hats. The prostitutes donned red, white, and blue, and Ellen saw Frieda flash a star-spangled garter at one of the cowboys. When Frieda realized Ellen had seen the gesture, she came over and asked, "You like ranching better than teaching now?"

"I like ranching with Charlie," Ellen replied, switching Billy from one hip to the other.

"Yeah, I guess if I'd snagged Charlie Bacon, I would, too." Frieda winked at her, and Ellen suddenly wondered if Charlie had known Frieda—if he had known her in the biblical sense, as Gladys had once put it. After all, the cowboys visited the Columbine. Charlie had been single for a long time. Wasn't it likely that he, too, was once a customer? Ellen remembered when Charlie had introduced her to Gladys. The two had acted like old friends. Maybe it had been more than that. *Good lord!* Ellen thought. She'd never considered such a thing. She looked at Gladys and found her chatting with Mutt. Mutt pointed at Ellen with her chin, and Gladys turned and waved. Mutt waved, too. Had the prostitutes hoped to marry Charlie? At first Ellen was shocked, and then amused. The idea that he had married *her* made her feel a little superior, and she smiled as she waved back.

As she glanced over the crowd, Ellen spotted Ruth. The woman was standing next to Wade Snyder. McGinty was no-where to be seen. Ellen made her way to her friend and said hello.

"Oh, Ellen," Ruth said. "I haven't seen you for so long."

"Let's find someplace to chat," Ellen said, sending Snyder a hard look.

"She's busy," Snyder said.

"It's Independence Day. No one's busy," Ellen told him.

"Come on, Ruth." He gripped her arm. "McGinty's look-ing for you."

"No." Ruth shook her head and pulled her arm away. "I'm going to talk to Ellen."

"McGinty ain't goinna like it."

"Are you saying Mr. McGinty doesn't want his wife to talk to a friend? Why in the world is that? And who are you to say such a thing?" Ellen asked.

Snyder scowled and told Ruth, "Have it your way. You'll be sorry." He disappeared into the crowd.

"What an odious man. He acts like he owns you. What did he mean by that?"

Ruth shrugged.

"Is he still boarding with you?" Ellen asked.

"He's living with us," Ruth replied.

That meant he was not paying room and board, Ellen thought. She turned to her friend, whose face was gray. Ellen looked for bruises on the woman's body, but Ruth wore long sleeves. *In all this heat*, Ellen thought. "Are you well?" she asked Ruth.

"Oh yes," the woman said. Then she brightened. "My, what a joy to see you. And little Billy. He has grown so much." It had been weeks since Ellen had stopped at the McGinty house to deliver Laura's last letter. "I have not heard again from your daughter," she said.

"She is too busy to write. She has a new baby, a little girl. She wishes I could be with her to help."

"Why can't you?"

"McGinty would never let me go."

"Why not just do it?"

"There is no money."

Ellen remembered how the old man controlled the purse strings. Ruth had to beg him for money to purchase foodstuffs. She started to ask if things were better with McGinty, but she saw him coming toward them, Snyder at his side. They reached Ruth, and McGinty gripped his wife's arm. "Wade told you I was looking for you. You come along," he said.

"I'll stop by with my quilting," Ellen said.

Ruth turned and went with her husband, not even saying good-bye. Ellen watched as her friend disappeared in the crowd. Then she sighed and looked for Charlie, who was listening to a speech. Among the activities celebrating the Fourth were speeches, footraces, a picnic, and a band concert. The band wasn't very good and the primary instrument was the harmonica, but it was a band nonetheless.

Charlie grinned at Ellen and said, "Come on; it's almost time."

The highlight of the day was the rodeo, and Charlie had signed up to compete in bronc riding with cowboys from the ranches around Wallace. Ellen was dubious. Charlie had broken horses for Mr. Gurley and knew what he was doing, but she feared he might be thrown and break a leg or even worse. "Are you sure you want to do this?" she asked.

"Hell, honey, I'm the best bronc rider here. They expect me to ride."

"I'm worried you might hurt yourself."

"Then why'd you marry a cowboy?"

Ellen bit her tongue as Gladys joined her. "You riding, Charlie?"

"Yeah."

"Morris says if you're competing, there ain't no reason for him to do it."

"He could come in second," Charlie said. "It pays ten dollars."

"That ain't much if he breaks his neck. How'm I going to raise these boys with no papa?"

"What does first place pay?" Ellen asked.

"Twenty-five," Charlie told her.

They could use the money, Ellen thought, although she still didn't want Charlie to compete. She started to protest again, then realized that if she stopped him Charlie would feel henpecked. He loved breaking horses. She'd fallen in love with a cowboy. Was she now trying to turn him into a granger? The unbroken horses represented the freedom of the open spaces that Charlie loved.

So Ellen joined the crowd waiting for the bronc riding to begin. Although she knew Charlie was a top hand with horses, she'd never seen him compete. She gripped Billy and pointed to Charlie. "Look at Daddy," she said. Billy grabbed a streamer on her hat and shoved it into his mouth. Then he clapped his hands with the rest of the crowd. Ellen watched as Charlie climbed onto a horse that danced around and snorted.

Two cowboys held the animal in place until Charlie was ready. Then they let go. The horse bucked as Charlie dug his spurs into it. He held on, one hand in the air, as the horse bucked again, trying to throw him. The horse fishtailed, and Charlie's hat flew off. A man yelled, "Pull leather!" and another called, "Jump off!" Then the horse suddenly turned sideways, and the move threw Charlie to the ground. The crowd cheered as he picked up his hat and slapped it against his leg to remove the dust. The announcer yelled, "Looks like old Fatback's in the skillet!"

"Tough luck," one of the cowboys said. "You sure drawed a devil horse."

"Worst thing about bronc riding is you have to get on the darn horse," another said.

"Nah, worst thing is getting off."

Charlie limped over to Ellen. "Sorry, honey. He used me up."

Ellen knew her husband's pride was hurt. After all, as he'd said, he was the best bronc buster in the county, and he'd just bragged to her that he would win the twenty-five dollars. "It's all right," she said. "That was a fine ride. I'm proud of you." And she was. Her heart had been in her throat while she watched Charlie ride the bronco, but she'd been exhilarated, too. *He is really something,* she'd thought. *And he's my husband!*

Charlie took Billy from her. They passed Morris as they walked to their wagon. "I guess I should have entered," Morris said. He was holding Ellis and told the boy, "Son, someday you'll win that prize money. You'll be as good as old Fatback."

THE DAY HAD been a fine one, the best in a long time, Ellen thought as they rode home, Billy asleep in her lap. They had eaten too much, and she'd seen Charlie taking a few nips from a bottle that the men passed around. She'd never asked Charlie to take the pledge, and she never would. Charlie didn't drink except when he was with the cowboys, and then he didn't get drunk. She looked over at her husband as he flicked the reins on the horses' backs. Charlie's hands were dark from the sun and leather-hard from the weather. She felt a thrill go through her as she thought of those hands touching her in the night. She thought of Gladys and how she had once said that Morris thought one woman was pretty much like another. Charlie wasn't like that. He didn't think of her as just any woman. He had married her because he loved her. They had a bond, the two of them. She thought back to the day she had decided to accept the teaching job in Wallace. How naïve she had been about the West.

Ellen slipped her hand into one of Charlie's. He looked over at her and smiled. "You sure do look pretty today," he said. She moved over on the wagon seat and put her head on his shoulder. "Pretty as daylight," he said.

It wasn't yet dark when they returned home. Charlie did the chores while Ellen fixed supper and put Billy down. After she and Charlie had eaten, they sat on the bench outside and looked at the sunset. The sky turned scarlet with streaks of gold through it, then faded into deep blue. Charlie leaned back on the bench and put his arm around Ellen.

They sat there until the sky turned black and was illuminated only by the pinpoint light of stars. There was no need for talk. Ellen was sleepy and rested her head on Charlie's shoulder. Then suddenly he leaned forward and said, "I smell smoke." He glanced at the barn, then turned to look at the house.

"I smell it, too," Ellen said, straightening up. "Is it a prairie fire?" There was nothing more frightening than a fire on

Twenty-two

By the time Ellen reached the Turnbull place, Charlie was using a wet burlap bag to put out small fires caused by flying embers. His face was dark from smoke. Sparks had burned holes in his shirt. He used his arm to wipe his forehead, smearing the grime, then smacked the sack against the ground, snuffing out an ember that smoldered in the prairie grass. The house was engulfed in flames, and nothing could be done to save it. No one was even trying to put them out. The fear was that the fire would spread onto the prairie.

Within minutes of smelling smoke, Charlie had saddled Huckleberry and mounted the horse.

"Maybe it's trash. Maybe Morris is burning trash!" Ellen had called.

"At night? Something's wrong. I'm going down there!" he'd yelled over his shoulder as he started off.

"I'm coming, too," Ellen said to Charlie's back. If the fire was serious, Gladys would need her. Maybe she could take the boys home with her. She hitched the horses to the wagon, then grabbed Billy and placed him in the Arbuckles' box in the wagon bed and started off for the Turnbull place. The smoke was thick when she reached it, and the horses fought her. She tied the wagon to a fence post, and settling her sleeping baby on her hip, she ran toward the fire.

"Stay back!" Charlie ordered. "It's dangerous." Embers were flying, and he swatted at a flame that sprang up. Two cowboys from the Gurley ranch were there, one of them stamping out flames that threatened the grasses, the other shoveling dirt onto the small fires.

The roof of the house had caved in, and fire had consumed the building. In a few minutes, it would be a charred mess. Ellen came close to see if anything had been saved, but there were no piles of belongings—no clothes, no dishes, not even a child's toy. Everything was burning.

"Stay back!" Charlie yelled again. A spark landed near her feet, and Ellen stamped it out before it could catch her skirt. "You shouldn't have come," Charlie said.

"Gladys? Where's Gladys?" Ellen shrieked, because it suddenly occurred to her that Gladys and her boys could have been in the house. Her knees were weak, and she nearly sank to the ground. Fires happened so fast. "Is Gladys all right?"

Charlie pointed at the barn with his chin. He slapped the burlap bag on the ground to smother a flame, then went to Ellen. "Don't go there, honey. Go on back home."

"Is she all right?" Ellen's voice was already raw from the smoke, and she turned Billy's face into her chest to keep the smoke from his eyes and mouth. The boy was whimpering. "Oh, Charlie, is she dead?" The idea that her friend had burned to death sickened Ellen, and she clutched her baby.

"Worse—" Charlie began to reply, but one of the cowboys yelled something and he rushed off to help contain a fire that threatened to spread.

"Tell me," Ellen said, but Charlie didn't hear her.

Other men had seen the smoke and were arriving to fight the fire, and Ellen moved out of their way. She looked toward the barn. The sky was black and the smoke obscured the stars, but firelight lit the barnyard. Ellen saw someone huddled near the corral. "Gladys?" she called. "Gladys?" Billy was crying now and Ellen soothed him as she hurried to the figure—two figures, she realized.

Gladys and Morris were huddled on the ground. Morris held Bailey, while Gladys cradled Ellis. Ellen sat down beside Gladys and touched her arm. Gladys turned to her. Tear trails ran through the soot and smoke on her face. Morris's face was black, too, and he shook with silent sobs. Ellen looked at the two little bodies that were soot covered and still. *Bodies*, Ellen thought. *The boys are gone.* "No," she said. "No!" She reached out a hand to touch Ellis's forehead. *Please God, no!* She glanced at Bailey, who was as still as his brother. *Not both of them! How could You take both of them?* She put her arm around Gladys, who did not seem to know she was there.

Morris lifted his head and stared at Ellen. "They're dead," he said. "My boys are dead."

Bailey will never be governor, Ellen thought remembering Morris's claims for his boys. *His brother will never be a champion bronc rider.* What was more horrifying than the death of a child? Ellen had mourned the loss of her unborn daughter, but this was so much worse. Ellis and Bailey had been living children, boys Gladys had given birth to and nursed and cared for. Ellen couldn't imagine a greater tragedy, and she grieved as if the child Gladys was holding were Billy. "Gladys?"

Instead of answering, Gladys used her skirt to wipe Ellis's face. "His face is dirty," she said in a daze. "Ellis, how'd you get such a dirty face? Boys are so naughty." She wiped the soot off her baby's cheeks and forehead, then kept on rubbing until

Ellen stilled her hand. "Wake up, Ellis," Gladys said. After a time, Gladys realized Ellen was there and said, "He won't wake up."

"Let me take him." Ellen shifted Billy onto her hip and held out her free arm.

"No," Gladys said. She began humming.

Ellen looked at Morris. "I'm sorry. Morris, I am so sorry."

Morris's back was to the fire, and he stared into the darkness. "They're gone. Both of them." A flame shot up into the sky, and in its light Ellen saw that Morris's shirt was burned.

"What happened?" Ellen thought of the stove in the house. It was a cheap one and might have ruptured. Perhaps the stovepipe had backed up. Morris might have been burning trash outside and let the fire get away from him. The shack was flimsy. Anything could have caused it to catch fire.

Ellen searched in the firelight for her husband. Nearly a dozen men were fighting the fire now. There were no telephones on the prairie, but neighbors seemed to know when they were needed. Maybe, like Charlie, they had smelled smoke, or perhaps they had a sixth sense that something was wrong. She saw Pike and Mr. Gurley and thought that Mrs. Gurley would be along soon. She would know what to do with Gladys and Morris and their boys.

Ellen turned back to Morris and asked again, "What happened? Was it the stove?"

"The lamp." He looked up at Ellen. "Bailey must have knocked it over."

If he did, the lamp would have broken. Kerosene would have spread over the wooden table and then the wooden floor, and the flame from the lamp would have set them on fire. The house must have gone up in minutes. The boys had been rescued but not before the smoke filled their little lungs.

"At least you and Gladys survived," Ellen said. She was sorry the second the words left her mouth. Gladys and Morris wouldn't be grateful. They would feel guilty. How did you go on knowing your children were dead, but you were alive? Ellen added. "It was a terrible accident. Nobody was at fault."

Morris turned his head to his wife and stared at her. "She left them alone. She went outside to smoke a cigarette."

"Oh my dear God," Ellen said. She'd never even seen Gladys smoke a cigarette.

"I tried to save them," Gladys said, although she was not speaking to Ellen. "Morris, I tried." She held out her arms, which were red and blistered. So were her hands. "I tried," she said.

"You left them alone," Morris told her. There was not criticism in his voice, or scorn. Only sorrow, sorrow deeper than anything Ellen had ever heard.

"I'm sorry," Gladys said over and over.

"My boys. You left them alone," Morris said.

MRS. GURLEY ARRIVED then. She had brought jugs of water and sandwiches for the firefighters. She handed them out, then went to where Ellen was sitting in the dirt with Gladys and Morris. "My dear friends, I grieve with you." She touched Gladys's face, then slowly took Ellis from her. "The loss of your boys is a loss for the entire community."

Ellen nodded. The deaths were indeed her loss, too. She would never again sit with Gladys in that little house, their quilting in their laps, as they watched the three boys.

She thought Mrs. Gurley might take the boys' bodies to the Gurley ranch to prepare them for burial, but instead, the woman asked, "May we take these precious little ones to your house, Ellen? Pike will help Charlie if he'll agree to make coffins for them." Then she whispered to Ellen, "I hope that is all right. I fear Lucy's reaction if she saw the bodies. Her puppy was kicked by a horse, and she does not yet know to deal with death."

"Who among us does?" Ellen asked, then added, "Of course we will take them. Gladys and Morris will come, too. They can stay until the house is rebuilt."

She looked to Mrs. Gurley for confirmation. "It will be rebuilt," the older woman said.

AND IT WAS. The funeral service was held at the church. The entire community attended, including Frances Ferguson. Ellen wondered how she knew about the deaths, but of course she did. Ellen had seen one of the cowboys from the Ferguson ranch fighting the fire. Miss Ferguson sat in the back pew, her weather-darkened face stern, not acknowledging the neighbors who stared at her with surprise. Ellen slid into the pew next to her. "I believe Gladys will be comforted that you are here."

"She will not. There is no comfort. I came because no one mourned with me for my boy. I would not be so callous," Miss Ferguson said.

The Turnbull boys were buried in the cemetery where Margaret and Charlie's brother and Ellen's baby rested. Ellen had picked wildflowers and stayed behind after the burial to put them on the graves. "It is an awful thing to end up in this spot with the coyotes howling over you," she told Charlie, who had waited for her, Billy in one arm. "It is the loneliest place in the world."

She shuddered, and Charlie put his other arm around her. "Come."

"Yes."

The two climbed into the wagon and drove to where the men were already constructing the new house, near the still-smoldering ruins of the old one. It was a simple shack covered with tarpaper, but it was as good as the first house had been. It went up quickly. The neighbors searched their own sparsely furnished homes for donations. The Gurleys brought an iron bed frame. Ellen stitched curtains on her sewing machine for the window. Others gave dishes and pots and pans, some cracked and chipped but still serviceable.

To Ellen's surprise, the McGintys attended the funeral and followed the others to the house-raising. Ruth brought one of her quilts for the couple. "Gladys will treasure it," Ellen told her. The two had moved away from McGinty, and they stood near the remains of the first house. As they talked, Ellen looked down and spotted part of a child's quilt that Gladys had made. It was burned, and only a block at the corner of the quilt was visible. Ellen wondered if Gladys would ever again stitch a boy's quilt.

ELLEN VISITED GLADYS whenever she could, sometimes neglecting her own chores to see her friend. Charlie understood. Ranchwomen supported each other in good times and bad. They would not have survived the prairie hardships without each other. Ellen remembered the day she met Gladys, when a bouquet of weeds had sat in a Mason jar on the kitchen table. So she brought flowers from her garden. More important, she brought food, because with her burnt hands Gladys could not

cook for a time. Eventually her hands healed, but they were
scarred, and Gladys would sit at the table staring at them.

The woman did not sit often, however. As if to make things
up to Morris, she kept the house spotless and spent hours at
the stove baking cakes and pies that her husband never ate.

"Wherever did you get the cherries?" Ellen asked one day
in late fall when she arrived just after dinner. Morris sat at the
table staring at a piece of cherry pie. He had not touched it.
He rose then and went outside without saying a word.

"He don't talk," Gladys says. "Sometimes I wish he would
yell at me or hit me, but he never does nothing. I grieve, too,
but if I say something, he just walks away. He stays outside
except for meals, but then, he don't eat much. And sleep."
She shook her head. "He ain't touched me in bed since the
boys . . . Used to be he'd want it every night. Now I try, but
he don't want nothing to do with me. He won't say my name.
He's never once said my name. It's as lonely here as if I was
living by myself."

Gladys began to cry, and Ellen clutched her friend's hand.
She didn't know any words to comfort Gladys. She had said,
"I'm sorry," so many times that the phrase no longer had
meaning.

"It wasn't your fault. He shouldn't blame you."

"It was my fault. That's it. Morris ordered me not to
smoke, but I done it anyway."

"There is forgiveness," Ellen said.

Gladys sniffed. "Not for me. Not from Morris. He hasn't
spoke five words all summer. He ain't ever going to forgive
me."

"How can you stand it?"

"I got to. It's my punishment."

"Maybe you can forgive yourself."

"I ain't never going to do that." The two were sitting at the table, and Gladys rose to clear the dishes and set them in the washbasin. She heated water on the new stove and began to wash the plates. Ellen settled Billy on the bed and picked up a towel to dry the dishes. "I had me a pretty good life," Gladys said. "Morris didn't care I worked at the Columbine. He come in there and swept me off my feet, said we was awful good together and maybe we ought to go to housekeeping. He never looked down on me for what I was. He set me up in that nice little house, and when the boys come, I thought I was the luckiest girl in Wyoming. I always said I was never going to have a dozen kids, but if that's what Morris wanted, I'd have done it. Lord knows, we tried. Sometimes Morris would come in here at dinnertime, and he'd pull me down on the bed . . ." Gladys glanced at Ellen and said, "I shouldn't be talking that way with you."

"That's all right." Ellen remembered when she and Charlie were first married and he thought of excuses to come into the house because he wanted her. He still did.

"Like I say, he ain't touched me at all. I think it would help us both if he did. When I try he moves away and pretends he's asleep. That's why I know he'll never forgive me. He won't throw me out. He won't even say he blames me. But when I see him staring at that rag dog I made for Bailey out of scraps—it's burnt, but Morris won't throw it out—I know he's never going to forget."

"Give it time," Ellen said, wondering if time would make a difference.

GLADYS DID GIVE it time. She waited the rest of the summer, the fall, and into the winter. One day Charlie came home from

Twenty-three

That was a hard winter for Ellen, even worse than the two previous ones because Gladys was gone. Ellen was glad when spring came and she was not confined to the ranch. The weather was warm enough now to take Billy and accompany Charlie when he went into town. She turned her head away from the Turnbull place when she passed, pretending she did not see Morris waving. Ellen had not stopped there since Gladys left.

Once when Ellen was at the mercantile, Gladys emerged from the Columbine. Her dress had a short skirt and low neckline, and she had on lipstick. Gladys looked away, but Ellen called to her and went across the street to speak. She didn't ask why Gladys had returned to the brothel. She knew. Instead, she said, "I miss you."

"I miss you, too. You was a good friend to me, Ellen. The best I ever had." Gladys thought that over. "Maybe you was the only friend I ever had—the only one that wasn't a hooker."

"You were a good friend, too. You helped me through the winters. I wish we could quilt again."

"You could come to the Columbine." Both women laughed.

Gladys was silent for a time, then put her hand to her eyes.

"I couldn't stand it," she said. "The last two weeks, the only thing Morris said to me was, 'Pass the salt.' I got to live with knowing I killed my babies. I couldn't look at him every day and see him blaming me, too. It'd never stop. I had to leave."

"It was an accident."

"It wasn't. I never told you, but I didn't have me just one cigarette. I had two. The boys wouldn't stop crying, and I needed a minute to myself. I smelled smoke, but I thought it was the cigarettes. Maybe if I'd been facing the house, I'd have seen the fire through the window, but I was turned away because the wind was blowing. If it hadn't been for the wind, the fire wouldn't have spread like it done. I tried to save them. Oh lord, I tried." Gladys held out her scarred hands as proof. "I got them out, but it was too late."

"You didn't have to come back here," Ellen told her.

"I did. I thought I was better than a whore, but I'm not." Gladys shook her head. "Don't speak next time you see me. It'll ruin your reputation."

"You know I wouldn't do that."

"Then *I* won't speak." Gladys turned and started back to the Columbine.

"Gladys?"

Gladys stopped, her back still to Ellen. "What?"

"Nothing. I wish you well."

"Was you going to tell me a woman's moved in with Morris?"

"No."

"But it's true. I already know about it. He got her out of a house in Cheyenne. She's going to have his baby. Maybe she'll have better luck than I did." Gladys turned to face Ellen. "I told you once that Morris thinks all women's about the same, so I ain't surprised. We had a good thing between us, but he never loved me, not the way Charlie loves you." Her voice broke. "The hard thing is I loved him." Gladys went inside and closed the door.

ELLEN HADN'T BEEN aware that the woman living with Morris was pregnant, because she'd never met her, never bothered to call. She knew she should put aside her resentment of Morris and visit her, but it was a long time before she steeled herself to do so. As far as she knew, Morris and Gladys were still married. Back east, an unmarried woman living with another woman's husband and pregnant with his child would have been shunned. In Wyoming, people only shrugged.

One afternoon when she could no longer put it off, Ellen mounted Little Betty, Billy in the saddle in front of her, and rode to the Turnbull place. The woman was a neighbor now, and Ellen couldn't ignore her forever.

"I'm Ellen Bacon, from north of here," Ellen said when the door opened.

"Yeah." The woman was noticeably pregnant. Since Gladys had been gone only three months, that meant Morris had dallied with her while he was still living with his wife, pleasured himself while Gladys was home mourning the loss of their boys. Ellen felt her hands curl into fists. Still, Ellen told herself, that was Morris's sin, not the woman's. Ellen shouldn't blame her.

"I've brought you some cookies to welcome you." Ellen held out a sugar sack. "I'm sorry I've been so slow, but it's been hard to get out in the winter." That was a lame excuse. Still, Ellen hoped the woman wasn't offended.

"I guess you can come in." The woman took the sack of cookies, then turned her back.

Ellen stepped inside. "I don't know your name."

"Mae. Mae Wilson."

At least she didn't call herself Mrs. Turnbull. Ellen looked around the room, which Gladys had kept spotless. The stove needed blackening; the curtains that Ellen had made for the house were dingy. The linoleum should be mopped. Dishes were stacked in the dry sink, and the bed was unmade.

"If I'd known you was coming, I'd have tidied up, but there's so much to do, and I'm feeling poorly," Mae said. That hadn't stopped Gladys from keeping up the house, Ellen thought. "You want coffee?"

Ellen shook her head. "Like you said, there's so much to do, and I must get back. I just came to say hello."

Mae nodded. "You come back anytime. I didn't know it'd be so lonesome out here."

"And you come to see me," Ellen said as she went back outside. There was a lump in her throat as she mounted Little Betty and Mae handed up Billy. She would be friendly with Mae—it was what was expected among ranchwomen—but Mae would never be the friend Gladys had been. Ellen wouldn't let her.

ELLEN CALLED ON Ruth whenever she went to town, taking letters from Laura when they arrived. If McGinty and his friend weren't around, Ruth would open them right then. "Those dear little children are doing well. Oh, how I would like to see them," Ruth said after she read one letter. "She has two, you know. Her husband is so good to her. Laura says he bought her a fur coat. And look, she sent me ten dollars again." Ruth's daughter almost always enclosed money. Ellen remembered how McGinty had thrown the letters into the stove without opening them and wondered how much money he had burned up. It didn't matter, because if he'd known about the money he'd have kept it for himself.

"Why don't you go see her?" Ellen asked, as she had before.

"Oh no." Ruth shrugged. "Laura is so busy. I'd just be in the way."

Perhaps Laura had never asked her mother to visit, Ellen thought. Maybe it wasn't just Ruth's fear that McGinty wouldn't let her go but that her daughter didn't want her. Laura had married well, and perhaps she was embarrassed by her mother. Ellen lifted her teacup to her mouth to hide her frown. She had bought tea at the mercantile for Ruth, and Ruth had insisted on sharing it with her.

"Well, I get to see little Billy, and that is almost like playing with my grandson," Ruth said, reaching out her hand to the boy, who had been sitting on the floor but used a table leg to pull himself up. He reached for Ellen's cup, and she let him have a sip of her tea. The boy made a face.

Billy let go of the table leg and nearly fell. Ruth reached out her hand to steady him, and Ellen saw the old scars from where her hand had been burned on the cookstove. The bruises on Ruth's arms were fresh, however. "You can't stay here. You must leave him before he kills you," Ellen blurted out.

She expected Ruth to deny that McGinty would ever do such a thing, but the woman only shook her head. "He wants me to sign over my land to him."

"What land?" Ellen hadn't known Ruth owned land.

"It's the only thing I have left from my folks. It's only scrub and not valuable, but McGinty has it in his head that he can use it in some scheme he and Snyder's thought up." Ellen frowned, and Ruth added, "He used to ride me about it, tell me it was as worthless as I am. He never cared about it before, but now he says it's his because he's my husband and what's mine belongs to him."

"That's not so."

"That's what I told him. He can beat me all he wants to, but I won't give it to him. It's special to me, and it will go to Laura someday. It's all I have to leave her."

"If he kills you, it will be his," Ellen said softly.

Ruth thought that over. "I reckon you're right."

"Is it worth it?"

"To me it is."

Ellen was about to say that Ruth could make out a will, giving the land to her daughter, but what good would that do? McGinty would have taken the land before Laura could claim it. Besides, would the daughter even want it? Did she care enough about her mother to claim the land for sentiment's sake?

RUTH HADN'T BEEN to see Ellen for a long time. So Ellen was delighted when the woman showed up at her door late one day. She was less pleased when she saw that Snyder was with her.

"We's on our way to the Bascom place. Her husband said take her along so's she could do her sewing with Miz Bascom." Snyder pointed to a bag that contained Ruth's quilt pieces.

Ellen looked at Ruth, whose head was down. There was no way McGinty would have cared enough about his wife to suggest she quilt with another woman. "Why, Ruth can stay here and quilt with me," Ellen said. "Why don't you go on and stop for her on the way back?"

Snyder shook his head. "Naw. McGinty wouldn't like it. But we got to stop here tonight because her horse is got lame and it won't go no further. I'm thinking we'll spend the night and go on tomorrow."

"Of course," Ellen said. "There's room for Ruth in here, but I'm afraid you'll have to sleep in the hay." She pointed to the barn.

Snyder nodded and started there with the horses, while Ruth went inside with Ellen, who asked what was going on. "Surely your husband isn't sending you to quilt with Mrs. Bascom."

Ruth shook her head. Ellen thought she had never seen her friend so dejected. "Snyder's going to kill me," Ruth said in a flat voice. "He only stopped because he's so drunk he can barely sit his horse. He fell off twice. It's too close to town for him to try anything on the way here, but out there"— she pointed at the window with her chin—"he'll just say my horse threw me or some such."

"Oh, Ruth, are you sure? That can't be true." But Ellen knew it was.

"I was foolish and even thought Wesley was trying to be nice to me after what he did last night. But then I knew that wasn't his way."

Ellen waited for an explanation, but there was none, and she said, "You're not going on with Mr. Snyder tomorrow."

Ruth shrugged. "Maybe it's best to be done with it all. I can't live like this anymore. Last night, he let Mr. Snyder have me." Ruth slid into a chair and put her face in her hands. "He's broke me for sure."

"He what?" Ellen asked, but then she knew. The idea that McGinty had shared his wife with his friend sickened her. "I will not let you go with Mr. Snyder," she said. She considered that. She could insist Ruth stay with her, but McGinty would only kill her later on. She had begun preparing dinner, but she sat down at the table with Ruth and took her friend's hand.

Silent tears ran down Ruth's face. "I just wish I could see Laura one more time."

The two were sitting there like that when Charlie came inside and asked why Snyder was passed out on a bale of hay, an empty bottle beside him. "You don't have to worry about supper for him. He'll be there all night."

"He's going to kill Ruth," Ellen told him.

"He's what?" Charlie pulled out a chair and sat down at the table.

Ellen nodded. "That's what Ruth says, and I'm sure she's right." She related what Ruth had told her.

"Well, we can't have that. Ruth'll stay with us. I'll tell Snyder to get the hell out."

Ellen shook her head. "That might work tonight, but she can't stay here forever. Mr. McGinty will come and get her and force her to go home. Still, I've been thinking, and I know what might work." She stood up. Billy was on the floor, and she cut off a slice of bread and handed it to him. "Our supper can wait. Charlie, get out that bottle of whiskey you keep in the cupboard and put it next to Mr. Snyder in case he wakes up. Then hitch up the wagon. I have a letter to write."

Twenty-four

It was dark when Ellen and Charlie set off. Billy was asleep in the back of the wagon, cuddled against Ruth, who was lying down under a blanket. They didn't want anyone to see her. Before they left, Charlie poured whiskey into Snyder's bottle in case he woke up. "The man will think he died and went to heaven when he finds it. He won't believe there was any left," Charlie said. Clouds covered the stars, making it difficult to see the road, but that was fine with Ellen. She felt they were on a dark errand and the fewer people they encountered the better.

Halfway into town, they passed a rider, who reined in his horse to have a talk. Charlie didn't stop but only waved at him and said, "Got to see the doc. Boy back there's sick."

"God go with you then!" the man called.

"Who was that?" Ellen asked.

"Saint Peter Jones."

"Is that his real name?"

"So he says. He told me his folks expected him to live up to it, and he does, if you don't count gambling and whoring. It's likely he'll say a prayer for Billy."

Ellen thought that was sweet and said a prayer for Ruth, too, although she wondered if Saint Peter's prayers would do more good than hers.

"You think this idea of yours will work?" Charlie asked after a time.

Ellen shrugged. Then because Charlie couldn't see her in the dark, she said, "Yes. I hope so anyway." In fact, she wasn't so sure, but Ruth might be listening and Ellen wanted to reassure her.

"It's a good thing this isn't Saturday night," Charlie said.

It was a Monday night, and while Wallace wasn't crowded, there were still people in town. The mercantile was open, and the saloon seemed to be doing a good business. Lights were on at the Columbine, too. Charlie drove past the buildings and parked the wagon on a dim side street. "Here goes," he said. "I just hope nobody notices me."

Ellen could see him grin. "Me, too." She watched as Charlie walked to the Columbine. He'd pulled down his hat and wrapped a bandana around his face, but anybody who knew him would recognize him by his size and walk.

In a few minutes, he was back. "Gladys just about fisted me when she opened the door and saw me standing there," he said. "She sure was mad. I had to put my hand over her mouth to keep her from yelling at me."

"Did she agree?" Suddenly Ellen was nervous. What if her plan didn't work? What would they do with Ruth then?

"You bet. She said we couldn't have picked a better night. They don't have a single customer, and they were in the kitchen making fudge. The girls all hate McGinty. They're a nice bunch, you know, Ellen. Folks look down on whores, but in my mind most of them are as fine as any women you could meet."

Ellen was startled by that. How did Charlie know? But she'd already realized her husband most likely hadn't been celibate when he met her. So maybe he did know.

Charlie looked up and down the street, which was deserted. "Come on before somebody sees us," he said. Ruth was wrapped in a blanket, and he lifted her out of the wagon while Ellen picked up Billy, and they hurried to the Columbine.

Gladys had turned off the outside light, and she opened the door as soon as they were on the doorstep. "I was never so disgusted in my life when I saw Charlie standing there," she told Ellen. "I just couldn't believe . . . Well, I'm glad I was wrong."

"You are good to do this," Ellen said. "You all are," she added, when she saw the two other prostitutes standing in the kitchen doorway."

"Oh, I'm glad to get back at old McGinty a little. All of us hate him," Frieda said. "We're a girl short, so there's an extra room. We'll hide her as long as you want."

"I hope it's not for too long, but I don't know."

Charlie set down Ruth, who looked around the room and at the three women. "I don't know how to thank you," she said

"It's okay," Mutt replied. "Your husband's not welcome here, but you are. I kind of like playing a trick on him."

Ruth smiled at that.

"You just stay in your room and keep the door locked so's nobody will go in when we're busy," Frieda added.

"You better get before somebody sees your wagon and thinks you're here on business," Gladys told Charlie.

Charlie blushed and took the sleeping Billy from Ellen. Gladys touched his arm. "Could I hold him?"

"Sure," Charlie said. He and Ellen watched as Gladys pressed the warm little boy to her breast. She rocked him for a minute before she handed him back. "I'll never forget how sweet they smell." Her voice wavered and she turned aside.

"Come and visit," Ellen said. "You'd be so welcome."

Gladys shook her head. "Them days are over."

BEFORE CHARLIE AND Ellen and Billy left Wallace, Charlie stopped the wagon at the mercantile and Ellen slid an envelope into the mailbox nailed to the front of the store. She wished she could have sent a telegram, but the stationmaster, who operated the telegraph, was a friend of McGinty's. She would have to trust the mail.

ELLEN THOUGHT SHE would wait five days before sending Charlie to Wallace for the mail. That would be long enough for her letter to reach Kansas City and the answer to come back. The letter she had sent to Laura was harsh and would have embarrassed Ruth if she'd read it, although it might save her life. After all, Ruth couldn't stay in the whorehouse forever—or with Ellen and Charlie, for that matter. McGinty would find her and either kill her or force her to go home. And of course, there was no place in Wallace where she could live. Laura was Ruth's only relative. Like it or not, Laura would have to step in. Ellen believed she would, because Laura's letters to Ruth were affectionate. Ellen had written Laura, telling her everything. "Your mother is hiding, but that won't be for long. If you do not help, I fear for her life," she wrote.

Now, the morning after she and Charlie had hidden Ruth at the Columbine, Ellen looked out the window and saw Mr.

Snyder coming toward the house, Ellen realized he was the flaw in her plan. What would they tell him when he discovered Ruth wasn't there?

The man was hungover and stumbled as he made his way across the barnyard. He held on to the doorframe of the house for a few seconds before coming inside and dropping onto a chair. He shook his head and mumbled something about being tired because the hay was a bad place to sleep. He smelled of whiskey, and Ellen wondered if he'd awakened that morning and finished off the liquor Charlie had poured into his bottle. Or maybe he'd drunk it the night before. She was sure it was gone.

"Well, good morning, Snyder," Charlie boomed, and the man winced.

"I have your breakfast," Ellen said. "How many eggs do you want?"

Snyder shook his head. "Ate too much last night. Don't want none," he said, although he hadn't had supper. He closed his eyes for a moment, then opened them and looked around the room. "Where's Ruth?"

Charlie looked at Ellen for an answer, and she thought for a few seconds before replying, "I guess she's wherever you took her."

"Huh?"

"Last night. You came inside and told her you were leaving. I said it was awfully late, but you insisted she go with you."

"Nah, I never did nothing like that. I'd of remembered."

Charlie moved in front of the man. "Are you calling my wife a liar?"

Snyder winced. "I don't remember it."

"I'm not surprised. You sure were drunk. You came in here and woke us up and said you were taking Ruth," Charlie told him.

"Where was I taking her?"

"That's what I asked. You said it wasn't our business," Ellen said. She looked at the man with loathing, remembering he had forced himself on Ruth.

Snyder considered that, then frowned trying to recall. He looked around the room, searching for Ruth.

"She's not here," Charlie said. "You can look in the barn, too."

Snyder went outside while Ellen and Charlie stood in the doorway watching him. "Do you think he believes us?" Ellen asked.

"Question is, will McGinty?"

As Ellen turned back in to the house, she spotted Ruth's bag with her piecework in it. "I better hide that. Ruth would never leave her quilting behind."

Charlie smiled. "I wouldn't worry. No man's ever going to think about that."

FIVE DAYS LATER, Ellen sent Charlie into Wallace for the mail. She was waiting outside when he returned. Charlie shook his head. "It's too early, honey. You know the mail isn't that fast. It'll be another week or two before you hear from her."

"Did you check the letter box in front of the mercantile? Maybe the letter wasn't picked up."

"I did. It was empty. It went out all right."

"I should have taken it inside to mail." She hadn't done so because she didn't want anyone to see her in town that late at night.

"Don't borrow trouble," Charlie told her.

"Was there any talk of Ruth missing?"

Charlie shook his head. "Not that I heard."

"Maybe that's good. It means Mr. Snyder must have told Mr. McGinty he'd done something with her and Mr. McGinty believes it. Maybe Mr. Snyder does, too."

"I got to go to see Mr. Gurley. I'll be back by suppertime."

"Maybe you should have waited for the train!" Ellen called. "You could go back!"

"Folks would sure wonder why I went for the mail twice in one day."

Charlie was right, Ellen thought as he rode off. It was too soon for Laura to respond. But what if she ignored the letter and never replied? What would happen to Ruth? Maybe Lizzie could help. Ellen was thinking about that as the dust settled behind Charlie. She watched until he was out of sight and was about to go inside when she saw a buggy in the distance. She thought it might be Mrs. Gurley with Lucy and walked toward the road to greet them. She didn't recognize the buggy, however, and decided it must belong to the homesteaders who had moved in to the north. She would invite them to stop and rest while she got them water.

The buggy stopped, and a woman asked, "Is this the Bacon ranch?"

"It is," Ellen said.

"Then I have come to the right place." The woman drove the buggy to the hitching post, then got out and tied up the horse. "This is the best the livery stable had to offer," she said. She turned, and Ellen saw that her clothes were even more fashionable than those of Julia Brownell's sisters.

"Are you Laura?" Ellen asked before the woman could introduce herself.

"I am. I would have been here earlier, but I could not leave immediately. I came as soon as I could."

"You are a good daughter."

Laura gave a tight smile but didn't agree.

"Come inside. There is tea. Your mother and I used to quilt over a cup of tea."

"Mama would have liked that."

Laura went ahead of Ellen, who studied her. The woman was conservatively dressed in a navy coat and matching tam-o'-shanter. Her black kid shoes—already covered with dust—looked expensive. After Laura took off her coat, Ellen was impressed with Laura's fine wool suit, its skirt stylishly short. Ellen thought of the long skirts and shirtwaists she had brought with her to Wyoming. She had considered them smart then, but now they were out of fashion. Laura's husband must indeed be wealthy—and generous.

"Until I received your letter, I did not know about Mama," Laura began. "She always wrote that she was happy and that Papa was good to her. I never knew. I blame myself for being so foolish."

Ellen's back was to the woman as she fed kindling into the cookstove and filled the kettle with water. She wished she had kept Lizzie's tea service polished so that she could use it then, but it was hopelessly tarnished. She did get out the good cups and saucers, however. She turned to Laura and saw she was crying. Ellen sat down at the table and took Laura's hands. "No, of course you didn't. Ruth would have been ashamed. She didn't have much, but she had her pride."

"I sent her money. I would have given her more, but she told me not to, that she didn't need it. I thought Papa would take it from her anyway." Laura dabbed at her eyes with an embroidered handkerchief.

"Your father burned your letters before Ruth could read them. He'd have burned up the money, too."

"I should have realized when Mama told me to send my letters to you that something was wrong. I knew Papa was a hard man, but Mama said he was better after I left."

"Why did you leave?"

Laura stared hard at Ellen. "My father was evil. I couldn't stay."

Ellen knew better than to pursue the question. She got up and poured water into a china pot and carried it and the cups to the table. "My sister gave me a beautiful silver tea service, but I haven't polished it in a long time."

"This awful land. It is no place for nice things." She paused. "Did Mama come here for tea often?"

Ellen shook her head. "She never came. Your father wouldn't let her. I stopped by at her house when I was in town or when you sent a letter. I brought the tea, and we drank it while Ruth read the letters. She was so proud of you and your children. She dreamed of seeing them one day."

Laura sighed. "And he tried to kill her?"

"That is what she thought. We managed to get her away when Mr. Snyder was drunk. In the morning we told him he had taken her away in the night." The tea had steeped, and Ellen poured it into cups.

"He believed you?"

"As far as we know. My husband was in town this morning and said there was no talk of Ruth missing."

"Surely someone would notice she was gone."

"She had few friends. At first, she attended church, but after that, she stayed home."

"Because Papa wouldn't let her go."

"So I assume."

While Laura sipped tea, Ellen wondered about the woman's plans for Ruth and she blurted out, "Did you come to fetch your mother?"

"Of course."

"You and your husband will take her in?"

"I have made plans for her." Laura's voice was firm, and Ellen knew the woman didn't care to discuss them. "Where is Mama?"

"She is safe." Ellen fidgeted. How could she tell this sophisticated woman that her mother was hiding in a whorehouse?

"Where? Not here, surely?"

"No."

"Where then?"

Ellen sighed. "I do not mean to offend you, but we have hidden her in a . . ." Ellen searched for a proper way to say "whorehouse." "In a house of assignation?" She looked away, embarrassed, when Laura gasped. "You must not think poorly of your mother," she added quickly. "She has her own room and the girls are kind to her. It does not reflect on Ruth at all. It was the safest place we could think of where your father couldn't find her. He's not allowed . . ." Ellen stopped when she saw that Laura was laughing. Ellen stared, not understanding what was so funny.

The woman took off her white gloves, which had been soiled from holding the horse's reins. Then she removed her hat, revealing beautiful auburn hair knotted at the back of her neck. "You've put up my mother in a whorehouse?"

Ellen was annoyed. After all, she and Charlie had done the best they could. "If you could have thought of a better place—"

Laura held up a hand that was fitted with gold rings.

"Ellen—may I call you Ellen?—I am only laughing at the irony of it. I don't have two children. I don't even have a husband. I made up that life so that my mother would not know what I did. You see, I run the finest brothel in Kansas City."

AFTER DARK THAT night, Ellen rode into town with Laura in the buggy. Charlie, Billy asleep in the wagon bed, drove behind them. Partway down the main street, Ellen gasped and pointed to a man entering the saloon. "There is your father."

Laura stared, and her lip curled. "The old bastard. He's the reason I turned out."

She became a prostitute because of her father? Ellen didn't understand.

"Good riddance," Laura said.

After they turned in the horse and buggy at the livery stable, Charlie tied the wagon to a post around the corner from the Columbine. Laura insisted on accompanying him to the hook house. When they returned, Ruth was with them. Laura helped her mother into the wagon, and Charlie drove them to the depot and bought two tickets. They would wait in the wagon until the train arrived, Laura holding her mother in her arms, because they did not want the stationmaster to see Ruth and tell McGinty that she had gone to Kansas City.

"Your daughter's lovely," Ellen told Ruth. She handed her friend the scrap bag with her quilt pieces that had been left behind.

"Yes," Ruth said.

"You don't mind . . ." Ellen stopped, not sure what Laura had told her. It would be a shock to Ruth, finding out Laura not only wasn't a married woman with two children but was the owner of a brothel.

"That she's a prostitute?" Ruth shook her head. "I figured it out a long time ago. I didn't want Laura to know that, so I went along with it. I'm sorry I wasn't honest with you."

Ellen chuckled, then stopped when she saw a figure hurrying toward the depot. She grasped Charlie's arm and pointed. "McGinty?" she whispered.

"Nope. Look."

In a minute Gladys reached the wagon. "What?" Ellen asked. "What's wrong?"

"Nothing," Gladys said. "Miss Laura offered me a job. I'm going to Kansas City, too."

Twenty-five

Those were even lonelier days now, with both Ruth and Gladys gone. Ellen was determined to be a friend to Mae, but it wasn't easy because Mae found little to like about life on a ranch. "I look out the door and see the same thing every day—nothing," she told Ellen.

Mae complained that she was bored, and when Ellen said that after the baby was born she might long for a little of that free time Mae only shrugged. She didn't seem excited about her pregnancy and remarked that she hoped it didn't spoil her figure. Mae did not keep up the house, but if Morris didn't mind, why should Ellen? She wondered if Morris missed Gladys, but of course he didn't say a word to Ellen about that. He never mentioned anything about the boys' deaths or about Gladys leaving Wallace. It was as if they had never been part of his life.

Ellen had not heard from Gladys. Ruth wrote to say she was living in a nice little house that Laura had bought for her and that Gladys sometimes accompanied Laura to Sunday night supper there. Laura sent Ellen a gold ring to thank her for caring for Ruth.

"We should visit Mrs. Hawkins. That would give you

something to do," Ellen told Mae. The Hawkinses had moved into the Brownell place and were trying to make a go of it. Ellen had called once to welcome them. Mr. Hawkins waved but did not stop working. He and his boys were adding a room onto the house. Mrs. Hawkins had tacked muslin to the ceiling to keep the dirt from falling down and whitewashed the walls. She'd hung a gold frame containing her marriage certificate over the bed. The house was as tidy as it could be with six people living in it—the couple plus two sons and two daughters. Mrs. Hawkins had been gracious and said she appreciated the call, but Ellen saw she was busy and stayed only a few minutes.

Now she thought she should introduce Mae to their new neighbor. Mae agreed to be at Ellen's place at eight one morning, and Ellen would drive them on north to their neighbors' house. She waited until ten before going by herself. She worried that Mae was sick or something was wrong with the baby, but if that was the case, surely Morris would have come for her. Mrs. Hawkins was in the midst of washing, so Ellen did not stay long. As she was leaving, she asked, "Do you quilt? Perhaps we could spend a few minutes one day piecing."

"Lord, no. Waste of time, if you ask me, putting all those bitty pieces together. Why'd anybody do that when you could just order a blanket from the catalogue?" The woman turned her back, and Ellen knew she had been dismissed. Mrs. Hawkins would not replace Gladys as a friend.

Later when Ellen told Mae they must have gotten their days mixed up, Mae replied, "I didn't feel like driving all the way up there just to see some woman in a soddy. I got better things to do than that." Ellen wondered what those things were.

As it turned out, Ellen did make a close friend—Hattie.

The girl had finished high school, and despite her desire to go to college and become a teacher, she had stayed home to help her family. When she wasn't caring for her own brothers and sisters, she worked as a hired girl for the Gurleys. Hattie hadn't given up the idea of becoming a teacher, however, and she stopped often to see Ellen, who took out her own normal-school books and went over the lessons with the young woman. Sometimes Hattie brought her piecing and the two women sat in the warmth of the cookstove, stitching.

Despite the hard work and her disappointment about college, Hattie was always cheerful, and Ellen's heart lightened when she saw her turn in to the yard. "I love this prairie, even on a day like this," Hattie said once when the sky was overcast and the wind blowing. "I guess I'd about die if I had to live where I couldn't see the horizon."

"Don't you ever feel lonely?"

"Well, sure I do. It's pretty lonesome sometimes, but I don't mind that. It's being in crowds of people that sets me off."

"When have you ever been in a crowd out here?" Ellen asked, and both women laughed. "The prairie does drive some women crazy. Julia Brownell, for instance," Ellen continued. "Sometimes I think it makes me a little looney." She'd never before told anybody about that.

Hattie didn't laugh. "Well, you wouldn't be a woman if it didn't. I think even Mrs. Gurley gets down sometimes. Wyoming's a man's place. That's for sure."

Billy, who had been crawling around on the floor, bumped his head and began to cry. Both women reached for him. Ellen scooped him up and held him. "He makes everything worthwhile," she said. "Billy keeps me from loneliness."

"And Charlie."

"Of course. I am doubly blessed." She thought of Gladys, who had lost both her husband and her babies, and remembered how she had clung to Billy when she had held him at the Columbine. After the fire, Gladys would have hated the prairie, hated the wind that had caused the blaze to spread. Perhaps it was a good thing she had left Morris. Even if Morris had been kind to her, Gladys never would have gotten over the horror of losing her boys. No matter how long she lived on that ranch, Gladys would not have looked at the spot where her house had stood without reliving the nightmare. Maybe one day she would marry again and have a family. Ellen hoped so.

"Have you heard from Gladys?" Hattie always seemed to know what Ellen was thinking. The young woman could keep a secret, and Ellen had confided in her that Laura had taken both Ruth and Gladys to Kansas City. She had not admitted that Laura ran a brothel, however.

"Not directly. But Ruth says Gladys is fine."

"She will not come back then?"

"Why would she? There's nothing for her here. After all, Morris has a new wife."

"Are they married?"

Ellen smiled. "Who knows. Probably not. It just seems like a nice thing to assume."

"I heard one of the Gurley cowboys say she's a hooker out of Cheyenne. I guess Morris knows how to pick them." Hattie covered her mouth. "That wasn't a nice thing to say," she added, but Ellen was smiling.

THE WEATHER WAS especially harsh that winter. Snow swept the prairie, and the wind blew it into drifts that were house high. Ellen went outside only to feed the chickens or milk the cow, and she dressed in a wool coat and mittens and wrapped a shawl around her head. It was too cold to take Billy with her, and if Charlie wasn't inside Ellen made sure the stove was cold and the kerosene lamps blown out before she hurried to perform her chores. She was that afraid of fire. She didn't complain about the cold because Charlie had it far worse than she did. He spent hours outside caring for the cattle, and when he came into the house he had icicles hanging from his hair and his face was red, burned by the sun and wind. Ellen worried that his ears would get frostbitten, but Charlie wrapped a scarf around his head under his Stetson. "Hell, honey, I'm used to the cold," he said one day as he rubbed charcoal under his eyes to keep the glare of sun on snow from making him snow-blind.

After days of being confined to the house with Billy, Ellen felt edgy. Her emotions went up and down. Her son was teething and cried. Mrs. Gurley told her to rub the boy's gums with whiskey to dull the pain, and that helped, although Ellen worried it would give him a taste for liquor. She even sipped it herself sometimes.

One day, Charlie brought home a dog he found on the prairie. "He'll die if we don't feed him," Charlie said.

"What if he's wild?" Ellen asked. Billy reached for the animal, but Ellen held him back. The dog might have rabies. Besides, he was filthy.

"I don't think so. He came up to me and wagged his tail. He must have run away from someplace."

"He's bound to have fleas."

"I'll scrub him good."

The dog lay down on the linoleum, and Billy curled up beside him. "I guess that's your answer," Ellen said. "What are you going to call him?"

Charlie shrugged. "'Dog,' I guess."

"That's no name for a dog."

"Let Billy name him."

"You mean when he learns to talk?"

"Then I guess you'll have to do it." Charlie went outside for the washtub. When he returned, the wind blew the door shut, sending snow over the floor. "Damn wind," Charlie said. "Winter wouldn't be so bad if it wasn't for the wind."

"There's his name then," Ellen said. "I guess we can call him Windy." She turned to the dog. "Is that all right with you, fellow?" The dog thumped his tail. Billy yanked it, but the dog didn't mind.

"I guess Billy's got him a friend," Charlie said.

Windy was a mongrel, not large as ranch dogs went, but he was ferocious in protecting Billy. He growled whenever anyone approached the boy and barked when Billy cried. He protected Ellen, too, keeping by her side when anyone turned in to the barnyard. Windy was a good rat dog, and when spring came Ellen would discover he killed rattlesnakes.

Both Ellen and Charlie doted on their little boy. Charlie loved to show him off, putting him on the saddle in front of him when he rode to the Gurleys' on an errand. Cowboys were a soft touch when it came to children, and Charlie said he could have charged a dime each to let them hold Billy. When he went to Wallace, Charlie bragged that Billy had walked before he was even a year old. The men sitting around the stove agreed that was remarkable, although, childless themselves, they had no idea if a child walked at birth or waited until he was five years old.

With both Ruth and Gladys gone, there was no one for Ellen to visit in Wallace, so she went to town less often now. Sometimes she stopped at the school, where there was a new teacher, because none of them—Ellen included, of course—stayed more than a year. The current teacher, Miss Evans, wouldn't either, she confided to Ellen, because she was engaged to a man back home in Minnesota. She had accepted the position because she wanted to make enough money to help with the down payment on a house. "Why don't *you* come back? The parents still talk about you," she asked Ellen. "You could bring your boy with you."

Ellen thought about that. She remembered the owner of the mercantile once approached her about resuming teaching. She'd told him she was a married woman and had a husband to care for. Now she had both husband and baby. Still, the idea intrigued her, not just because she was lonely without Gladys but because they needed the money.

One evening, she broached the subject with Charlie. "Miss Evans is leaving," she said.

"Who?"

"The teacher in Wallace."

"Found her a cowboy, did she? I remember one teacher that was sweet on a cowboy. Handsome fellow he was."

"Oh, I doubt there's another cowboy around here who's that good-looking."

"That's about right. He was smart, too."

"Not as smart as she was. *She* married *him*."

Charlie grinned and reached across the table and took Ellen's hand. "I guess that cowboy's about the luckiest fellow around."

Ellen squeezed his hand. "They'll be looking for a new teacher."

"Well, I hope they get a good one. Billy'll be starting school before long." He glanced at his son, who was sleeping in the red bed now.

She paused. "I know of a good teacher."

"Who's that?"

"Me."

Charlie laughed. "You're a married woman."

"I don't believe there's anything that says a married woman can't teach school. I've thought about it, Charlie. I miss teaching, and I could take Billy with me. He doesn't have anyone to play with, and it would be good for him to be around other children. Besides, we could use the money."

"Are you saying I can't provide for us?"

"Of course not. But a little extra money wouldn't hurt. You know as well as I do that we could use it."

"What would folks say?" He stood and looked out the window at the dark barnyard.

"I think they'd say they were glad I'd gone back."

"About me. What would they say about me? I'm thinking they'd say Charlie Bacon can't provide for his family. That's what."

Ellen stood and went to her husband. "Nobody would think that. Everyone knows it's hard to make a living out here. We're partners, and I want to help."

"You'd shame me," Charlie said.

Ellen started to protest but stopped. The two stood side by side, looking out the window. "We'll make it, honey," Charlie said, putting his arm around his wife's shoulders.

BILLY WAS FUSSY, and Ellen was rocking him back and forth in hopes he would go to sleep, when she heard a wagon outside. She put Billy on his bed and went to the door to see Mae sitting on the wagon seat. It was early, not yet eight o'clock, and Ellen knew Mae often slept till noon. "Come on in. I'll just heat the coffee," she told Mae.

"Don't barely have time. I just come because you've been real nice to me and I didn't want to leave without saying good-bye."

"You're going on a trip?"

"I'm leaving permanent."

"Morris is giving up his ranch?" Ellen couldn't believe it. Morris would have terrible memories of what had happened on his place, but he'd worked hard, as hard as Charlie, to make a go of it. Why would he leave?

"Morris ain't going."

"Not going? You're leaving without him?"

Mae shook her head. "I tried to make a go of it, but it's too bare out here. The wind drives me crazy, and you can't see nothing human, just cows, for miles around. Cheyenne maybe ain't the finest place in the world, but there's people. I tried, but I can't spend my life looking out the window at a bunch of cows." Mae tightened her hands on the reins. "I just come to say thanks for being neighborly. You're about the only thing out here I'm going to miss."

"I'll miss you, too," Ellen said, then glanced at Mae's burgeoning figure and asked suddenly, "How does Morris feel about this?"

"Oh, he don't care none. He didn't try to stop me."

"About the baby, I mean. I can't believe Morris would let you leave when you're about to have a baby."

"Oh, that's all right. He don't mind. It ain't his."

Twenty-six

In March, a blizzard swept down out of Canada, bringing the coldest weather yet. The temperature dropped below zero and stayed there for days. Snowdrifts covered the windows, keeping the inside of the house gloomy, and the wind blew so hard that it shook the little structure. Ellen remembered Charlie telling her once that sod was warmer than lumber, and she was almost sorry she'd insisted he build a house for her. The shack was so cold inside that she dressed Billy in his coat and mittens and wrapped shawls around herself. She was cold even when she was bent over the cookstove, although she didn't do much cooking now. The larder was all but empty and had been for a month. Now hunger gnawed at her.

They were eating mostly potatoes again. She and Charlie didn't complain, but Billy wouldn't eat them. Ellen mashed the potatoes and added a little sugar, but the boy spit them out. He wasn't gaining weight, and Ellen worried about him. She worried about Charlie, too, because he was thinner, and Ellen's own clothes were loose on her. She didn't blame Charlie. He was doing the best he could. She had married him for better or for worse, and these days of want would pass, she told herself.

She thought up games for Billy to keep him warm. She chased him around the room and played pat-a-cake and hide-and-seek, with the little boy covering his eyes while she pretended to look for him, calling, "Where's Billy?" She was glad for the dog now, because he played with Billy on the cold linoleum floor. Windy slept with the boy, keeping him warm. There weren't many scraps to feed the dog, and he, too, was hungry. His ribs showed.

Charlie shoveled a pathway to the barn, and Ellen insisted on milking the cow, although her hands cramped with the cold. Charlie offered to do the milking, but Ellen said she needed to get out of the house twice a day. Besides, Billy was excited when she came back inside with a pail of warm milk. Milk was about the only thing the boy would consume.

Ellen did not tell Charlie—she did not want to add to his worries—but she was concerned about Billy. It wasn't just his weight. It seemed that every day he was a little more lethargic. He grew fussy, and although she rocked him back and forth, he didn't sleep well. He cried more, until Charlie finally complained, "We got us a crybaby cowboy." He thought that over, then asked, "You think he's okay?"

"It's just the cold. When spring comes, he'll be fine. He needs to run around outside in the sunshine. We're all tired of being cooped up."

When the storm abated, Charlie saddled Huckleberry and went to check on the cattle. "Only one dead," he said when he returned. "I guess we're lucky."

Not so lucky, Ellen thought. After the loss of cattle the year before, they couldn't afford to lose even one animal. But she only smiled and said, "Yes, lucky."

Charlie picked up Billy, who was sleeping on the floor. The boy fretted when Charlie put his cold face next to Billy's.

"He's nice and warm," Charlie said, handing the boy to Ellen while he shrugged off his coat.

Ellen took Billy and felt his forehead. "Too warm. I think he's catching cold."

"Give him a little hot whiskey. That's the best thing for a cold."

"Charlie!"

"That's what they do at the Gurley ranch. Seems to work, and if it doesn't you don't much care."

"That may be fine for a tough old cowboy, but Billy's a little boy. We'll have to think of something else."

Hattie came by and told Ellen that her family, too, was down with what her mother called the catarrh. "Keep a tea-kettle of water boiling on the stove, and let Billy sit near it. Ma says the steam's as good as anything," Hattie suggested. "If that doesn't work, I'll bring a tincture Ma mixes up. One of us is all the time getting the catarrh."

Billy had a dry cough, and then congestion that settled in his lungs. Hattie brought her mother's concoction, but that didn't help. "Mrs. Gurley said she'd come, but Lucy's down sick, too, and Mrs. Gurley is afraid to leave her. Lucy gets upset when she doesn't know where her mother is." Hattie smiled. "Mrs. Gurley loves that little girl as much as Margaret. It was a nice thing you letting her raise her. She's trying to teach Lucy her letters. Mrs. Gurley said she learned how from you."

Billy did not get better. His eyes were red, and his nose ran. He had trouble breathing. The fever was worse, and Ellen put a cold cloth on his forehead to try to bring it down. That didn't help either. At first, Billy cried all the time, but after a while, he was too tired—or too sick—and only sent out pathetic wails. Charlie suggested they take Billy to the doctor, but the cold outside was intense and the wind fierce. Ellen feared the trip into town would only worsen Billy's catarrh. "Maybe you should fetch the doctor," Ellen said at last.

Charlie bundled up in his overcoat and buffalo mittens and rode through the drifts into town. He returned hours later, his face red from the cold and his mouth so frozen he could hardly mumble. "Doc's with a woman having a baby. I went out to where he was at, but he says he can't leave. He'll come as soon as the baby's born. He told me you're doing everything you can. I said it was serious, but he says women always think that with their firstborn. Says we won't worry so much when we have three or four." Charlie took off his coat and shook out the snow. Flakes landed on the stove and sizzled. "Maybe we will, and maybe we won't. Is Billy any better?"

"About the same." In fact, he was worse, but Ellen didn't want to worry Charlie any more than she had to. "I suppose the doctor's right. One day we'll look back on this and laugh about how worried we were."

"Only not now." Charlie sat down beside Billy, who was in a fitful sleep. He put his cold hand on the boy's forehead. "He seems hotter."

"That's because you're so cold."

"Maybe," he said. "Did you give him milk?"

"I heated it the way he likes it and added a little sugar and cinnamon, but he won't drink it." She pointed to the silver cup with Billy's initials on it that Lizzie had sent when the boy was born. "I poured the milk into Windy's dish. Poor dog is worried."

"What about an egg?"

Ellen shook her head. Billy whimpered, and Ellen picked him up. Windy jumped off the bed and went up to her. He'd barely left Billy's side since the boy had gotten sick. She was tired. Billy had been sick for almost a week, and she hadn't slept any more than he had. She had been up all night, smoothing his forehead with a cloth she dipped into cold water. The steam had helped Billy breathe better, but she'd taken the teakettle off the stove, because the heat in the room made the little boy hotter.

She jiggled him up and down, then handed him to Charlie, while she went to the stove and stirred the soup—potato soup. She wished she had something better to feed her husband, but there would be no meat until they butchered one of the cows. Even then, that wouldn't provide much, because the cows were as starved as they were. She wondered if she should send Charlie to the Gurleys' to ask for a piece of beef so that she could make beef tea for Billy. But he might not take it, and Charlie would be humiliated at having to beg his neighbors for food. Ellen dished up the soup and placed it on the table with a loaf of bread that was two days old. Then she took Billy and held him, hoping Charlie wouldn't notice that her soup bowl was only half-full, because although Ellen had thinned the soup with water, there wasn't much of it. Charlie was working outside in the cold, and he needed it more than she did. What if he, too, came down with the catarrh? It would be up to her to do Charlie's chores. Besides caring for Charlie and Billy, she'd have to hitch up the team and deliver hay to the cattle, and Ellen wasn't sure she could do it. She did not consider that she, too, might get sick.

The little boy's whimpers were worse than his cries, because Ellen knew they meant he was growing weaker. After a time, they were so faint that Ellen could have slept through them, but she didn't. Billy had been in his bed, but she picked him up and held him against her as she rocked him back and forth. She hummed softly, hoping she wouldn't wake Charlie, but he sat up and asked about Billy and she realized he hadn't slept either. "He's just so sick, Charlie. We're never going to laugh about this."

"Let me hold him. You rest." Charlie took the boy and sat down in the rocker, which creaked under his weight. The boy sent out little cries and arched his back, and Charlie said, "I'm sorry, honey. He's just like a calf. He wants his mama, not his papa." He stood and handed the boy to Ellen.

Ellen sat down again in the rocker, and the boy fell asleep. "Go to bed, Charlie," Ellen said.

Charlie was too restless. He walked around the room, beating the fist of one hand against the palm of the other. "There's got to be something we can do," he said. "I'll go ask Mrs. Gurley. Maybe she knows."

"Hattie already did. I've tried everything she suggested. We just have to let him get well."

"You think he will?"

Ellen stopped rocking. "What?"

"I didn't mean anything."

"Don't say that, Charlie. He'll get well. He has to."

Charlie went behind Ellen and put his hand on her head. "Sure he will."

But what if he didn't? Ellen thought. What if she lost him, just like she had lost the baby girl she had carried, just like Gladys had lost her boys? Ellen tried to put the thought behind her, but there it was. She tried to push it from her mind, but Charlie now had said it out loud. She kissed Billy's forehead and hummed to him. "Nothing's going to happen to Billy," she told Charlie.

"Of course not." Charlie lit the kerosene lamp, then turned it low. He pulled out a chair and sat down, his elbows on his knees, his head bowed.

Ellen wondered if he was praying. She'd never known him to pray. After a moment he raised his head and looked at her. His eyes glinted with tears. Clutching Billy, Ellen went to her husband. Charlie was still seated, and she stood in front of him, holding their son between them. Charlie put his arms around her waist. "He'll get better. It's just the catarrh. Our boy will be all right."

They stayed like that for a long time; then Charlie stood up. "You want me to make you some coffee?"

"That would be nice."

Charlie fed cow chips into the banked fire in the cook-stove. They had collected the fuel in the fall to supplement the wood. The circles of dung burned quickly, but they made a hot fire. Charlie set the pot with yesterday's coffee on the stove and when it boiled he poured it into two cups then doctored it with sugar and Pet milk. "Here, honey," he said, handing one of the cups to Ellen. She was holding Billy with both hands rocking back and forth. When she didn't take the cup, Charlie said, "I'll put it on the table."

Ellen didn't respond, only held on to Billy. She wasn't humming anymore.

"Ellen?" Charlie said. When his wife didn't answer, Charlie said again, "Ellen?"

The dog began to howl, and Charlie told him to shush.

Ellen looked up at Charlie, tears streaming down her face. "What?"

"Our boy's gone."

Charlie stared at her, open-mouthed. "He's gone?"

"He's dead, Charlie."

Charlie stared down at his silent son. "No," he whispered. Then louder: "No!" He was racked with sobs. Ellen had never before heard him cry. He paced the room, then hit his fist against the door and screamed, "No! God damn it, no!" He went back to Ellen. "Are you sure?"

She was still rocking the baby. "I should have known better. I'm his mother. It's my fault."

Charlie shook his head. "It's mine. This house is no better than a line shack. I should have built a decent one that wouldn't get so cold. I would have, but I was worried about getting the planting done. Potatoes. Damn potatoes. I thought they were more important than my boy."

"No, Charlie. It's not the house. It's the catarrh. We couldn't have done anything." She began to cry, and Charlie knelt beside her, putting his arms around his wife and the dead boy. They were there like that when Hattie came.

SHE KNOCKED AT the door, then opened it and peered in. "Mrs. Gurley sent beef tea. She made it last night. She's sorry she didn't think of it before." The sun had come out, and the glare on the snow affected Hattie's eyesight for a moment. At first, she didn't see Ellen and Charlie. When she finally spotted them huddled together, she gasped. "Oh no." Hattie was a devout girl, and she dropped to her knees. "I'll pray for him," she said, "and for you."

Ellen wished she, too, could pray, but she was too numb. Besides, if she did, she would blame the Lord—blame Him for Billy's death and the shabby house and the snow and for Wyoming. It was the devil's land. But she didn't pray. All she could do was hold the little body against her breast to keep it from growing cold.

Charlie stood then, his eyes red and his face haggard. "He died in the night. He just stopped breathing."

"He won't cry anymore," Hattie said. She set the jar she'd

been holding on the table. "Make Ellen drink it. It'll help her get her strength back. I'll go for Mrs. Gurley. Don't worry about the milking. I'll ask Pike to do it."

After Hattie left, Charlie stared at the door. Then he put on his coat and mittens and told Ellen *he* would do the milking. At that moment, he couldn't bear to be inside the house, knowing he couldn't do anything to help his dead son and his weeping wife. When Ellen finally looked up, Charlie was gone. She rose then, thinking she ought to fix his breakfast, but she wouldn't. Instead, she set Billy on his bed, then poured water into the teakettle and built up the fire in the stove. When the water was warm, she washed the boy, then dressed him in a sailor suit that Miss Ferguson had given her. She put the tiny cowboy boots on his feet. Charlie had splurged on them at Christmas. She wrapped him in a quilt she had made so that even in death he would be warm.

She wondered where Charlie was. He should have finished the milking by now. She heard pounding and went outside, following his footsteps to the barn. Tears streaming down his face, he turned to her and said, "I'm making a coffin for Billy."

"Pike will help you," Ellen told him."

Charlie shook his head and said fiercely, "I'll do it. He's my son."

DESPITE THE WEATHER, the little church was filled for the funeral service. Charlie sat in the front row with Ellen. She was sure Charlie blamed God for the death of one more person he loved and was not sure he'd go inside the church with her. "He was there for *you*," Hattie explained later.

Ellen barely noticed the friends who had come to mourn with her. Her eyes were on the little coffin that Charlie had

made and sanded and stained. When the service was over and
the mourners had filed past to say their good-byes to the little
boy, Charlie put the lid on the casket. But Ellen took his arm.
"No," she said. She leaned over her son, crying, her tears falling on the quilt wrapped around the little body, until Charlie
led her away.

"I'll take Ellen home," Mrs. Gurley said, but Ellen refused.
She insisted on going with Charlie as well as the minister,
Hattie, and the Gurleys to the cemetery. Morris, who had
attended the service, followed after them. Pike and Charlie
had already cleared the snow from the grave site next to Ellen's baby girl and blasted a grave in the frozen earth. Charlie held Ellen as the coffin was lowered into the ground, and
the minister said a prayer. She looked out across the prairie,
which chilled her heart with its terrible vastness. Then Charlie led her to the wagon for the cold drive home. There was
food on the table that the neighbors had brought, but Ellen
would not eat. Charlie helped her into bed and covered her
with quilts. Only then did he remember the dog. He saddled
Huckleberry and returned to the cemetery, where Windy was
keeping watch over his young master's grave. Charlie picked
up the dog and put him in front of him on the saddle. As they
rode home, coyotes began to howl.

Twenty-seven

Now came the worst of the hard times.

Spring arrived, greening the prairie, blooming the wild-flowers, and bringing home the birds. Ellen barely saw them. Neighbors called with food and condolences, but Ellen was mute, hardly noticing their attempts to console her.

She did her chores and kept the house clean. She kept up with the milking and the washing. This was not like the time following the loss of her baby girl when she was unable to do the slightest things. Back then, it was her body that was responding to the depression. She hadn't really known that child. But Billy, the baby born on Christmas morning, was a living, breathing boy who she had held and nursed and played with. Now her heart and mind were dealing with a terrible sadness that was caused by the loss of a child she had nurtured for more than a year, someone she had loved as much as she did Charlie.

Why Billy? Why not her? she asked over and over again. Why couldn't she have been the one to die? She had lived a good life, and while she would not have wanted to leave it, she would have given it up willingly if her son could have lived. But she hadn't had that choice. God had made the choice for her, and she blamed Him. She understood now why Morris had turned on Gladys. He'd had to blame someone. Gladys had accepted his censure, because there was no one she could blame but herself.

Other people Ellen knew had lost children. She thought of Margaret Gurley's death, but the Gurleys had had Pike and now they had Lucy. Ellen had no one. She did not take comfort in knowing that others had grieved.

There was a terrible loneliness on the prairie then, and Ellen felt crushed by the sky. She wondered what her life would be like if she'd never seen the newspaper advertisement for the teaching job in Wallace.

The minister called to console her, but he represented the God who had taken her little boy. Ellen could barely invite him inside. She merely stood aside to let him enter the house, then steeled herself to hear him repeat the foolish things said by others. Still, propriety dictated that a ranchwoman be hospitable to whomever called. Without asking, she went to the stove and put the coffeepot on the burner to reheat the morning's coffee. She did not bother to take down the good china but poured the coffee into a tin cup and handed it to him. "Milk?" she asked, but he shook his head.

"I stopped on the way to pick flowers." He held them out. Ellen had not noticed he was carrying a bouquet. "I don't know their names. It's possible they are weeds."

Ellen softened a little at the kindness. She took the flowers and set them in a canning jar that she filled with water. She pointed to a chair, then sat down herself at the table.

"You do not care for coffee?" he asked.

"No."

"It is a difficult time," he said. It was not a question but a statement of understanding.

"Yes."

"I realize how unqualified I am to be a minister at moments like this. I try, but I do not have the words to make a person feel better. I can only say I am sorry."

Ellen nodded.

"Sometimes it is hard to understand the Lord. Sometimes you might even hate Him."

Ellen had been staring at her hands, but now she looked up at the minister. "Sometimes."

"I believe God understands that." He sipped the coffee. "Mrs. Bacon, I do not know why God chose to let Billy die. I wish I could tell you. I wish I could say something that would bring you peace."

Ellen liked that the minister had used the word "die." Others had said Billy was called or chosen or had—the word she hated most—passed, as if he'd only been passing by.

"I don't know the reason for death, but I know there is reason for life." He raised the cup again but only stared into the dark brew. "I had a brother who died."

Ellen looked away. She was not consoled by stories of others' losses.

"I asked myself if I would have been better off if he had never lived at all. The answer was no, and that helped me deal with the grief." He set down the cup and stood. "You have already thought too much about death. Come outside with me." He held out his hand and led Ellen to the door. "There is such beauty on the prairie this morning," he said, pointing at the vast stretch of land around them. The sky was a brilliant blue, and the earth was alive with green. "This land always revives

me. I pray you will find hope in it." Then he added, "I was
at the cemetery yesterday. There are wildflowers near Billy's
marker. Is that your work?"

Ellen shook her head. She had refused to visit the grave.
Charlie must have planted them there.

ELLEN APPRECIATED THE minister's visit, and the visits
from Hattie and Mrs. Gurley. Still, she grieved. Charlie was
cheerful. He talked of the new calves and his hope for a good
hay crop. At dinner one night, he told her of finding a hawk
with a broken wing. He'd tried to catch it, hoping he might
mend the wing, but the bird had hopped off. "I was afraid I'd
frighten it to death," he said.

Ellen merely nodded, then stood and cleared the plates.
She did not stop to think that her husband was trying to as-
suage not only her grief but his own, too.

Charlie tried to be upbeat around Ellen, although he was
burdened with a sense of guilt that he had not brought the
doctor in time. It didn't matter that the doctor couldn't have
helped. Like Ellen, Charlie brooded over what he could have
done to save his son's life. He did not let Ellen see that, however.
Sometimes when he was working the cattle, he felt his eyes brim
over with tears.

Once Hattie came into the barn to find him bent over,
crying. She started to back away, but Charlie heard her and,
thinking she was Ellen, held out his hand. She did not take it
but mumbled an apology for intruding. Charlie was startled
and wiped his eyes, and Hattie, embarrassed at such a sign of
raw sorrow, turned and went to the house.

Lizzie wrote, asking if she should come, but Ellen told her

282   SANDRA DALLAS

no. She did not want to go visiting with Lizzie, did not want a sewing machine or any other expensive gift.

THEY CARRIED ON as they had in previous years. Charlie insisted they attend an ice-cream social at the church held to raise money to add a steeple. Ellen was dutiful and baked a cake to be auctioned off. Charlie bid four dollars for it—four dollars they couldn't afford. He said nobody else was going to eat what he knew was the best cake at the social. He reminded Ellen how he had bought her box supper at the schoolhouse auction just after they'd met, and Ellen gave a small smile as she remembered how embarrassed—and proud—she had been that he'd paid more than anyone else did to purchase a meal. "I needed to get your attention, because I already knew I was going to marry you," he said as he set the cake in the wagon. "You were the prettiest girl I ever saw. And you still are." Then he whispered, "I'll always remember how you looked on our wedding night. I thought maybe I'd married an angel by mistake."

Expressing his feelings came hard for Charlie, and he didn't do it often. Ellen should have been touched, but instead she only shrugged. She didn't notice that Charlie's face fell.

In July, Charlie took her to the Independence Day celebration. He put a tiny flag in his hatband, and when Ellen put on her worn housedress he insisted she change into her best dress. He even suggested she wear the horseshoe brooch he had given her that first Christmas. As they rode into Wallace, she thought of July Fourth the year before, when Billy had been with them. The little boy hadn't known what was going on, but he had been excited. She remembered how his face had lit up with wonder when he heard the band and how he had smiled when he saw his father on a bucking bronco. When

Charlie was thrown from the horse, Billy had clapped his hands with the rest of the crowd, although he hadn't known what he was doing.

When they reached Wallace, Charlie tied up the horses, then left Ellen with a group of women. He joined the men, who were passing around a bottle. When Ellen saw Charlie take a swig, she wondered if he had started drinking. Perhaps he kept a bottle of whiskey in the barn. She hadn't noticed if he stumbled or slurred his words, but then she hadn't paid much attention.

"I could use a drink myself," a woman said. Ellen turned to see that Miss Ferguson had come up beside her. The old woman pointed with her chin at the men. "I never thought God made whiskey just for them."

One of the women frowned and said, "God didn't make whiskey, Miss Ferguson. Satan did."

Ellen might have smiled at the exchange, but she only looked from one woman to the other.

"Ha!" another woman put in. "Now, Edna, I can think of more than one night with a blizzard howling outside that whiskey did a better job than the cookstove of keeping me warm."

"Well, I can't help but remember Mr. Brownell, who drank up his wife's money, and look what happened to her," Edna told her.

"She still at the asylum?" someone asked.

"She's dead," Miss Ferguson said. "She jumped out of a window and killed herself. The way I see it, they should have arrested her husband for murder."

"Julia's dead?" Ellen asked.

Miss Ferguson studied her. "I'm surprised you didn't know, you being her friend and all. I heard it was announced at the church."

Ellen looked away. Despite the minister's kindness, she had not been to church since Billy died.

"Mr. Brownell's dead, too. They found him up north of here in a cabin. The rats chewed off his ears."

"What happened to the boy?" Ellen asked.

"He ran off, I guess. Nobody knows where. I thought you knew about it. You don't get out much, do you?" Miss Ferguson asked.

That was none of the old woman's business, and Ellen didn't reply.

Miss Ferguson stared at Ellen a moment, then left. When she was out of earshot, one of the women said, "She's a strange old bird. You ever heard how she got that way?"

Ellen didn't care to gossip about the woman, but she hadn't the energy to defend her. She was glad when Charlie came up and took her arm and said the speeches were about to start.

The two walked to the bandstand, where a group of musicians was finishing "The Stars and Stripes Forever." Their playing was poor, but the crowd cheered anyway. Boys tried to climb a greased pole to snatch the silver dollar that was on top. There were patriotic speeches; then a boy recited "The Flag Goes By." The program ended with "The Star-Spangled Banner," and Charlie and the other men took off their hats and held them over their hearts.

The women had filled picnic tables with food, and as soon as the program was over people rushed to eat. The men made sure to take some of what their wives had brought. Husbands knew that a woman would be embarrassed if her pie or chili or deviled eggs was left over. Charlie nudged Ellen to show that the cake she'd brought was gone by the time he reached it. Ellen was still picking at her food when it was time for the rodeo.

"I'm going to win this year. You wait and see," Charlie told Ellen. He took her arm. "Come on, honey. I want you to watch me."

"Of course," Ellen said without enthusiasm. She followed Charlie to where the rodeo was taking place and stood beside Miss Ferguson.

"I'm going to beat you this year!" Morris called.

"In a pig's eye," Charlie told him. "Right, Ellen?"

Ellen smiled but didn't reply. But Miss Ferguson yelled, "Morris Turnbull, you're a fool. Can't anybody outride Charlie Bacon!"

The two women watched as one rider after another was bucked off. Charlie had drawn a mean bronco named Shooting Star. "Climb on him, cowboy," a man said as he helped Charlie into the saddle. Then he yelled, "Let 'er rip!" as he opened the gate. Charlie on his back, the bronco bucked and snorted. He twisted and fishtailed. Miss Ferguson yelled, "Ride 'em, Charlie!"

Charlie slipped a little in the saddle, but he held on. When time was called, Charlie slid off the horse, then picked up his hat, which had sailed off during the ride. He came over to Ellen and gave her a sheepish look, waiting for praise.

Ellen smiled, but it was Miss Ferguson who said, "That was a hell of a ride, cowboy! Maybe the best I ever saw. Shooting Star is a devil horse all right. I thought for sure you wouldn't last. I guess you must be pretty proud of him, Ellen."

"Of course," Ellen said. She patted Charlie's arm.

"I reckon I won the twenty-five dollars," Charlie said.

"We could use it," Ellen told him.

Charlie slumped, and Miss Ferguson gave Ellen a long stare. "I'd sure be proud if that was my man," she said.

Both Charlie and Ellen were silent on the way home.

When she stepped out of the wagon, Ellen looked down at her dress and realized the horseshoe brooch was gone.

TOWARD FALL, THEY knew it would be another bad year. The crops were failing, and Charlie sold off some of his cattle. "Hell isn't but a mile from here," Charlie muttered one night at supper. He had made arrangements to work for the Gurleys and Miss Ferguson during fall roundup, for seventy-five cents a day. He didn't tell Ellen how poorly they were doing. At first, he didn't want to worry her. Then he wondered if she cared.

ONE MORNING WHEN Charlie was working at the Gurley ranch, Miss Ferguson rode into the barnyard on a beautiful red horse. She had an eye for horseflesh and had told Charlie more than once that he ought to let her buy Huckleberry. "He's too good to be hitched to a plow," she'd said.

"I'd hitch up myself before I'd do that. It'd break his spirit," Charlie had replied.

Now Miss Ferguson dismounted and tied her horse to a hitching post. She ran a hand over his nose with affection, then turned to Ellen, who was standing in the doorway. "Charlie's not here," Ellen said, hoping the woman wouldn't stay.

"Didn't come to see Charlie. You got coffee, do you?"

Ellen turned and walked into the house. She took out a tin cup and filled it with coffee from the pot on the stove, not caring that it was only lukewarm.

Miss Ferguson took a sip and set down her cup. "Not feeling very hospitable, are we?"

"Isn't it hot enough for you?" Ellen asked.

"You know it isn't."

"I'm not feeling up to company."

"You're not up to much of anything, are you?" Ellen started to protest, but Miss Ferguson held up her hand. "Oh, I know, you think it's none of my business, but somebody has to straighten you out."

"You're right. It's none of your business."

"Matter of fact, it is."

"My son is dead," Ellen said. She turned her back on the woman, wishing she would leave.

"Of course he is, and we're all sorry about that. I lost a child, too, you know."

"Is that supposed to make me feel better?" Ellen bit her lip. Miss Ferguson didn't deserve that. She turned around to apologize.

"I'm not here to grieve or to try to explain away why your boy died. I wouldn't know how. I want to tell you that you feeling sorry for yourself is going to ruin your life. You want to turn into a bitter old woman like me, you just keep on the way you are. If you do, you'll take poor Charlie right along with you, turn that sweet cowboy into a mean son of a bitch. And that's a pity, because there's not a man in Wyoming who loves his wife as much as Charlie does you. He's grieving, too, you know, but he doesn't want you to see it. Times are hard just now, and a man needs his wife beside him. But she's not thinking about anything but herself."

Ellen looked away. "That's between Charlie and me."

"And me. Charlie came to me yesterday. Nearly made me cry."

Ellen frowned. What did the woman mean?

Miss Ferguson nodded. She'd been sitting at the table, but now she stood up. "He wanted to sell Huckleberry."

"His horse?" Ellen was stunned. Next to her and Billy, Charlie loved that horse more than anything in the world.

"That's right. I asked him if he needed the money that bad. He told me things were tough, but that wasn't the reason he wanted to sell. It was because of you."

"Me?"

"He said he wished to Christ he could do something to make you better. He thought maybe he could buy you some stylish new clothes and a trunk to put them in and a ticket to Chicago to see your sister. He said maybe that was what you needed." Miss Ferguson scoffed, "Fancy duds! What's a man know about what a woman needs? But I believe he'll try anything. He loves you that much."

Ellen was shocked. "Did you buy Huckleberry?"

"I told him I'd think about it. I thought I'd let that be up to you."

Ellen went to the stove and poured the last of the cold coffee into a cup. But she didn't drink it, only stared at the thick brew. "Is it that bad?"

"It is."

"Am I that bad?"

"You're grieving. That's understandable. But it's time you get over it. You're a lucky woman, Mrs. Bacon. There aren't many men as good as Charlie. It breaks my heart to see him grieving just like you are, and you not doing a thing to help him. He lost his son, too." She set the cup on the table, and without saying more she mounted her horse and rode off.

THAT AFTERNOON, WHEN Charlie rode into the barnyard, Ellen was waiting for him, Little Betty already saddled. "It's time you took me to see Billy's grave," she said.

Charlie nodded. "I expect so."

Ellen put her hand on Charlie's arm, clinging to him a little too long. Then he helped her mount Little Betty, and together the two rode across the prairie to the cemetery. Charlie led the way to the grave, then lifted Ellen off her horse. "There," he said. He pointed to a little mound of dirt that was covered with wildflowers. At the head of the grave was a huge rock with "Our Boy Billy Bacon" carved in it.

Ellen thought of her husband kneeling there with a chisel. It would have taken him a long time to chip out the words, and tears would have clouded his eyes as he worked. She turned to Charlie and put her arms around him. The two of them held each other as they cried.

Twenty-eight

Ellen had shut herself off from the world around her, and now she realized how poorly the ranch was doing. Hail had wiped out the hay crop, and bugs had nearly destroyed the potatoes. All they had were the cattle, and it was likely that come spring, Charlie would have to top out the herd in order to get a little cash. Ellen prayed that they would make it through the winter. Charlie still had Huckleberry. Ellen never told him she knew he had tried to sell the horse, and she had made Miss Ferguson promise to let her know if Charlie approached her again. No matter how bad things got, Ellen would never let him give up Huckleberry. That would be an awful blow to Charlie's pride.

Now Ellen did her part. She shortened the outdated skirts she had brought for her teacher year and mended blouses so that she wouldn't have to buy new ones. She sold butter for fifteen cents a pound and eggs for five cents a dozen. When she discovered the bill at the mercantile was so large that the storekeeper warned he might have to limit her purchases, Ellen gave him the ring that Laura had sent her. When that wasn't enough, Ellen traded in her sewing machine as payment.

Charlie objected. "Your sister gave it to you. That's the nicest thing you have."

Ellen shrugged. "It's not such a sacrifice. I never wanted it. I keep running the needle into my finger. It's easier to stitch by hand. Besides, it takes up too much room and I have to dust it." She smiled at her husband. "I've been looking for an excuse to get rid of it." Charlie loaded it into the wagon for her, and she drove into Wallace to deliver it. She was glad Charlie hadn't come with her and seen the tears in her eyes when she relinquished the sewing machine. It was indeed the best thing she had.

Food was scarce. They weren't starving, but they ate mostly sowbelly, boiled beans, and bread now, and not much of that. They both grew thin. Sometimes Charlie shot a rabbit and Ellen made rabbit stew. She'd stop baking cakes and instead served biscuits and syrup for dessert. She couldn't afford lemons, so she substituted vinegar for lemon juice in a pie. When Charlie inquired what kind of pie it was, she remembered that he had asked her never to serve him vinegar pie. Vinegar pie would mean he couldn't provide for her.

"Lemonette," she replied, holding her breath for a minute. "It's lemonette pie."

"Lemonette?"

Ellen nodded.

"Well, it's awful good."

Ellen didn't mind the sacrifices. Eating simply, wearing mended clothes, even giving up the sewing machine weren't important when she considered how fortunate she was. Miss Ferguson had been right. There weren't many women as lucky as Ellen. Who else had a husband who'd consider selling his prize horse for his wife's benefit? She realized the depth of Charlie's love for her, and she loved him right back. Those days were almost like the first ones of their marriage. Her eyes lit up when she saw Charlie riding in from working the cattle. She lingered a little too long in the doorway, her dish towel in her hands, as he grinned at her. She watched him dismount, admiring how straight his back was, and his hips. She'd always liked his hips. She'd walk over to him and ask him how his day had been, not caring so much for the answer but loving the way he put his arm around her and rested his chin on her head. Then he'd touch her belly, and the two of them would smile, because neither one of them was surprised that she was pregnant again.

AFTER THE LOSS of two children, she might have been apprehensive, but instead, Ellen was thrilled. She was content, as she had not been since Billy died. This baby would live, she thought as she polished the cradle that Miss Ferguson had given her and that Charlie had retrieved from the barn. She would be healthy, and she would be a companion for her parents in their old age. Ellen was sure the baby would be a girl, and she made plans for her. Charlie would show her how to ride, and she would love horses the way he did. She might even learn to brand and castrate and earmark cattle. Ellen would teach the girl her letters and how to cipher. By the time she was ready for school, she would be able to read and do arithmetic. Maybe she'd go off to normal school one day, the way Ellen had, and become a teacher. She might live with Lizzie in Chicago for a time, but her heart would always be in Wyoming.

"You're pretty sure it'll be a girl then?" Charlie asked one evening when Ellen sat beside the kerosene lamp, crocheting a baby cap from store string. "I wouldn't mind, as long as she looks like you."

Ellen looked up and smiled. A girl would be easier for Charlie, she thought. A boy might remind him too much of Billy. Not that they would ever forget Billy. There would always be an ache when they thought of him. Ellen couldn't help but think how Billy would have been a big brother to his sister, how the two would have played together, Billy always protecting her, just the way Pike looked after Margaret. Billy's death would be the girl's loss, too.

Still, Ellen had begun to accept her son's death. She would always regret it, but now she was aware of how fortunate she was to have Charlie—and this baby to look forward to. "She'll be our ray of sunshine," Ellen said.

"That's what you want to call her?"

"What, Sunshine?"

"Ray."

"We could."

Charlie laughed. "Folks would think she's a man."

Ellen shook her head. "We'd spell it *R-a-e*. That's a girl's name. Oh, Charlie, let's do."

Charlie didn't think much of the name, but if that was what Ellen wanted, he'd go along with it. "What if it's a boy?"

"Then we'll name him Ray."

Ellen put down her knitting and held out her hand, and Charlie took it. "Rae," he said and nodded.

ELLEN WAS EVEN healthier than she had been with the first two babies. The only thing that marred her pregnancy was the measles. She saw Charlie staring at her one morning and asked what he was looking at.

"You've got spots all over your face."

Ellen picked up the mirror. "Measles," she said. "I have the measles." She'd seen enough schoolchildren with measles to be sure. "You better keep away from me."

"I had them when I was a kid."

When Hattie called, Charlie told her to stay away for fear of catching the illness, but Hattie, too, had had measles. "You think in a household of kids we wouldn't have come down with them? Ma gave us chicken manure tea. Cured them right up."

"Chicken manure tea," Charlie repeated to Ellen.

"I'll take my chances."

Ellen recovered quickly, and she used that as proof she would have a healthy pregnancy and easy childbirth. It pleased her that the baby would come in the summer. The other two had been born—and died—during snowstorms. This baby would arrive in the sunshine. Ellen dreamed of lying in bed with her newborn, looking out the open door at the green prairie and the blue sky, watching as a fiery sunset lit the heavens.

"What if it rains?" Charlie asked, after Ellen told him the sun would be shining when the baby was born.

"What better omen than rain?" she asked, because the rain was scarce again that year.

"I got another one of those omens," he told her. He reached into his shirt pocket and told Ellen to close her eyes and hold out her hand. When she did, Ellen felt him drop something sharp into it and opened her eyes to see the gold horseshoe brooch with the green shamrock. "I found it when I was cleaning out the wagon," Charlie told her. "It was stuck in a crack under the seat."

ELLEN AND HATTIE had grown even closer. They were confidantes. Hattie had fallen in love and was unsure whether to marry or pursue further education. Ellen advised the girl to get her teaching certificate first, then marry, just as she herself had. If the boy truly loved her, he would wait. Teaching for a year or so and then marrying would be a good life, just as hers was, Ellen said, confiding details of her marriage. She told Hattie about the day she'd first seen Charlie riding into the schoolyard and how she had fallen in love with him right then.

Hattie was visiting when the labor pains began. The two were weeding Ellen's flower garden when Ellen rose and said, "I think the baby's coming."

"I'll ring the dinner bell," Hattie said. Charlie had installed the bell that spring, not so much for Ellen to call him to dinner but in case she needed him in an emergency. Charlie was not far away. He heard the bell and rode to the house. "It's time," Hattie told him. "I'll stay with Ellen. You go for Mrs. Gurley and send Pike for the doctor."

Charlie didn't bother to dismount. He rushed off, while Hattie went inside where Ellen had changed into her nightdress and was sitting in the rocking chair. When a pain hit her, she clutched her stomach. "Is it bad?" Hattie asked.

"Not so bad yet," Ellen replied. "I think there's time for the doctor."

"If there isn't, me and Mrs. Gurley will deliver it. With all the kids at home, I've been around birthing more than you have."

The two laughed until Ellen felt another pain. There were several before they heard someone pull into the barnyard. "Mrs. Gurley," Hattie said, peering out the door. She frowned. "She has Lucy with her."

The older woman came into the house by herself. "Pike's off somewheres, so he couldn't fetch the doctor. I offered to go, but Charlie said he'd get there quicker. He was so nervous you'd think Ellen had never had a baby before. I had to bring Lucy, since there's no one at home to tend to her and I don't dare leave her alone." Mrs. Gurley laughed. "I thought it might not be a good thing for her to see a birth, but when I told her about it, she just shrugged and said she'd seen babies before. She's outside playing with Windy. She's seen dogs, too, but I guess she thinks they're more fun." She studied Ellen, then said, "I think we'd better get you in bed."

"I took off the quilts and put a tarp under the sheet," Hattie told her. "There's water heated on the stove, and I boiled string."

"Then you don't have any need for me."

"For either of us, I expect. Ellen had an easy delivery with Billy. Remember there wasn't time to fetch the doctor and Charlie had to deliver him. But I'm glad that this time Charlie's rode for the doctor, just in case."

"Just in case," Mrs. Gurley repeated.

Ellen groaned and doubled over, and Mrs. Gurley said, "Looks like this baby's not going to wait for any doctor." The two women washed their hands, and Hattie tied one of Ellen's big aprons around Mrs. Gurley. "It shouldn't take long. It's a good thing you were here, Hattie, or Charlie might have had to deliver this one, too." She turned her attention to the woman on the bed, and when the pains hit Ellen, Mrs. Gurley ordered, "Push." Each time, Ellen strained and pushed as hard as she could. But the baby wouldn't be born.

The pains went on for a long time—for hours—and the women kept glancing at the door, hoping to see Charlie and the doctor. Ellen screamed, and perspiration ran down Mrs. Gurley's forehead as she tried to aid in the birth. "It's not coming," she whispered to Hattie. "Something's wrong."

"What?"

Mrs. Gurley shook her head. "I don't know. I think the head's too big."

"The head?"

"Ellen's a small woman. The baby's head might be too big to come out."

The pain had ended, and Ellen asked, "What's wrong?" Her voice was low and strained.

"Nothing, only this baby's stubborn. I guess that's because it's Charlie's," Mrs. Gurley replied. She and Hattie exchanged a glance. "You see if you can help this baby get out, Hattie. You've got tiny hands. Mine are big as plowshares."

"I've never done that. Ma's babies all slipped out."

"Well, you have to try."

Hattie shrank back.

"Do it, girl. You want her to die?"

Hattie looked at Mrs. Gurley, stunned, and the older woman nodded. Her glance softened as she studied Hattie, perhaps thinking it was a pity a girl so young had to see such things. But then this was woman's sin, as the Bible said. Maybe it was time enough for Hattie to know what she might be in for if she married. "This is serious. We have to get that baby out of there. It could die, too."

Hattie swallowed hard. Because she had been present when her mother delivered her babies, Hattie knew the pain of childbirth. Still, her brothers and sisters had emerged squalling.

"It's Ellen we got to think of. Now see what you can do."

Hattie slid her hands into Ellen, but she couldn't extract the baby.

"Might be the only way is to crush its head," Mrs. Gurley said at last.

"You mean kill it? No!" Hattie was horrified.

Mrs. Gurley glanced over at Lucy. The girl had come into the house and was sleeping on a quilt on the floor. The moans and screams hadn't awakened her. Mrs. Gurley arched her back, then used her apron to wipe her face, which was red and covered with perspiration. "Sometimes you have to choose, the mother or the baby. But it's not my choice. It's Charlie's."

"He'd want to save Ellen," Hattie said.

"That's what I think, too, but it's not for me to say. I couldn't crush this baby's head without him saying so." She shuddered. "I'm not even sure I could do it then."

"Where is he?" Hattie asked, suddenly angry. "He ought to be here. He probably stopped at the saloon to celebrate."

"You know he didn't. He's off somewheres looking for the doctor."

"He should have come back."

"He'd just be in the way. Maybe it's a good thing he doesn't see this."

"Maybe he ought to."

Mrs. Gurley nodded. "That's the way of it with men. They ought to see what taking their pleasure does to a woman." She studied Hattie, thinking again that the girl was too young to know a woman's burden. She turned to Ellen and tried again to help with the birth. "We're not giving up, Hattie," she said.

"No," Hattie replied. Her face was wet with tears. "She's Ellen. We have to do something. What?"

"That's the thing of it. I don't know." Mrs. Gurley closed her eyes, and Hattie thought she was praying.

Ellen gasped then. The cry was weak, and Mrs. Gurley shook her head. "Poor thing. She's wore out. She can't hold out much longer." She bit her lip, then said, "Where's that doctor? Where's Charlie? Damn men! They ought to be here."

Hattie went to the door. She was surprised it was dark out. Maybe it had been dark for a long time. She had no idea how long Ellen had been in labor. The sky was lit by stars, millions of them. The peaceful night did not calm her, however. She stared off into the distance and thought she saw something. "Mrs. Gurley!" she called. "Someone's coming!"

"The doctor?" Mrs. Gurley looked up from the bed.

"I don't know. Maybe. It looks like two men." Then she murmured, "Please, God."

The men were riding fast, and in a minute they turned in. Charlie jumped down from his horse, without bothering to tie him to the hitching post. "How's Ellen?" he said, then grinned. "Is the baby here yet? Is it a girl?" When Hattie didn't answer, he explained, "I'd have been back sooner, but Doc was all the way out at the Kruger place. The Kruger boy nearly got his leg cut off when he fell on a plow blade, and Doc wouldn't leave till he was sure the boy would live. He said if I helped him, he'd get here faster." He stopped when he saw Hattie's face. "Ellen?" he asked, then rushed inside, not waiting for a reply. The doctor was behind him, a bag in his hand.

"Ellen?" Charlie said, kneeling beside his wife. "Honey?"

"Charlie?" she muttered.

Mrs. Gurley used her sleeve to wipe her eyes as she explained to the doctor what was wrong. He nodded, then examined Ellen. "How long has she been like this?" he asked.

"Hours," Mrs. Gurley said. "Will she be all right?"

The doctor didn't answer. He took a pair of forceps from his bag, then went to work on Ellen. She screamed, but the screams were soft now, as if she'd expended all her energy. Charlie gripped her hands and said, "You got to save her, Doc. I don't care about the baby."

The doctor didn't answer, didn't seem to hear Ellen's cries as he went to work and after a time extracted the baby. He handed it to Mrs. Gurley, while he tended to Ellen. "She's torn up pretty bad. I have to try and stop the bleeding."

Charlie looked up at the baby, but Mrs. Gurley shook her head. "She didn't make it. She was a girl," she said.

"A girl," Charlie whispered to Ellen. "You have a little girl." He didn't tell her that the baby was dead. Ellen was too weak to smile. She closed her eyes, and her breathing was soft.

Charlie sat beside her until the sun was up, and then all the next day as Ellen lay unconscious. The doctor had stopped the bleeding but told Charlie to prepare himself. Too much had gone wrong.

Morris stopped. He'd seen Charlie ride past with the doctor and come to see if the baby had arrived. When Mrs. Gurley told him that Ellen wasn't going to make it, he said he'd do the milking and feed the animals. Pike came, too, and took Lucy home.

Hattie and Mrs. Gurley remained, along with the doctor. They stayed until Ellen took a deep breath and lay still.

The doctor had been sitting in the rocking chair, and he stood and examined Ellen. Then he pulled the sheet over Ellen's face and said, "It's over, Charlie. Ellen's gone."

Epilogue

The two women finished their coffee, and the older woman screwed the cap back onto the thermos and set it beside her on the running board of the Packard.

"Oh my, Hattie, Charlie must have been devastated," her friend said.

"It was a terrible thing to see, Martha. He didn't cry. It would have been better if he had. I remember tears ran down his face when Mother Gurley told him the baby was dead, but with Ellen . . . He just stood up and went outside. He didn't say a word. It was all bottled up inside him. The rage on his face . . . I've never seen anything like it. He went to the barn, and for a minute, I wondered if he might find a gun and shoot himself." Hattie studied her hands a moment, remembering.

"Mother Gurley and I washed the baby and wrapped her in a quilt. Then we washed Ellen and dressed her in that Japanese silk dress she wore at her wedding. Charlie gave me the horseshoe brooch to pin to her dress. Then we laid them out. Miss Ferguson came along then—Morris had stopped her on the road to let her know about Ellen—and told us to go home, that she'd sit up with the body that night. We'd have stayed, but we were both so tired. We'd been up for two nights."

"She was buried in Wallace?" Martha asked.

Hattie nodded. "In the cemetery. We passed it down the road. Ellen never wanted to be buried in such a lonely place, but where else could she be laid to rest? Besides, that's where Billy was. The service was outside. Charlie never could abide churches. When I got there, I saw he'd chipped Ellen's name in the rock beside Billy's grave. Rae's name was there, too. Charlie must have spent a day chipping away at that marker. The minister gave a real nice talk, said as how she was a good woman. Then Johnny Dare played 'Going Home' on his violin. I never hear that song without shedding a tear."

Hattie stood and brushed off her skirt as she looked back toward the house. There were tears in her eyes. "I can't ever stop here at this old house without crying either," she said, brushing away the dampness with the sleeve of her coat.

"Everybody was at the funeral. It wasn't held for a couple of days. We waited until Ellen's sister arrived. She was devastated, poor thing. Gladys was there, too."

"Gladys?" Martha asked. "How did she know?"

Hattie smiled. "Well, that was the one nice thing. I never was sure how Morris found her, but he sent her a telegram. She came, and she never went back to Kansas City. You see, they hadn't gotten around to getting a divorce and were still married. They are yet. I guess Morris realized that one woman wasn't just like the next one, that Gladys was something special, and he loved her after all. They've been a loving couple all these years. Ellen would have been pleased if she knew the two of them had got back together. We passed their ranch just a mile or so back, the house with all the flowers around it. Gladys always was a hand at growing them. She taught Ellen, and she taught me. Their girls are grown now. They had three. One's married to the governor."

Hattie opened the car door. "We best get on home. Pike'll think I've got a puncture, although he knows I can change a tire as good as he can."

"Did you ever get the teaching degree?"

Hattie shook her head. "I knew when Ellen died that happiness was fragile. I didn't care so much about being a teacher after that. I just wanted Pike. I was never sorry we got married right away." She smiled. "Come along. If I'm not back before long, Lucy'll start supper, and we'll have bread and butter and canned pineapple."

"It must have been a burden, taking her on."

"No burden at all. I knew when I married Pike that they were a package, that someday he'd have the care of her. She's as sweet a woman as she was a little girl. I've never minded a bit."

Hattie leaned against the open car door and stared at the remains of the house. "There are lots of deserted shacks like this on the prairie. Lots of folks couldn't make it out here. Those were bad times, and they failed. Ellen and Charlie were ordinary, just like everybody else. There was nothing different about them, except for the way they loved each other." She looked away, then said softly, "I like to think that's the way with Pike and me."

Hattie started to get into the Packard, but Martha took her arm. "What happened to Charlie? Did he stay on?"

Hattie looked out across the prairie. The wind had come up and was whipping the grass back and forth. A hawk dropped out of the sky, then rose again with his prey in his mouth. "At the burying, folks came up to him and said how sorry they were, but Charlie didn't hear them, didn't even mumble a reply. He watched while the men lowered the coffin into the grave—Ellen and little Rae were buried together in one coffin. Charlie insisted on shoveling the dirt over the box himself. Then he stood there, clutching his hat, staring at that mound. People left, but Charlie stayed on. I remember because Pike and I waited, thinking how we'd take him to the Gurley house for supper. The sun was low down, and still Charlie didn't move. Then the coyotes began to howl, and I remember Ellen saying that was the loneliest sound she'd ever heard. It made me shiver to think she'd hear them forevermore.

"It was dark by the time Charlie put his hat on his head. He called to the dog, but Windy wouldn't leave the grave. Charlie leaned down and petted him and told him to keep watch. Then he walked past us, and touched my arm. 'She'll save a place for you,' I told him, and he smiled a little.

"Pike started to say he was welcome for supper, but I put my hand on Pike's arm, and he was still. We watched Charlie as he went to his horse. He mounted Huckleberry and sat in the saddle for long time, staring at the grave. Then rode off. We never saw him again."

Acknowledgments

Many years ago, I wrote a *Denver Post* review of the autobiography of a cowboy. The author told about working on ranches, then marrying and settling down on a small spread of his own. His wife kept the house and garden and he ran the cattle, and together, they had a few good years. Then the wife died. Dispirited and unable to make a go of the ranch by himself, the cowboy drifted off.

What struck me about the small volume was how ordinary the couple's life was. Theirs was the story of so many settlers in the West. They were decent people who worked hard to scratch a living from the land, but in the end, they died or moved away, leaving behind little to show they had ever been there.

Although I gave away the book, I never forgot the story. I began thinking about it a few years ago and wondering if it would make a novel. In fact, I had the last line of the novel in the back of my mind. So, I set out to find another copy of the autobiography. That was a bit difficult, because I couldn't remember the title or the author's name or even the time period. I thought the story took pace in Wyoming, but I wasn't sure. Little surprise that I never did get another copy. So, knowing the search was hopeless, I went ahead and wrote my story, without the help of the book that had inspired it.

Where Coyotes Howl is one of my favorites—perhaps the favorite—of all my books. I like writing about the women who settled the West. The story reminds me of one of my early books, *The Diary of Mattie Spenser*. And I loved doing the research, which included reading scores of journals and narratives written by early western women. Still, the reason I was so emotionally involved in *Where Coyotes Howl* is because the bulk of the writing was done when my husband, Bob, was in the ICU at Rose Medical Center in Denver, and later in a rehabilitation facility. I woke early each morning and wrote before I went to spend the day at his side. The writing kept me centered, as we both struggled with the physical and mental effects of his illness. He was dismissed from rehab just as COVID-19 got under way, then confined to the house for the long healing process. I continued to write during those days and weeks, and completed the book about the time my husband was fully recovered. Bob was an integral part of my writing *Where Coyotes Howl,* so it's appropriate that I dedicate the book to him.

We are both grateful for the support of our family during that ordeal. Kendal was always there with soup and good humor (and the idea for Miss Ferguson's story). Dana was there—in spirit, since COVID-19 kept her from being with us in person. Forrest and Lloyd supported us with their love for Bobob.

Others contributed more directly to *Where Coyotes Howl*. Danielle Egan-Miller, my agent, is always upbeat about my work. You prop me up, Danielle. Executive Editor Elisabeth Dyssegaard, my first-rate editor at St. Martin's Press, worked with me to strengthen the story. Thanks, Elisabeth, and thanks, too, to Assistant Editor Alex Brown, for handling so many details.

I was apprehensive about asking Candy Moulton to read my manuscript. After all, she is a distinguished Wyoming historian as well as executive director of Western Writers of America. It was my good fortune that she agreed. Your critical eye saved me from making errors about Wyoming and ranching, Candy.

Finally, thanks to my readers, some of whom have been with me for more than thirty years. You lift my spirits at any time.